THE TANGLEWOODS' SECRET

THE TANGLEWOODS' SECRET

Titles by Patricia M. St. John
STAR OF LIGHT
TREASURES OF THE SNOW
THE TANGLEWOODS' SECRET
RAINBOW GARDEN
THE SECRET OF THE FOURTH CANDLE
THE MYSTERY OF PHEASANT COTTAGE

For older readers:
NOTHING ELSE MATTERS
THE VICTOR

THE TANGLEWOODS' SECRET

Patricia M. St. John

with Scenes from the Film
Produced by Intamedia

Scripture Union

130 City Road, London EC1V 2NJ

© Patricia M. St. John 1948
First published 1948
Reprinted 1959, 1962, 1967
First published in paperback 1964
Reprinted 1969
New paperback edition 1971
Reprinted 1974, 1976
This edition 1980
Reprinted 1981 with pictures courtesy
International Films
Reprinted 1982, 1983 (twice)

ISBN 0 85421 880 7

Made and printed in Great Britain by
Purnell and Sons (Book Production) Ltd.,
Member of the BPCC Group, Paulton, Bristol

CONTENTS

1

HOLIDAY PLANS

It was a beautiful home where Philip and I lived with Aunt Margaret—a white house on the slope of the hill behind which the sun set, with a garden and an orchard where cowslips and clovers ran riot under the apple trees. Philip and I slept in the two top attics, with the doors open so that we could shout across, and I could never quite make up my mind which window I loved best, Philip's or mine. Philip's gave me a feeling of security, for it looked out on the garden hedged in with pines and the shelter of the dear green hills with their bracken and gorse rising beyond; but mine gave me a thrill of adventure, for it looked out on the great Worcestershire plain with its fields and its cherry blossom, and its far, far hills, somewhere away in Herefordshire, where I had never been.

I loved those hills; sometimes they looked so green and near, sometimes so misty and far away. I looked on them as a sort of fairyland where I might go some day when I was grown up. And when Philip came in to sit on my bed in the morning to listen to the first bird songs, or to watch the flaming sunrise over the plain, we used to tell each other stories about them, and about the strange beasts that lived upon their slopes.

Philip was nearly eleven, a year-and-a-half older than I,

and I loved him more than anyone else on earth. He was a gentle, thoughtful boy, slow in coming to conclusions, but completely dogged in carrying them out. Ever since I could remember he had been my friend, my protector and my comforter; and, except at day school, we had never been apart. We were about as different as a brother and sister could be. Philip was well-built, with serious blue eyes and a round, placid face; while I was small and thin, with dark, untidy hair and a sharp chin. Philip was good and obedient; I was wild and contrary. Aunt Margaret openly loved Philip, but she shook her head over me and said that I took years off her life.

At the time of my story we had been five years with Aunt Margaret, and had forgotten what Mother and Father looked like. I was four years old when they had sailed for India; of course, Mother had meant to come home long ago, but the war had stopped her. I don't think I really wanted her to come back; Aunt Margaret was so fond of telling me what a disappointment I should be to my poor mother, that I hoped to put off the discovery as long as possible. In her letters she always sounded as though she loved me very much, but that, I supposed, was because she did not know me. In any case, when she came she would like Philip much better than me, because grown-ups always did, and Philip would like her, because Philip liked everybody; and I would much rather have Philip all to myself. So I pushed away the thought of Mother's home-coming, and thought about it as little as possible.

This story begins on the first day of our Easter holidays, when Philip came into my room in his pyjamas at half-past six in the morning, and curled up on the end of my bed with his notebook and pencil in his hand; together we leaned our elbows on the window-sill to watch birds and to make plans.

Bird-watching was our great hobby that holiday. We had a notebook in which we recorded each different kind of bird we saw, and everything we noticed about it—its song, its nest, its habits. Philip had made the book himself, and it was beautifully neat and accurate. He did all the writing and I painted the eggs when we found them; but my drawings were not particularly life-like.

Philip longed for a camera with which to photograph his nests. " If only I could take photographs of them," he would say, over and over again, " I might be a great naturalist—my book might even be printed."

But the cheapest camera in the shop windows cost pounds, and our money-box held exactly forty five pence, even though we had been saving for weeks and weeks. We emptied the coins on to the quilt, and counted them over again, just in case we'd made a mistake the time before. But we hadn't. Philip sighed deeply.

" I shall nearly be going to boarding school by the time I get that camera," he said sadly. " I wish we could earn some money, Ruth."

We gazed out into the garden rather sadly, racking our brains for some plan; but nothing brilliant suggested itself to us. Below us, April had touched the fruit trees, and blossom foamed like a soft white sea over the plain. Our own damson trees were white and lacy, and I could see nests of primroses around their roots and golden daffodil trumpets resplendent in the sun. I looked across to my own hills, but they were hidden in the early haze of a spring morning. All of a sudden I felt Philip's body stiffen beside me, and he half dived out of the window in his eagerness.

" Tree creeper!" he hissed. " On the plum!"

I leaned out beside him and we watched together—a neat brown bird running up the tree, tapping the bark for insects. Philip was all alert now, noting every slightest pose and gesture—hardly drawing his breath until the little creature had spread his wings and disappeared round the corner. Then out came pen and notebook, and my brother was absorbed for five minutes.

"Ruth," he said eagerly, looking up at the end of that time, "we must get to the woods early today and have plenty of time—and Ruth, I was thinking in bed last night, we ought to have a naturalist's headquarters. We ought to build a place where we could keep pencils and rough paper and provisions in tins, instead of always carrying them with us—because we shall go every day all the holidays. And we must escape early before Aunt Margaret thinks of things we ought to do."

I nearly tumbled out of bed in my eagerness.

"We'll race through our holiday jobs," I announced, "and I'll be as good as gold, so she'll hardly notice me, and she won't watch me, and when I've swept and dusted in the drawing-room I'll just slip out before she thinks of anything else, and if she asks where we've been we'll say we've been getting wood—and we'll bring a little back with us to make it true—but I don't see why we should have to work at all in our holidays! I know what I'll do—I'll dress quick, and go down now and help Aunt Margaret with breakfast to make her think how good I'm being!"

I was out of bed in a flash, and in ten minutes' time I duly presented myself in the scullery, arrayed in a clean pinny, with my hair in perfect order.

"Can I help you, Aunt Margaret?" I enquired meekly. "I got up early in case you might need me."

As I was noted for my lateness in the mornings, my aunt looked rather astonished.

"Thank you, Ruth," she answered pleasantly, hiding her amazement, "you can lay the table for me. I should be very glad."

Everything went smoothly. Philip and I bolted our breakfast and sat bottling up our impatience while Uncle Peter and Aunt Margaret sipped their second cups of coffee, discussing the day ahead. Then Uncle Peter went off, and Aunt Margaret turned to us.

"And what plans have you two made?" she asked. Philip had the answer all ready. "As soon as we've done our holiday jobs, we're going to get wood in the Cowleighs, Aunt Margaret," he replied, in his sweetest voice.

"Very well," answered my aunt a little doubtfully, "but you must remember I need your help in the mornings. Ruth is old enough to assist in the house now; she shall start with wiping-up and doing the drawing-room, and then we'll see."

I could be quick when I liked, and I wiped up the breakfast things in an astonishingly short time. Then, without any further consultation with my aunt, I seized the broom and duster and made for the drawing-room. I poked the dust wildly round the linoleum with the broom, and flicked it off the ledges at top speed. I could not see the dustpan, but wasted no time about it—I gathered up my little heap and shoved it under the carpet. Then I tiptoed back to the kitchen, replaced the broom and duster, and was out of the front door like a streak of lightning.

Out and free on an April morning, with the sun shining, and the birds singing, and the lambs bleating! I tore round the back like a whirlwind and pounced upon Philip all unexpectedly, nearly knocking him over; but he was quite used to me by now, and was not much alarmed.

"Finished already?" he enquired, rather surprised.

"Yes; haven't you?"

"No," he answered. "I've got to chop these sticks into little bundles for kindling wood. It will take ages."

"Oh," I cried, "we can't wait! You've made quite

enough of those silly bundles. No one will know we haven't chopped them all up if they can't see the rest. Quick—give those sticks to me!"

And before my more conscientious brother could protest, I had heaved the remainder into the ditch and was kicking the dead leaves over them.

"And think," I shouted, prancing up and down, "how quickly we shall find them when we are sent to get more!" —and with a final leap I was away across the orchard— away through the clean wet grass all starred with primroses and flecked with blossom petals, and out through the gap in the back hedge like a young rabbit, with Philip at my heels.

The gap in the hedge was our own special right of way, and no one else knew about it. Aunt Margaret could see the gate from the kitchen window, and sometimes we preferred to keep our comings and goings to ourselves. So we had found a gap, behind the hen house, invisible to anyone else on account of the overhanging branches which we brushed aside. It led out into another meadow which led to the road, which in turn led to our dear woods.

Once in the road I danced and shouted like a young mad thing; it was sheer joy to be alive on such a morning. Philip followed more soberly, his eyes glued to the hedges, now and then stopping to listen or to watch. I did not wait for him; I felt as though spring had got into my feet; I think I scared away most of the birds before Philip came anywhere near them.

I vaulted the gate that led through the meadow, and stood still for a minute watching the staid mother sheep with their merry long-legged lambs, leaping, like me, among the daisies. And as I watched, one of the lambs with a smudged nose and black stockings suddenly saw me and came rushing towards me, uttering little bleats of welcome. I squatted down and held out my arms; he ran straight into them, and started licking my face with his eager warm tongue.

"Philip!" I cried. "Philip, look what's happening!"

Philip was beside me by this time, and together we knelt in the grass while the lamb prodded us, licked us, and leaped from one lap to another. As we played, an old shepherd came and leaned over the gate, smiling at us.

"That's the little orphan," he explained. "He's bottle fed, and he's not afraid of anyone. The other sheep push him away, so off he goes on his own. He's always in mischief, the wee rascal!"

The lamb at this moment leaped from my knee and ran to the gate; the old man stooped and picked it up.

"He knows my voice all right, don't he?" he remarked, smilingly. Then, tucking it inside his coat, he turned away towards the farm.

"That's a new shepherd," I said to Philip. "I've never seen him before."

"I have," answered Philip. "He's over from Cradley for the lambing season. Come on, Ruth! We're wasting time."

He jumped up, and we raced across the open meadow with the wind blowing my plaits out behind me; then over a stile, and we were standing in our woods.

2

THE WIGWAM

PHILIP and I left the path and fought our way through the young trees which seemed all bound together with honeysuckle tendrils. At last we paused to look round, and Philip took a seat on some moss while I squatted beside him.

"We'd better build our headquarters here," he announced. "It's a good home base for further excavations."

Philip liked long words, and sometimes read the newspaper in search of them, though he did not always understand them.

"How?" I enquired.

"Like a wigwam," explained Philip. "Look, can you see that little mountain ash tree just there? That will be our centre prop. Now we'll collect branches, and lean them up against the middle, close together; then we'll bind them together with honeysuckle binding, and just leave a little doorway to creep through—and we'll have a floor of dead bracken and moss, very soft and comfortable—it will be almost like building a nest. Then at the back we'll dig a hole and line it with sticks and stones; we'll bury our supplies there, and cover them with bracken so you won't be able to see anything; it will look just like a floor."

I was thrilled, and set to work immediately; we worked hard all the morning, dragging dead boughs through the

14

undergrowth and cutting long stakes with Philip's clasp knife. Before long we had the skeleton wigwam firmly fixed, with a little doorway just large enough to admit a child—though it was a tight squeeze even for Philip.

It took us some days to complete our wigwam; every morning I rushed through my jobs and we made a bee-line for the woods. Every morning the pile of dust under the carpet grew bigger and bigger, but as Aunt Margaret had done the spring-cleaning my laziness was not noticed.

Oh, those mornings in the woods! We seldom kept together; we both wandered off on our own trail, happy with our own fancies, returning to the home base with armfuls of bracken and binding—each of us finding our own treasures and adventures and sharing them on our return.

Perhaps our best find lay in the beech tree just above our wigwam. One day, when I was quietly weaving the wall, I heard a rush of great wings—a brown owl swooped close past me. I was up the trunk in an instant, like an excited squirrel, hoisting myself from branch to branch and searching every hollow and crevice for the nest. My search was rewarded, for there, in the topmost fork of the tree, cradled in straw and fluffy brown feathers, lay one pure white egg, hot from the mother's breast.

I climbed down a little way so as not to disturb the mother, and sat swinging my legs and looking about me. The slopes behind the woods were misty with bluebells, and through the thin veil of young green I caught the glint of kingcups. I was so happy that it almost hurt—and then I saw Philip, looking very small, moving slowly through the trees, his arms full of bracken.

"Phil!" I called. "Come up here!"

He was up in a minute; together we gazed in deep delight at the pure, precious thing. Then we caught sight of the mother sitting in the next beech, snapping her yellow eyes angrily, and we thought we had better go down. Instantly she spread her great brown pinions and dropped on to her nest; we slid down and discussed baby owls, lying on our tummies in the wigwam.

Everything went well for a week, and Aunt Margaret seemed content enough to let us go our own way. If ever I noticed her looking tired and overworked, I told myself that it was not my business. My holidays were my own; I was going to spend them how I pleased, and in any case I wasn't much good at housework. So it was rather annoying to me one morning when my aunt stopped me, just as I was tearing out of the house, and asked me where I was going.

"Out with Philip," I answered, wriggling a little under her restraining hand. "I've done my jobs, honestly I have, Aunt Margaret. Please let me go; Phil's waiting for me."

"Well," replied my aunt quietly, "I think Philip must be content to go alone this morning. I need you, Ruth. I've got a big wash this morning, and you can help me in pegging out the clothes and turning the wringer. It's time you did a lot more than you do."

I kicked the ground and looked just about as sullen as it's possible for a child to look.

"But I specially wanted to go out today," I whined.

Aunt Margaret gave me a little shake.

"Well, you can just do what somebody else wants, for a change," she replied. "And if you can't do as you're told cheerfully, you can stay in this afternoon as well. You are getting more lazy and selfish every day; the sooner you take yourself in hand, the better."

She marched off to the kitchen and I followed, scuffling my feet and scowling. I was furious; why, the owl egg might hatch today, and I should miss it! The tits might come out of their nest, and Philip would see them alone.

It wasn't fair! I hated Aunt Margaret at that moment, and I made up my mind I wasn't going to help her; I'd be as naughty as I could and then she'd be sorry she'd ever asked me to stay.

My thoughts were interrupted by the back door being flung open and Philip's head appearing. He had been working for Uncle Peter in the garden, and looked somewhat flushed and tousled.

" Coming, Ruth?" he asked eagerly.

" No, she's not coming," replied my aunt shortly. " She's going to make herself useful for a change. You run away and play by yourself this morning, Philip. Ruth can join you this afternoon, if she behaves herself."

We both had a miserable morning. I made ugly faces at the table and vented my wrath on the mangle. I sighed, and yawned, and scuffled; I kicked the furniture, and scowled at my aunt's back; but she was working hard at the wash-tub and pretended not to notice. She often pretended not to notice my tempers, and nothing annoyed me more; what was the good of being sulky when she would not even look at me? I grew crosser and crosser.

She noticed me all right in the end, however, because she told me to carry out a basin of clean handkerchiefs and hang them on the line. I did not really mean to drop them, but I was so busy slamming the back door and rattling the clothes pegs that the basin slipped from my hands, and all the handkerchiefs were scattered in the yard; it had rained in the night, too, and the yard was very muddy.

My aunt was very angry indeed. I think she would have liked to box my ears, for I saw her clasp her hands very tightly together. She told me the truth about myself in no uncertain terms and said I might go now, as I was more trouble than I was worth on a busy morning, but that for a whole week I was to stay in every morning and work in the house, and by the end of that time she hoped I would have learned how to be a little more pleasant and useful, and a little less clumsy. She spoke about my selfishness, and what a disappointment I should be to my mother; then she took the basin of muddy handkerchiefs out of my hands and went into the house.

I stamped my foot, gulped back my tears, and marched out of the gate with my head in the air; I had lost my mornings for a week, but there was an hour left before dinner—I would go to meet Philip, and walk home with him.

It was a very quiet morning, clouded and hazy and warm after rain; all the world smelt sweet and fresh and fragrant, and I felt strangely out of place with my ugly, angry thoughts and my tear-stained face; so much so, that I even stopped to think about it, and looked about me. There were the trees doing their work without haste or clamour, each leaf perfect in its unfolding, each opening bud a miracle; and there was no fret or needless hurry— just the peace of doing something well; I couldn't have put it into words at the time, but that peace seemed to enter into me for a few minutes, and I stood thinking how perfect life could be if only I could be good.

I did not often want to be good, but I wanted it then— wanted with all my heart to be good, and happy, and useful—in harmony with God's world. I even clasped my hands together and spoke aloud, because I wanted it so badly.

" I want to be good," I whispered. " I don't want to lose my temper and be selfish. Oh! why can't I be good? "

But my words seemed to float away into the empty air, for I knew nothing of Someone who stood so close to me, longing to help and change me. To me He was nothing more than a Person who had lived long ago, and about whom I read in church. So after a few minutes I shrugged my shoulders and went on.

"I never shall be," I muttered. "I shall always be horrid and cross, and nobody will ever like me."

I met Philip, absolutely beside himself with joy; he did not seem to have missed me at all!

"I watched the egg hatch," he announced. "I went up and she flew off; when I looked, the shell was cracked and I could see the membrane heaving up and down; I daren't stay in case it got cold and the owlet died. She's back now, brooding on it, and I shouldn't go up if I were you, because she might peck you."

There wasn't time to go up, in any case, as it was high time to go home to dinner. On the way I told Philip of my tragic morning. He was comforting and sympathetic, and I felt better, even though knowing perfectly well that I deserved no sympathy. Then, in his own thoughtful way, he stopped talking about the mornings and we spent the rest of our walk home planning the afternoons.

3

TERRY

IT was only three days later that we had our first adventure and made a new friend; and this is how it happened.

The wigwam was well and truly finished and as snug a little house as anyone could wish, with its secret hiding-place where we hid our tea and other belongings when we went exploring. The tits had left the nest, we had watched their first uncertain flight, and had seen them flounder on to the moss, screaming for their mother. The owlet, too, was growing; he now resembled a ball of soft grey cotton wool, with a hooked beak and round yellow eyes, and he seemed to have no objection to our holding him in our hands.

This particular afternoon the wind was behind us, blowing strongly from the hills. We had been caught up in it and had run all the way. Being carried along like that had made us laugh, and we reached the wigwam quite breathless with running and laughter, ready to fling ourselves down on the mossy floor and recover our breath in the cool, dark shade of its walls. So it was quite a shock to me when Philip, who had dived half-way through the entrance, suddenly backed out on to his haunches, his eyes wide with astonishment, and whispered dramatically.

" The wigwam is occupied!"

" Who by?" I enquired indignantly, backing a step or two.

" Well, I couldn't exactly see," replied Philip, " but I think it's a boy."

" Well," I said loudly, " it's our wigwam, and he'd better come out, because we want to go in."

There was a dead silence.

" You'd better come out!" said Philip, very loudly and clearly.

Still no answer.

" Perhaps it's a dead body?" I suggested.

" No it isn't," answered Philip. " I saw it scratch itself."

There was a long, uncertain silence; Philip began to giggle.

" I think I'd better go in and look again," he said. " Perhaps he's deaf."

He went down on all fours and approached the entrance with extreme caution; his front half disappeared into the doorway, and another long silence ensued.

" Hurry up!" I exclaimed impatiently, taking hold of his back legs in my excitement. " Who is he? And what is he doing?"

" We're just staring," said Philip with another giggle. " It's a boy, as I said—I say, boy, this is *our* wigwam, and we're coming in, so you'd better get out."

" Shan't!" said a voice from within.

" Then I shall pull you out," said Philip, with perfect good humour.

" Then I shall catch hold o' the wall and pull it down with me," answered the voice coolly.

Another silence, while the rivals eyed each other narrowly, and I danced up and down with excitement and indignation.

Philip broke the silence.

"I know," he said, "let's have a tournament, like in the history book!"

"A how much?" enquired the voice; its owner seemed unfamiliar with history books.

"A tournament," repeated Philip. "It's like a fight between two people who are having a quarrel. Whoever wins the fight wins the quarrel. You come out and fight, and if I win you go away, but if you win you can share the hut. Because, after all, you know, we *did* build it."

Our uninvited visitor seemed to like this idea, for I saw Philip wriggle out of the entrance backwards and roll merrily over on to the ground, thus making room for him to come out. And, angry as I was, the minute I saw his face in the gap I liked him, and wanted to know him.

"I hope Philip wins," I thought to myself. "But all the same, I hope he'll stay and play. I like him."

He was a little boy, about as big as I, but the same age as Philip. His clothes were ragged and rather too small for him, but his eyes were as bright as a blackbird's, and his thin face was brown and powdered with freckles. His thick hair fell down over his forehead, and reminded me of an untidy thatch; in his arms he held an enormous bunch of kingcups and cowslips. He laid them carefully on the moss and bade me 'let 'em alone while he knocked out that toff'.

The tournament began in a highly irregular fashion, before anyone was ready for it, for the boy suddenly ran at Philip and punched him on the jaw. Philip, taken by surprise, had not the time to hit back before he was punched again on the ear; and even then he stood and blinked several times before making up his mind what to do about it.

"*Hit* him, Phil!" I yelled, nearly joining in myself, and beating the nearest tree to relieve my feelings.

It was a good fight to watch, once Philip got fairly started; Philip was as strong and as determined as an ox, but the boy reminded me of a little ferret. He twisted and turned, and leaped and wriggled, his thin brown arms bulging with muscle, and his lips pressed tightly together. Back and back he came, while Philip stood his ground and measured out slow, relentless blows. It was a very exciting tournament indeed, and I behaved like a whole gallery of spectators rolled into one.

The boy won; he pretended to spring at Philip's neck, and then suddenly changed his tactics, and dived between his feet, bringing him to the ground with an alarming crash; by the time Philip had realized what was happening, the boy was sitting on his chest, thumping him with all his might.

"Stop it!" said Philip, coolly; "you've won."

"Beat yer 'ollow!" said the boy, getting up. "But I don't want yer silly ol' hut. I could build a better one meself."

He was gathering up his flowers and making off, when Philip ran over to him and held him by the braces.

"Don't go!" he said. "We'd quite like you to share the hut, and then perhaps one day we'll have another fight. I love fighting, don't you?"

"Not bad," said the boy.

"We're going to have tea now," urged Philip. "Come and have it with us. There's room for all three inside."

It was not nearly tea-time really, but we both felt we must do something to hang on to the boy—and at the word 'tea', a remarkable change came over him. He stopped looking sullen and bored, and suddenly became interested. Without even troubling to say yes, he squatted down on the mosss with an expectant smile on his face, and held out his grubby hand.

He must have been terribly hungry, for I had never seen anyone eat at such a speed either before or since! We opened our packet of sandwiches, and without so much as a Please or Thank-you he fell upon them and finished three while Philip and I were still eating our first; although our appetites were fairly healthy, too! Then, when the last crumb had disappeared and he had licked the jam off the paper, he gave a sigh of relief and we all settled down to get to know each other.

We lay on our tummies, our faces cupped in our hands, and the bluebells tickling our chins pleasantly. The afternoon sun came slanting through the trees in golden bars and made leaf-shadow patterns on the ground; up above, the wind murmured in the tree-tops; but we were sheltered and warm and peaceful.

" What's your name?" asked Philip.

" Terry," he replied, and went on chewing a piece of grass.

" How old are you?"

" Eleven come August."

" Where do you live?"

" At the cottage in the 'ollow by the stream down Tanglewoods way."

" Have you any brothers and sisters?"

" No— there's only me and Mum."

" Where's your father?"

" 'Aven't got none."

" What are all those flowers for?"

" Me Mum sells 'em in the town—she's a flower-seller."

" Do you pick them all for her?"

" Yes, when I can cut school."

Nobody spoke for a time; then I suddenly had an idea. I put my hand on his arm.

" Would you like to see an owl's nest?" I asked.

For answer he pointed upwards to the tree. " That one?" he asked. " I've seen 'im once today; got a little tame one from that nest last year; it stopped with me wellnigh on two months."

I felt a little bit annoyed; it was *our* owl's nest, and he had no business to get there first; but Philip was before me. He leaned eagerly over towards the boy.

" Do you know lots of nests?" he asked. " Could you show us any more?"

He looked at us rather scornfully.

" I could show yer wellnigh on every nest in this 'ere wood," he replied.

Philip jumped to his feet. " Come on!" he cried. " Let's go and see! Show us them all, Terry!"

Terry got up slowly and looked us up and down, as though making up his mind as to whether we were the sort of children to be trusted with nests. Then he nodded.

" Right!" he answered briefly, and dived into the bushes.

A breathless hour followed, at the end of which I was quite exhausted and nearly torn to pieces, for Terry never stopped at an obstacle. We waded knee-deep in a pond to inspect a reed-warbler's woven home, and we swarmed impossible trees in search of crows' nests. We inspected holes in trunks, and watched a starling fly in and out. The wood was opened up to us, and we found out more about it in that hour than ever before. The sun was setting when we turned home.

" Good-bye," we said, and then we hesitated. Must this

be the end? Would such a wonderful boy want to see us again?

"Coming again?" said Terry casually, and we heaved a great sigh of relief. From that moment Terry was our friend; and, better still, we knew that he looked upon us as his friends.

4

THE LOST LAMB

WE saw Terry nearly every day after that, and the time passed only too quickly; he led us all over the countryside and showed us his secret nests and lairs and burrows; we learned to identify and track the footprints of little animals, and to recognize the different cries of birds and what they meant. He dragged us through swamps and marshes and brambles in search of the earliest flowers, and showed us where to gather rare orchids. It was as though he had opened up to us a new world of wonder, and we both loved and admired him for his amazing knowledge of woodland life. Before, I had always disliked Philip's friends, because I thought they took him away from me, but Terry seemed to think us both equally his friends, and never looked down on me for being a girl, and younger.

So it was a disappointment to us all when Philip twisted his ankle while swinging from a tree, and, after hobbling home, had to lie upon a couch for three days.

I stayed at home at first to help amuse Philip; I believe my efforts were quite successful, but they nearly drove Aunt Margaret to distraction. I started by catching a duck and bringing him in, dressed up in a doll's bonnet, to call on the invalid, and then letting him loose on the dining-room carpet. We forgot him after a little while; he waddled out into the passage, where he met my aunt, who was *not* pleased to see him; we heard him being shown out of the front door in a great hurry, squawking angrily, after which we watched him waddling across the lawn, the pink silk bonnet turning from side to side as the duck looked about him.

That diversion having been stopped, we decided to play soldiers, and settled ourselves one at each end of the dining-room with a lead army and a dozen marbles each; we bombed each other quite happily for a time, till it suddenly struck us that the kittens in the woodshed would make excellent army cavalry; so off I trotted, returning with an armful of soft, purring, black and tabby fur, which I dropped on the ground; four blue-eyed kittens with twitching tails and whiskers sorted themselves out and rushed into corners.

I selected a tabby and a black-and-white, and Philip had two coal-blacks to represent his army. We let fire on the leaden infantry, and then the cavalry charge began.

It was a marvellous game, and the kittens loved it; they tore after the marbles in all directions, slaughtering the soldiers right and left; Philip and I shrieked with laughter and scuttled round on all fours collecting our ammunition and recapturing the cavalry. Faster and faster ran the kittens, fiercer and fiercer grew the battle, when suddenly there was a crash and a splash; the tabby had leaped on to a dangling tablecloth and pulled it, together with a vase of flowers, over on top of himself. Of course, at that moment the door opened and Aunt Margaret came in.

The kittens instantly rushed between her feet; one stopped and dug his tiny claws into her stocking; the wicked tabby, unable to disentangle himself, rolled over and over all wrapped up in the tablecloth. The flower water streamed across the carpet, and Philip and I lay flat on the floor and laughed until the tears ran down our cheeks.

My aunt was not amused; I will not describe the scene that followed, but it finished up with four very excited little kittens being banished to the coal cellar, and one very cross little girl being turned out of the house. Philip was given a book, and put back on the sofa.

I spent the next ten minutes or so sitting on the wood-pile sulking; it wasn't fair! Aunt Margaret had said it was all my fault, and it had been Philip's fault just as much as mine that time, so I told myself. I had actually suggested the kittens, but Philip had thought it an awfully good idea, and, anyhow, why shouldn't we play together? I didn't like being sent off alone like that. I hated Aunt Margaret—and, when you came to think of it, it wasn't me at all, it was the kitten. At that point I suddenly thought of that wet tabby rolling round inside the tablecloth; I began to giggle, and felt better.

I got up and went over to smell some early lilies-of-the-valley that were coming out under the wall; by this time I was quite happy again. After all, it was very nice to be out of doors on a sunny spring day, even if I was alone. I decided to go to the woods and see if I could find Terry anywhere, so I squeezed through the gap in the hedge and strolled down the road.

I didn't go far into the wood, for the sun was pleasant on the outskirts and I wanted to pick flowers. The bracken was already beginning to shoot up and hide the bluebells, but the vetches were rambling over the ditches, and orchids and woodruff grew in the clearings; so I wandered round, dreaming of Philip and Terry. and Mother, and nests, and the far-away hills, and blue bells, and wigwams, until I had almost forgotten where I was, and it gave me quite a surprise to hear a man's voice quite close to me.

I looked up quickly, but he was not calling me; he was standing with his back to me, peering into the thickets; he had not seen me at all. But I recognized him at once; it was the Cradley shepherd who had picked up the orphan lamb and carried it under his coat.

Being rather an inquisitive child, I wanted to know what he was doing, so I went and stood where he could see me. As soon as he caught sight of me, he smiled broadly.

" Why!" he exclaimed, " you're the little maid as played with the lamb t'other day—and here you are a-turning up again just at the right moment. One of the little rascals 'as strayed, and I'm thinking as how he's caught somewhere here in these bushes, but I can't just see where. Maybe you'll stop and help find him."

I was only too delighted. Here was something nice to do, and a pleasant companion to do it with, so I set to work with great goodwill. I liked this old man with his white hair and his rosy face, and I felt he liked me; we were soon talking away as though we had known each other all our lives.

" Why did he stray?" I asked, as we parted the bushes and searched the ditches.

" Well," answered the old man, with a smile, " I reckon he's just like the rest of us; he likes his own way, and his own way's led him into trouble, poor little chap!"

" Well," I remarked, " I expect he's sorry for it now— all tied up in the bushes, and wishing he'd stayed in his meadow."

" Aye," agreed the old man, thoughtfully. " It takes a deal of thorns and briers to teach them lambs as their own way isn't the best one—he'll be crying his heart out for me now, maybe, if only I could find the place."

" Won't he be glad to see us!" I observed. " Oh! I'm longing to find him! I expect he'll be awfully tired and hungry. Have you anything for him to eat?"

He put his hand into his pocket, and drew out a bottle.

" You'll see!" he said. " The minute I pick him up in my arms, he'll have his nose in my pocket. He knows I wouldn't forget 'im—the little sinner!"

He chuckled softly, and we moved farther into the wood.

" He's strayed a long way, hasn't he?" I remarked.

" True," answered the old man, " but I'll find him yet. I've never yet had a lamb go astray, but what I've found him and brought him home; I always hear them crying out somewhere or other, although at times 'tis a long search."

" What's the longest you've ever searched for?" I asked.

" 'Most one night," he replied, " but that was in a storm, and I could scarce hear her cryings for the wind and the thunder. She was caught fast in a bramble bush, and I found her at dawn by lantern light—wellnigh dead with cold and hunger and crying."

" And what did you do?" I asked again.

" Do?" repeated the old man. " Why, I set her free and quietened her, and wrapped her in my coat, and carried her home; she was like a mad thing when we found her, but once she felt my arms round her she lay as quiet as a baby —she knew there was nothing more to be a-feared of then!"

I was about to ask another question, but he suddenly held up his hand and stood perfectly still, listening.

I had heard nothing, but his practised shepherd's ear had caught the sound at once—the faint cry of a tired lamb calling for help.

" That'll be him," he said simply, " in those bushes." And he made straight for the sound.

It was a wonder to me, when we saw him, how the little

creature had ever got in. The hedge was so matted and the briers so thick; and it was a still greater wonder to me that the shepherd ever got him out. But we started off, parting the boughs, and as he worked he spoke to the lamb as a mother might speak to a frightened little child.

I don't suppose the lamb understood the words, but he knew the voice in an instant—knew in a flash that he was sought and found and loved, and at the sound of it ceased his weak struggles and fretful crying; he gave one joyful bleat and then lay still and waited.

It took a long time to reach him. I stood and watched while the old man patiently worked at the tangle, thorn by thorn, and brier by brier; when he finally picked up the little prodigal his hands were dreadfully scratched and bleeding, but he didn't seem to notice; he just held that trembling lamb close and let it nuzzle its black nose trustfully into his pocket.

" Are ye ready to come home?" he whispered, playfully lifting the little smudged face to his own.

" Baaa!" said the lamb, and put its nose back into the shepherd's pocket.

We walked home quietly, my small hand clasped in his large horny one, and the lamb lying in the crook of his arm. He seemed to be thinking deeply and his face looked very happy. I longed to share his thoughts, but did not like to ask, so I said nothing.

When we reached the field, the sun was setting and the sky behind the bluebell slopes was the colour of pink shells. We laid the lamb among the others, and he gave a bleat of content and fell fast asleep.

" Well," I said slowly, " I suppose I'd better be getting home now; thank you for letting me help, and I hope I'll see you again soon."

But he drew me down beside him on the wooden bench

that ran round the outside of the fold. " Before you go, little maid," he said, " I'll read you a bit of a story about another sheep as strayed." And as he spoke, he took a small, worn New Testament from his pocket, and opened it at Luke, chapter fifteen; then he began to read, in his slow, kind, country voice.

I suppose I had heard the story before, but it had never interested me. But tonight it was different; it seemed to belong to the sloping buttercup fields, and the long evening shadows and the pink sky, and the sleeping folded sheep. I rested my head against the shepherd's shoulders and listened with all my heart.

" And when He hath found it, He layeth it on His shoulders, rejoicing.

" And when He cometh home, He calleth together His friends and neighbours, saying unto them, Rejoice with Me; for I have found My sheep which was lost.

" I say unto you, that likewise joy shall be in Heaven over one sinner that repenteth."

He closed his Testament, and I looked up at him.

" Good night, little maid," he said.

" Good night," I answered, " and thank you very much." And I walked slowly home through the buttercups.

5

A BRILLIANT IDEA

I NEVER told Philip about the shepherd—at least, not about the last bit—because I was afraid he would laugh and think it queer, and I should not have liked that. In any case, I almost forgot about it next day, because I had one of my brain-waves, and when I had a brain-wave I could never think of anything else until I had carried it out.

It came about next day, when Philip was hobbling round the garden, not yet being able to walk to the woods. We had played all our usual games, and were lying under the apple trees wondering what to do next. As there wasn't anything much to do, we just lay and chatted, and Philip started talking about his book again.

"It's getting very fat, Ruth," he assured me, "and it's full of useful information about birds. All I'm waiting for now is the camera to take the pictures—and I shan't get it for years. Just think," he went on dreamily, "what a beautiful picture that baby owl would have made when he sat on our hands!—and those tits sitting in a row on the hawthorn bush."

"Never mind," I said comfortingly, "we've got twenty five pence more than when we last counted, so we're getting on!"

"But it's so slow," sighed Philip. "I shall soon be nearly

grown up, and I expect I shall be sent to boarding school, and there won't be much chance to take pictures. I wish Auntie would let me be an errand boy, and earn something in my spare time."

I interrupted his thoughts by suddenly pouncing on him and slapping him violently on the back.

"Philip!" I shouted, "I've had a most marvellous idea!"

"What is it?" he asked, doubtfully; he was a little suspicious of my good ideas—they so often turned out badly, and ended up with punishments.

"It really is a good idea this time, Philip," I urged, "and Aunt Margaret could never discover. We'll pick flowers, like Terry's mother does, and sell them; we'll earn pounds and pounds. Do say yes, Phil! It would be such fun!"

Philip was still extremely doubtful.

"But Terry's mother wouldn't like it," he objected, "because if they bought our flowers, they wouldn't buy hers as well, and then she wouldn't get so much money."

"Oh, but we shan't go to the same places," I assured him. "She sells hers in the street in the town; we'll go to people's back doors—and we'll dress up a bit to look like gipsies."

Philip's eyes danced; he was coming round fast, as I knew he would sooner or later.

"Let's go to the big houses half-way up the hill, where they have big iron gates and drives," he said. "We'll dress up in our oldest clothes like gipsy children, and we'll make our faces a bit dirty and wear our muddiest shoes; you tie your plaits up in your red hanky, and we'll get pounds and pounds. Let's start soon!"

I always liked to carry out all my plans instantly, and leaped to my feet immediately. Then I remembered Philip's ankle, and tried to curb my impatience.

"You'll be able to walk tomorrow, won't you?" I

pleaded. "Although, even if you couldn't, a little limp would be quite helpful. It would make people sorry for you. We could say, 'Pity the poor lame beggar!' and hold out a hat, and you could put a big white hanky round your ankle and look as though it hurt you; only you wouldn't have to do it too much, because it would make me laugh."

I laughed delightedly at the very thought, and rolled about joyfully in the grass.

Philip's ankle was much better next day, and we escaped early and made for the woods with a big wicker shopping-basket. We were going to pick all the morning and sell all the afternoon; we had no idea of prices, which rather worried us, but we were trusting to luck rather than to judgment, and hoped for the best.

"Where are you going?" I asked Philip, as we reached the stile.

"Down to the swamp in the hollow," he replied. "I'm going to pick lots of cowslips, and there are some late king-cups out, and the valerian's in bud. I might find some orchids, too, to put in with the cowslips; the colours go well together."

"We can get some wild cherry blossom, too," I added, "and I'm going to pick little bunches of wood sorrel and violets for tiny pots. We'll sell them cheap—about three-pence each—to the people who don't want big bunches. Oh, Phil! What fun it will be!"

I was dancing down the sloping path that led to the swamp, and nearly collided with a swinging bough of cherry blossom swaying low across the path. I stopped to pick some, and Philip caught me up. He did not help me, but stood quietly staring up at the pure clusters.

"Isn't it beautiful?" he remarked slowly. "It's like great snowdrifts up there."

"Yes," I answered absently. "Pick some, Philip! I'm doing all the work."

"Isn't it a pity," went on Philip, taking no notice of me, "that it doesn't last? It will all have fallen in a few days, and the blossom will be all brown and ugly. Nothing beautiful really lasts, does it?"

"Oh, there'll be some bird cherries later on, I expect," I answered, in a matter-of-fact voice. "Stop staring, Philip! It's silly to think about things like that; get on and pick some flowers."

Philip stooped down and started gathering large late violets but his blue eyes were sober. I marched on rather crossly, for I didn't like Philip in these melancholy moods. But although I tried to forget them, his last words kept ringing in my ears: 'Nothing beautiful really lasts, does it?'

It was quite true. All the nasty things like tempers and rows with Aunt Margaret went on and on, and you couldn't get rid of them; they might stop for a time, but you knew they would always come back; while beautiful things like holidays, and blossom, and sunsets, and birds singing, faded and died, and left you empty. Certainly other beautiful things came and took their places, but it didn't comfort you for the ones that had gone.

"Not one single thing," I said aloud to Philip, who had caught me up.

"Not one single what?" enquired my brother; he had seen a jay, and had forgotten all about everything else.

"Beautiful thing lasting," I explained, rather vaguely.

"Oh!" said Philip. "No, I suppose not, but it doesn't really matter, because more come. Jays usually nest low down, so keep your eyes open."

As he had not yet told me about the jay, I could not see what that had to do with it, but I was quite used to my brother's one-track mind, and said no more. In any case, we had nearly reached the swamp, so we turned our serious attention to the flowers.

We picked hard all the morning, and quite filled the shopping-basket with our bunches. There were golden balls of cowslips mixed with vivid purple orchids and lacy white woodruff. The dazzling brightness of the buttercups we veiled with cow parsley, and mingled the kingcups with cotton grass and valerian. The blossom we left by itself, for we felt that its perfect whiteness was best unadorned. I carried it separately, while Philip carried the basket. We hid all our flowers in the orchard, and went in to dinner, inwardly bubbling over with excitement, but outwardly quite calm.

Aunt Margaret looked rather hard at Philip, who was gobbling his dinner at a tremendous pace. She was a little suspicious of our haste to be off again.

"Philip," she said rather severely, "I think you should rest that foot this afternoon. You've done enough walking on it this morning."

Philip turned injured blue eyes upon her.

"Why, Auntie," he assured her, in his most polite voice, "I've been standing still nearly all the morning. I just went to the bog and stayed there and picked a few flowers. I think, too," he added seriously, "that a lot of exercise makes it feel better. It stops it getting stiff. In fact, I had planned to walk on it as much as possible this afternoon."

And Philip, as usual, had his way, as he always did with my aunt.

"Very well," she agreed, "but don't overdo it—and keep out of that bog; your sister's shoes are a perfect disgrace."

Philip looked at my shoes and sighed. He, of course had remembered to change his before Aunt Margaret noticed them; I, of course, had not. How calm life would be, I thought rather bitterly, if I had been born like Philip!

Aunt Margaret went into the kitchen to wash up after dinner. She did not ask me to help her, and I certainly did not offer. I was always full of excuses and arguments when asked to help, and my aunt was rather tired today, so she let it be.

Once the door was firmly closed, I fled upstairs. I untwisted my plaits and my hair fell dark and loose to my waist. Then I tied up my head in my Indian handkerchief that Mother had sent me, and put on a dirty pinafore. My muddy shoes needed no touching up. I looked a perfect little vagabond. Philip in his bird's-nesting coat and Wellington boots looked a fit companion for me.

"Don't let Aunt Margaret see us," he whispered cautiously, as we slipped out of the door. "She'd have fifty fits! We'd better go through the gap."

We climbed the hill that led to the big houses rather slowly, for the day was hot and the basket was heavy; also Philip's ankle hurt quite a bit, although he would not admit it. What really worried us was the fact that the flowers were drooping so. Of course, we should have put them in water overnight, but we had been too impatient to wait till next day. Yet, in spite of our impatience, when we actually reached the first pair of iron double gates we seemed in no hurry to go in.

"What are you going to say?" asked Philip, rather nervously.

"Me?" I replied indignantly. "I'm not going to say anything. You've got to say it; you're much better at all that sort of thing than me."

"Oh, well," said Philip peaceably, "perhaps we shan't have to say anything. Perhaps the person who lives here will come to the door and say, 'What beautiful bunches of flowers! I'll buy two'—and then we shall just smile and hand them over, and she'll give us some money and we'll go away."

This charming prospect cheered us up a lot, and we walked rather quicker until the path divided; the left-hand path ran round the front between beautiful lawns, flower-beds and cedar trees; the right-hand one ran around to the back.

" Do we go front or back?" I asked.

" Back, I think," said Philip. " After all, we mustn't forget we're gipsies."

Our timid knock at the back door sounded dreadfully loud—so loud that we both jumped. We had hardly had time to recover ourselves before the door was flung open and a housemaid appeared. She was a very grand house-maid with dyed hair and a permanent wave, and there was a heavy smell of scent about her.

" Well?" she asked, sharply.

It all happened so suddenly that we were both quite taken aback, and simply looked at each other. There was a moment's silence, then a violent desire to scream with laughter seized me. I could *not* speak. I turned away from Philip with shaking shoulders, but not before I had seen that he was feeling as bad as I was. He whisked out his handkerchief and pretended to sneeze into it, but the result was a sort of cross between a snore and a roar, which set me off worse than ever. The tears streamed down my cheeks and I turned my back on the housemaid.

" Well?" she asked again. This time she sounded down-right angry, so Philip controlled himself and answered in a very shaky voice.

" Would you like to buy some flowers?" he quavered.

" Good gracious, no!" replied the girl. " What in the world should we be buying flowers for here? Didn't you see the gardens? The mistress has more flowers than she knows what to do with. Besides, those what you've got in the basket are all dead."

"Oh, they'll be all right in water . . ." I began, but she had already slammed the door in our faces, and we were left giggling feebly on the steps.

I wiped my eyes on my pinafore, because I had forgotten my handkerchief, and we made off down the drive between beautiful beds of lilies of the valley and wallflowers which we had been too excited to notice on the way up. We kept relapsing into peals of laughter, and were too amused to feel disappointed. Anyhow, we were certain we should be more fortunate next door. After all, the girl had been rather funny; her lips were so scarlet, and her nose was so big.

The next house certainly looked less grand; the garden was smaller, and we could see the front door from the road. We stopped a minute to read the notice on the gate. It said: 'NO HAWKERS, NO CIRCULARS', in large capital letters.

"What does that mean?" I asked.

"I don't know," answered Philip. "It sounds like a man that sells hawks. Anyhow, it couldn't mean us, so come on!"

We walked purposefully up the path, holding the basket between us. "Whatever happens, we mustn't laugh this time," said Philip. "Don't let's look at each other at all; let's just both talk fast, and we shall be all right. And let's go to the front door, because perhaps the masters and mistresses will be nicer than the maids."

We climbed a flight of stone steps, and I pulled the bell handle rather harder than I meant to. It rang so loudly that Philip put his hands over his ears and went quite pale; it seemed awful to have made such a noise on such a quiet afternoon. We gave each other a desperate look, and at that moment the door opened; an elderly lady with an eye-glass and a very straight back opened the door and stood looking down at us as though she didn't like us much.

We were so determined to have no awkward pauses this time that we both started talking at once, very fast and loud:

" We've picked some flowers," said Philip.

" And we thought you might like to buy them," said I.

"They are about six pence, I think," said Philip.

" Unless you think it's too much," said I.

" They look a bit dead," added Philip.

" But they'll be quite all right when you put them in water," said I.

" Because they are really quite fresh," said Philip.

" We only picked them today," said I.

During this surprising flood of conversation, the old lady stood staring at us in indignant astonishment. She took no notice of the withered bunch of cowslips that I was feverishly trying to push into her hand, and asked in an icy voice:

" Little boy and girl, did you not read the notice on the gate?"

" Yes," admitted Philip, rather puzzled, " but I'm not a hawker."

" And I'm sure I'm not a circular," I chimed in, rather pertly.

" Little boy and girl," went on the old lady in an awful voice, " if you are too young to understand the English language, you are certainly too young to be doing this sort of thing. Go home to your mother!"

And for the second time that day we found ourselves standing on the steps with the door shut in our faces.

Philip was discouraged, and suggested going home; but I was more persevering, and urged him on.

" Let's try again!" I pleaded. " They can't all be as nasty

as this. Look, this next gate says nothing about circulars, so it must be all right."

"Neither did the first one," murmured Philip, but he followed obediently inside, and we set off up the drive, the basket growing heavier and the day growing hotter every minute.

There was a beautiful rock garden on one side of the path. I was, walking a little ahead when I suddenly noticed a clump of brilliant bell gentians nestling in a crevice; never before had I seen such a heavenly blue, and in an instant I had squatted down on the path to examine them more closely. At the same moment, Philip, trudging along behind me, saw a skylark soar upwards and remain poised and motionless. He threw his head back and walked on, forgetful of everything else, and of course tripped right over me, head first. I rolled over, with my legs waving wildly; the basket upset and scattered the flowers in all directions, and we both screamed at the top of our voices.

It was at this point that a man came round the corner, and nearly fell over us as well.

"What on earth . . .!" he began; but by this time we had sorted ourselves out, and were sitting up.

"Sorry!" said Philip, rubbing his nose.

"You tripped over me," I remarked indignantly.

"Well, you shouldn't have squatted down like that," protested Philip.

"Well, you shouldn't have had your head in the air!" I argued.

"Well, I was watching a skylark," explained my brother peaceably, "and, oh, listen!—I can hear it now!"

"Are you interested in birds?" asked the man suddenly.

"Yes," replied Philip, coming out of his dream and lifting serious blue eyes to his questioner. "Are you?"

"Very," answered the man soberly. "I have all sorts of

birds nesting in this garden. I'll show you some if you get up—unless you and your sister wish to sit in the middle of the path all the afternoon."

Philip jumped to his feet and walked away with the man. I gathered up the flowers and followed; they were already deep in conversation on the subject of golden-crested wrens.

We had a very happy half-hour, for he showed us four or five rare nests, and Philip was in his seventh heaven. Then, when we had been all round the garden, he took us on to the verandah and gave us each a drink of lemonade; and as we drank it, he suddenly remarked, " By the way, why did you come?"

Philip had quite forgotten our real errand, and looked quite startled for a moment. So I answered for him, holding out the basket.

" We came to sell flowers," I explained, " but we fell over. Would you like to buy some?"

He selected three bunches of withered cowslips.

" Is this how you earn your living?" he asked gravely.

" Oh, no," I replied, " not really; we wanted to earn some money for something very particular, so we thought we'd sell some flowers—but nobody seems to want them."

" Nonsense!" said the man. " Cowslips are my favourite flowers. I'd pay a lot for a scent like that "—and he pressed fifteen pence into my hand.

Philip went rather pink. Then, laying his hand on the man's sleeve, he said earnestly, " We should like to give them to you. You have given us such a lovely afternoon, and . . . and . . . we are very much obliged to you."

The last words came out with a rush, as though he was reading a speech. The man's eyes twinkled, but he still spoke gravely.

" Not at all," he replied. " It's been a pleasure to meet you, and I should like your little sister to keep all the money. You have an extraordinary knowledge of birds for one so young, and I should like you to come again."

I put the two coins in my pocket in a great hurry. I was dreadfully afraid the man would take Philip at his word, but he didn't. He walked to the gate with us, and we all shook hands and said Thank-you. Then he turned back up the drive and we stood once again in the road.

" Let's go home," said Philip.

"All right," I agreed. "Fifteen pence isn't bad for a first day, and we will try again tomorrow."

But Philip did not answer; he was walking down the road in a happy dream. He had been in Paradise.

6

AN UNFORTUNATE TEA-PARTY

WE went out flower-selling nearly every afternoon after that, for a week, and earned nearly fifteen shillings. We never again met anyone quite so nice as the bird man, but quite a lot of people seemed pleased with our flowers and bought bunches; they looked better now, too, because we remembered to put them in water overnight instead of selling them at once, and the basket of fresh, wild bunches made a good show.

We took Terry into our confidence, and he did not mind at all; in fact, he helped us quite a lot, for he had a gift of selecting the right colours and arranging them to perfection. In order that Aunt Margaret should not see the flowers, we kept the bucket by the gap in the hedge, and Terry would sometimes arrive there late in the evenings and add a few of his finds to ours. We had shown him our private gap as a mark of friendship, and he used to creep in and out like a small weasel, and leave notes for us, stuck on the apple boughs. His spelling was shaky, but that did not worry us at all—and anyhow we had invented a code, in case Uncle Peter ever found them when attending to the hens. Aunt Margaret we felt quite safe about; she never went into the orchard.

Most mornings we found a scrap of paper which said,

"Cum to △—bring ooooo." This meant that Terry would be waiting for us at the wigwam, and would require feeding; and where Terry commanded, we always obeyed. Aunt Margaret almost gave up the unequal struggle of trying to make me help in the house, and I became really gifted at getting out of doing my jobs. If I ever had a twinge of conscience about her tired and rather sad face, I managed to forget it the minute I had dived through the gap in the hedge and was out in the world again.

It was towards the end of the week, when we were sitting at dinner, that my aunt remarked:

"I'm going out to tea this afternoon, Philip and Ruth, and I shan't be back till about six. You may take yours out, and not come back till supper, if you like."

We both *did* like, very much, and we kicked each other joyfully under the table.

"Who are you going out to tea with, Auntie?" enquired Philip, who always took a polite interest in other people's affairs.

"With an old friend of mine who has come to live here just lately," answered my aunt. "Later on, I should like to introduce you to her; she is very fond of children, and has often asked about you. She knew your mother, too."

"Will she ask us out to tea, too?" I enquired with interest. I liked going out to tea because we always had such nice things to eat.

"If she did, you would have to behave yourself rather better than you usually do," replied my aunt dryly, and I frowned and wriggled with annoyance. Why should she always spoil even nice, good things like going out to tea, with silly remarks like that? Of course I always behaved nicely out to tea! I was far too shy not to, and in any case it was rather fun having grown-ups say how well-mannered we were; quite a change, too, as far as I was concerned.

Dinner over, my aunt carried me off to the kitchen to help dry up the dishes, which I did at lightning speed, and made off the instant I'd finished. Aunt Margaret called after me to come back and put the cloth away tidily, but I pretended not to hear, and scuttled through the front door. I knew she could not possibly catch me, for I was as fleet-footed as a little rabbit, and I hoped she might have forgotten by the evening. Going out to tea would drive it out of her memory.

Philip was waiting near the gap, looking rather anxious, with the basket in his hand.

"Come along," he said, "we must get well away before Auntie starts. We might meet her—and we forgot to ask which way she was going."

"Oh, I think she's going down the town way," I answered carelessly. "I heard her say something to Uncle Peter about it—someone she was going to see down Beech Road."

"But perhaps it was somebody else," objected Philip.

"No, no," I replied reassuringly, "it was sure to be the same one. She doesn't go and see many people; she's too busy."

Philip chewed a piece of grass thoughtfully.

"She's always working, isn't she?" he remarked at last. "Sometimes I think we might help her a bit more than we do. After all, it's quite kind of her to have us to live with her; we're not her children."

"Oh, I don't know," I answered quickly, for this sort of talk was not at all to my liking. "I help with the drying and dusting sometimes, and you do the wood for Uncle Peter, and we both pick fruit in summer, and shell peas and things. After all, we're not grown-ups, and children shouldn't have to work in the holidays. We do quite enough work in the term."

But I could see by the look on Philip's face that he was not quite satisfied, so I changed the subject as soon as possible.

We went down a country road today, to a collection of rather pretty cottages mostly inhabited by retired, elderly ladies. The may was beginning to come out, and the boughs of the hedges were weighed down with the heavy blossom. Underneath, on the banks, buttercups, vetches, dead nettles, speedwells, and cow parsley grew in sweet-scented riot, all stretching up towards the sunshine; it was the high tide of early summer, and the birds sang as though they would burst their throttles with song. It was a peaceful sort of day on which no one would expect anything to happen; and so we were taken completely by surprise, never dreaming that the afternoon would turn out as it did.

The old ladies were unusually nice, too, and at the first four houses everyone bought something, and we earned over twenty pence. Most old ladies fell in love with Philip and did whatever he wanted; I suppose it was his blue eyes and his polite, serious way of speaking. One of them patted him on the head and called him ' Little man,' which he did not like at all, and one of them gave us a chocolate each, which we liked very much indeed.

We wandered up a lane to have tea, and sat on a gate looking over a radiant buttercup field, where sleepy brown cows chewed their cud and switched their tails lazily. We munched our bread and jam as peacefully as the cows and almost as silently, for Philip was not really a talkative boy. He had a good deal to think about, as he sometimes told me when I chattered more than he liked.

Tea finished, we lay down in the grass and drank from

a pipe, which was spurting water out of the bank. It wasn't very nice, and I thought it had a distinct flavour of cows; Philip drank a great deal, and then remarked that he only hoped it wasn't the drains.

It was still only four o'clock, so we decided to go back to the road and try some more cottages. We were going to do our best today, and then go back to Terry and the woods tomorrow, for we were getting a little tired of flower-selling; still, it was encouraging to be finishing up so well, and on reaching the road we approached the next cottage hopefully enough.

It was a very nice one, long, low and built of grey stone, with beds of tulips massed against it. It stood on a little rise, and a pink and white apple orchard sloped away from one side of it. We pattered up the path and along to the front door; on our way we passed under a window, and heard the clink of china and the sound of ladies' voices. It sounded as if some sort of a tea-party was going on, and ladies at tea-parties are usually in rather a good mood, as Philip wisely remarked.

We rang the bell, and the drawing-room door opened immediately. A young lady came out and stood looking at us for a moment before asking us what we wanted. When we held out the basket and asked her to buy some flowers, her face dimpled with amusement; I had noticed that a good many people looked amused when we told them we were flower-sellers, but I never quite understood why.

" Wait a minute," she said, instead of answering our question, " I must ask my mother, and then you must come in and show us what you've picked."

She disappeared back into the drawing-room, and we heard her merry laugh as she told her mother about us.

" Such a picturesque little couple, pretending to be flower-sellers," we heard her say. " The boy has a face like an angel, and the girl looks like a little wild gipsy. You must see them for yourselves; I'll bring them in."

She reappeared, all smiles, and held out her hand.

"Come in a moment," she said, "and show my mother and aunt your basket; I'm sure they would like to buy some cowslips. You shall have a biscuit each, too; we're just having tea."

We trotted in after her, suspecting nothing, and then both stopped dead in the doorway, transfixed with horror.

There were four chairs placed round a little table in the window so that the ladies were sitting with their backs to us. In the first chair sat a tall, elderly lady who was evidently the mother, for she was pouring out; next to her sat the aunt, and next to her was the empty seat which was about to be occupied by the young lady.

And next to that was a high-backed armchair, with large sides, and from the depths of it came the perfectly unmistakable voice of my aunt.

"The little girl is very unruly," said the voice, confidentially. "I shall be only too glad when her mother comes and takes her off my hands."

"Run!" I whispered to Philip. "Oh, Phil, run quick!"

But Philip in his usual slow fashion had not yet realized what had happened; he stood there blinking as though he were in some puzzling dream. I knew he would be several minutes making up his mind to run, and by that time it would be too late, so I cast about in my mind for some other way of escape.

There was one slender hope; if we walked in and stood behind my aunt's chair, it was quite impossible for her to see us without doing extraordinary gymnastics, for the chair was very big; and if we were required to speak, she would certainly know it was us; however, it was our only chance; as the young lady was beckoning us to come forward, wondering why we were hesitating, I took Philip's hand and led him straight to the only safe spot in the room.

Old Mrs. Sheridan and her sister smiled and tried to put us at our ease. She held out her hand for a bunch of cowslips; I took two steps forward, leaned right over, thrust them at her, and scuttled back to my hiding-place like a frightened rabbit to its burrow; the girl looked rather surprised, for we had not seemed shy on the doorstep; yet here we were behaving in the most peculiar fashion, and Philip was standing like a stuffed image, with his mouth open, looking as though he were seeing a ghost.

"What beautiful big flowers!" said Mrs. Sheridan, examining the clusters, "we shall have to go exploring and find some, too; whereabouts did you pick these, children?"

There was dead silence; neither of us dared speak. I heard a rustle in the armchair as though my aunt was about to turn round and examine these strange dumb specimens behind her—and if her head suddenly appeared over the top I knew I should scream. So I replied, in a hoarse whisper, "In the hollow, by the stream."

"By the stream," repeated Mrs. Sheridan. "Yes, I might have known these had grown near water; I shall certainly buy a bunch; fetch my purse, Isabel, and give these two children a biscuit each before they go."

The girl held out the plate, but to reach it we should have to walk out in the open; we shook our heads frantically, and lifted imploring eyes, but she merely thought we were being polite.

"Come along," she said, laughing, "they're very nice biscuits."

Hopelessly I took two steps forward, and leaned over as far as I could to grab two biscuits; but as I did so I saw my aunt's hat move, and I leaped backwards; in so doing, I bumped into a small cake stand and sent it flying.

At which point my aunt's head came right round the arm of the chair, and she saw me.

I can only dimly remember what happened next; I heard my aunt say, " Philip and Ruth, what is the meaning of this?" in a voice that reminded me of a bugle blast, and I heard Mrs. Sheridan say, " Pick them up, Isabel— they are butter-side down, all over the carpet—don't let them get trodden in." I saw Philip move back and trip over Isabel, who was picking up buttered buns, and I noticed that her face looked as though she were trying not to laugh. I remember everybody apologizing for everybody, and my aunt saying she could not understand it, a great many times, and Mrs. Sheridan saying it was nothing to worry about, and we were to forget all about it.

The next thing that comes back clearly to me was my aunt's turning to us when the commotion had died down, and telling us she was taking us home to punish us most severely; but before we went we were to come forward and tell Mrs. Sheridan how sorry we were for behaving so badly.

Philip had regained his senses by now, and he stepped forward immediately and looked up into Mrs. Sheridan's face. He was truly sorry for having spoilt such a nice tea-party, especially when Aunt Margaret went to so few, and he said so, so earnestly and politely that everyone was charmed; even my aunt looked pleased, and if only she could have stopped there, all would have ended peacefully; but now she turned to me and asked me coldly what I had to say for myself.

I don't quite understand to this day why I was so angry, but while Philip was talking I had decided that my aunt was an idiot; there was no need to have recognized and owned us—we should never have shown we belonged to her, and then no one would have known. Therefore, I argued, she had brought all this trouble on herself, and here we were being told *we* were naughty, in front of everyone—and we weren't naughty—why shouldn't we sell flowers? Anyone would think we were stealing!

All this was flashing through my rebellious little heart when my aunt spoke to me; for answer, I stuck my hands in my pockets and stamped my muddy boot.

"I'm not a bit sorry," I stormed. "We're not doing anything wrong, and no one called us naughty till we met you. We've earned the money and it belongs to us, and we shall go on doing it if we want. You always spoil everything, Aunt Margaret."

My aunt went quite white; never in my worst moments at home had I spoken to her like this, and here I was disgracing us all in somebody else's drawing-room. I suddenly felt terrified and miserable, and ran out into the garden, leaving them all standing looking at each other.

I wanted to dash on, but realized that they might think I was running away, and I was far too proud to run away. So I walked off towards home with my hands in my pockets and my head held very high in the air; I knew my aunt and Philip were coming down the hill behind me, so I pretended to whistle, but I was too miserable to keep it up for long. When I reached home I went and stared out of the kitchen window, and tried to whistle again; I wanted to look as if nothing had happened and as though I didn't care if it had; above all, I wasn't going to be sorry.

My aunt came in slowly, as though she was very, very tired; she crossed the room and stood beside me, looking out of the window.

"Ruth," she said, rather heavily, "I'm not going to

punish you, because it doesn't seem much good, but I've been thinking it out on the way home. I don't seem able to manage you, or bring you up as I should; you have ten days' more holiday, and then if they can take you, I am going to send you to boarding school. Your mother suggested it at Christmas, but I wanted to keep you then. Of course, it will be a big extra expense, but anything is better than have you grow up as selfish and obstinate and ill-mannered as you are now."

She turned away without looking at me, and I went on staring out of the window; I felt as though the whole world was falling down round me, and I wanted to run to Philip, and bury my face in his jersey and cry, as I used to when a tiny girl. But Philip had been sent straight upstairs to bed, and I was alone.

"I shan't go," I said, in what was meant to be a defiant voice, but which only sounded small and shaky.

"You won't be asked," replied my aunt, quietly.

There was a long silence, and I stood perfectly still, thinking furiously. Then I spoke again in the same small, trembling voice that tried so hard to be proud:

"Very well," I announced, "I shall run away, and I shan't come back," and with that I ran straight out of the door, and into the road.

My aunt took no notice. It was very early, and I often rushed off like this in a temper. No doubt I would come back before dark; she sighed heavily and went slowly up to her room.

7

RUNNING AWAY

I DID not stop for a minute when I got out into the road; I just went on running. It did not matter to me where I went so long as I got away, and in my angry heart I decided that I would never, never go back again. I would be a gipsy's little girl, or get some kind lady to adopt me, or ask someone to let me be their little servant, and then perhaps Aunt Margaret would be sorry. I knew Uncle Peter would miss me when he came home every night, and of course Philip would be dreadfully sad; at the thought of Philip my eyes brimmed over, and I went on running and running with the tears streaming down my cheeks, quite breathless, and sobbing.

"You're going away to boarding school." I kept whispering the horrid words to myself, and trying to take it all in; I saw myself going away in disgrace, alone in a train to a building which I imagined would be rather like Worcester gaol. And I imagined Terry and Philip sitting in the wigwam together, with the birds singing and the foxgloves sprouting up above the bracken and the wild roses uncurling in the hedges—and I should not be there. Then other pictures seemed to dance before my eyes: Philip kneeling alone at the bedroom window with the sun rising over the Ankerdines—and my little bed empty;

Philip lying on his tummy in the hayfields, writing his book—and I should not be there to draw the pictures.

It was quiet all round me as I trotted along; I had met no one, and except for the cries of birds going to bed and my own sobbing, the world had seemed quite silent. But now I suddenly became aware of the sound of children's voices and the barking of a dog, so I rubbed away the tears with the back of my hand and looked about me.

I had reached the entrance to a village where I had been once or twice before. It was a very little village; only a few cottages, a white square school, a village shop, and a church. It nestled in a dip of the low hills just where the country road met a larger main road with a signpost pointing to Bromyard.

I stood for some little time wondering what to do; I did not want to walk through the village just yet, for I knew that everyone would think I had been crying. Besides, I was hot and dreadfully tired, and my head was beginning to ache; I wanted to sit somewhere cool and quiet, where I could rest, and think where to go next. I looked all round me, and then realized that I was standing by a little brown wooden gate that led into the churchyard, and the church door was open. No one was likely to go into church as late as this, and even if they did I could crouch down in a pew, and they would not see me; so I went up the path between the rows of quiet gravestones, reading the names as I went past.

One stone interested me specially, and I stopped to read it again; it was a little white cross, marking a garden of forget-me-nots; on it was graven, " Jane Collins, aged nine years; went to be with the Lord, April 5th, 1900."

I read it through several times, and then shivered at the thought of poor little Jane Collins who had had to leave this world on an April day with its sunshine and its lambs, its singing birds and first flowers. Death had always seemed a distant thing, to be thought about by old people and clergymen, but Jane Collins was only nine years old when she went to be with the Lord. What if I, aged nine, had suddenly to go and be with the Lord? what would He say to me about all my tempers, and the lies I'd told, and the times I'd run away instead of helping, and the dust under the carpet? It would be far, far worse than going to boarding school; for the first time in my life I began to feel really frightened about being so naughty.

I walked on into the church porch, and peeped cautiously inside; it was quite empty, so I slipped through the door and began wandering round looking at the inscriptions, and the pictures, and the daffodils in vases; one thing pleased me most of all—and that was the evening light streaming through the stained-glass windows and falling in coloured patterns on the stone floor, making a sort of fairy track all up the western side of the church.

As I stood watching, it suddenly came over me how dreadfully tired I was. The church was so quiet and cool and friendly, with its sunset light and its daffodils, that I thought I would lie down and rest a little before deciding what to do next; so I collected some footstools, made a little mattress, wrapped myself up in an old black cassock that hung near the door, and cuddled down inside one of the pews where I could watch the beautiful patterns and think things out.

But I had not realized how sleepy I was; I had been out in the open air all day; I had been very frightened and very angry and very miserable, and I had run nearly three miles on a warm spring evening; in fact, I was so tired that I hardly remember laying my head down on the footstool. But just as I was dropping off, I thought I saw Jane Collins standing in the sunset light of the west window, pointing upwards along the golden rays; she was a little girl just like me, with dark plaits and a pinafore and blue socks, and the moment I saw her face I knew I had made a mistake in pitying her, for never before, either in dreams or real life, had I seen a child look so radiantly happy. Her arms were full of Easter flowers, and somehow I knew perfectly well that they would never fade or die. Then the light grew dim and blurred and I fell into a deep, deep sleep.

When I woke up I was lying in the dark, and for a long time I could not imagine where I was. I was very stiff, and cold, and sore, for the footstools had come apart and I was lying partly on the stone floor.

I sat up and changed my position. Directly I lifted my face I found that a wonderful thing had happened; the day was beginning to dawn, and a grey light was stealing through the eastern windows on the other side of the church; the darkness had scattered, and with it all my terrors and nightmares. I gave a great sigh of relief, and sat quite still with my small white face turned towards the morning.

And as I sat there waiting and listening, the dreadful silence was broken by the clear call of one bird, and I realized with a thrill of joy that the world was waking up again after the terrible night. Then another bird woke and answered, then another, until it seemed as though every bird in Herefordshire must be singing itself hoarse; and as I sat listening, the grey light gave place to gold, and the whole bird choir seemed to go mad with joy: the sun was rising, and morning had come again.

The relief was so great that I did not want to move. I forgot that I was cold and hungry and only remembered that the night was over, and that I was no longer alone, because the birds had woken up. Soon I would slip out of the church and run home to Philip, but for the moment I was content to sit and listen.

But I did not sit and listen for long, for somehow my head fell over on to the footstools and I dropped fast asleep again; when I woke the next time it was very suddenly, for the church was flooded with light, and there were heavy footsteps coming up the aisle.

I sat quite still and waited as the footsteps came nearer, and then my curiosity got the better of me; I crawled to the edge of the pew and peeped over. It was the clergyman; he was walking slowly up the church, looking up at the eastern windows. He need not have seen me at all, for his head was turned away and I was quite small enough to creep under the seat; I was just about to do this, for I did not want to be seen. Children were not allowed to sleep in churches, I was sure, and there was a County Police Station just down the road. But I had been lying all night in a draughty church with my legs on a stone floor, and I had caught a cold, so I was only half out of sight when a dreadful thing happened.

I sneezed!

I tried to stop, but it was no use; out it came with a loud explosion, and the clergyman jumped. Then he came and looked over the side of the pew; there he saw half a little girl, wrapped up in a cassock, sticking out from under the seat.

He said nothing, but came inside and sat down; then he leaned over and spoke very gently:

" Come out," he said. " There's no need to hide under the seat. I don't mind children in my church."

I uncurled slowly, sat down on the seat beside him, and looked up into his face. He was not very young and not very old, and his eyes were blue and kind; he reminded me of the old shepherd, somehow, only he was not wrinkled and whiskery; it was just that he was the sort of man I was not afraid of talking to.

"I couldn't help being here," I explained. "I came in last night when the door was open, and I went to sleep by mistake; I put on your clothes because I was cold, but I didn't mean to stay all night. Only when I woke up the first time it was too dark to move, and when I woke up the second time it was morning."

He looked rather startled. "Do you mean that you have been here all night?" he asked. "Whatever is your mother thinking? We must let her know where you are at once."

I sat silent a moment, twisting my hands together. I had a sudden funny feeling that I wanted to tell someone all about it, and I thought this man would do. Quite un-invited, I leaned my weary head against his shoulder.

"It's not my mother," I whispered, "it's my aunt; I wouldn't have done it with my mother; I've been very, very naughty, and she's going to send me away to boarding school because she can't manage me, and I didn't want to go, so I ran away, and here I am."

I looked up to see if he was very shocked, but he didn't seem to be so. He just looked very interested and rather sorry for me.

"I'm glad you told me that," he said gravely, "and I should like you to tell me a great deal more about it. But first of all we must tell your aunt where you are; then, perhaps, when she knows you're safe, she will let you stay a little, and we can talk. Are you on the 'phone?"

We were, and I knew the number.

"Good," said my friend. "We'll go straight back to the vicarage, ring up your aunt, and tell her all about it."

I put my small hand into his large one and we walked out of the church together. The world was radiant with song and light and colour, but I knew it must be very early morning, because the flower petals were still closed.

"Why did you come to church so early?" I asked suddenly.

"I came to say my prayers," answered the clergyman. "I often come out early, because everything looks so beautiful. Don't you think that these buttercups are enough to make anyone feel good and happy?"

I looked at the buttercups, but I did not feel happy, and I was quite certain I should never be good.

8

I MAKE A NEW FRIEND

WE went into the vicarage and he took me straight to his study; it was a big sunny room, full of books, and while I sat and rested in a big armchair he went away to telephone. He was gone a long time, and having nothing else to do I wandered round the room looking at the pictures; they were mostly photographs and not very interesting, but there was one that I liked so much that I moved my chair over in front of it so that I could gaze at it.

It was the picture of a sheep lost on a rocky mountainside. Overhead hovers a fierce bird, waiting for it to die, and the sheep looks up and cries to be rescued; someone has heard its cry, for the shepherd with his crook is leaning over the precipice; in another moment he will pick it up and carry it safe home in his arms.

I was so intent on the picture that I never noticed that the clergyman had come back; now he stood in front of me with a tray which he laid down beside me.

" I've telephoned your aunt," he said. " She's been very anxious about you, and the police and your uncle have been out looking for you all night. However, now she knows you're safe she doesn't mind your staying to breakfast with me, and afterwards you must run home and tell her how sorry you are."

63

I fell upon the tray of food with a tremendous appetite, for I had had nothing to eat since the day before; it was such a nice breakfast, too, with a boiled egg and strawberry jam and a teapot all to myself. I munched away most contentedly; he sat down on the sofa while I ate my breakfast, and we talked. I told him all about Philip and Terry, and the bird book, and the wigwam, and the camera, and the flower-selling. He asked a great many questions, and seemed really interested in it all.

But when I had finished my last mouthful of bread and jam, I realized that now I should probably be sent straight home; and I didn't want to go just yet for I thought my new friend was one of the nicest men I had ever met, except perhaps Mr. Tandy the old shepherd. So I laid down my tray and went over and sat down beside him on the sofa; once again I found myself staring at the picture on the wall.

" Isn't that a nice picture?" I remarked. " It reminds me of the shepherd at home. One of his lambs escaped, like the one in the picture, and he went to look for it. I went, too; we looked for ever so long, and then we found it all tangled up in a thorn bush, crying, and it took Mr. Tandy ages to get it out; his hands got all scratched to bits in the thorns."

My friend was looking at the picture, also; he did not answer for a minute.

" Ruth," he said suddenly, " how did the lamb get into such a place? Why did he ever get lost?"

" Well," I replied, " I suppose he ran away; they often do."

" Yes," went on the clergyman—and he was speaking very earnestly now. " But why did he run away? He had a kind shepherd and a very nice green field. Why didn't he stay there?"

"Well," I answered thoughtfully, "I expect he thought it looked nicer outside, and went to see. Then I expect he got lost, and when he wanted to go back he just couldn't find the way."

"You're quite right," said my new friend. "Just look at the lamb in the picture. I expect he had been trying to find his way back all night; but he was lost, and the farther he went, the steeper the rocks became, and the more hopeless he felt. So I think he stopped trying at last, and just stood quite still at the edge of the precipice; and what did he do then, Ruth?"

I looked up at him; I was beginning to understand that he was not talking about a real sheep any longer.

"I don't know," I whispered, rather shyly.

"Well, then, I'll tell you," went on my friend. "I think he looks round and sees a precipice underneath him, and big rocks above him, and he says to himself, 'It's no good, I can't possibly get back by myself. There's only one Person who can take me home—and that's the Shepherd.' So he opens his mouth and gives a little cry; the shepherd has been waiting all night for that little cry; directly He hears it He leans over and picks up the lamb, and carries it safe back to His own pasture—and I don't know who is the happier, the lamb or the Shepherd."

My eyes were fixed on him; I knew now that he was talking about me.

"I ran away, too, and got lost last night, didn't I?" I whispered again.

"You did," answered the clergyman, "and, do you know, when I found you hiding in the church and you told me that you'd run away and you didn't know how to be good, I thought to myself, 'Here's one of God's lost lambs trying to get back by herself'—and you'll never do it, Ruth. There's only one Person who can take you back into

God's way and keep you there, and that is the Lord Jesus Christ, who called Himself the Good Shepherd."

"Then why doesn't He do it?" I asked.

"Because you are still trying to get back without Him," came the answer. "You tell me you try to be good, but you keep being naughty instead. Well, every time you are naughty you are getting a little bit farther away from God's way, and a little bit more lost than you were before. What you've to do is to stop trying to make yourself good; you've got to tell the Shepherd that you are quite lost, and ask Him to find you and take you back into God's way, and to make you one of His own obedient lambs."

"Will He really do it?" I asked.

"Ruth," said the clergyman suddenly, "how old are you?"

"Nine," I answered, wondering what that had to do with it.

"Well then, He's been loving you and looking for you for nine whole years; don't you think He'll be glad to hear you call to Him, when He's been waiting for such a long time?"

I sat very still, thinking hard.

"Is it really all I've got to do to be good?" I asked at last. "I thought it was very difficult to be good."

"It's all you must do at first," he answered; "that's the wonderful part. You see, the Good Shepherd has done it all for you. He took away sin when He died for sinners on the Cross, so that you can be forgiven without any punishment. You told me that your friend's hands got dreadfully torn and scratched as he rescued that lamb—but he lifted the lamb out of the thorns without hurting it at all. And in just the same way the Good Shepherd was wounded and hurt when He came to look for you; He has done everything, and all you've to do is to say Thank You, and to believe that His wounded hands can lift you up and carry you back to God's fold directly you ask Him."

"And what happens then?" I asked. "Shall I always be good after that?"

He smiled.

"You won't always be good all at once," he replied, "but you will always belong to the Good Shepherd, and He will begin to teach you how to be good. He will often speak to you in your heart, and you must learn to listen to His voice; when He speaks you must always obey. And you must learn to talk to Him about everything, too; we call it praying, but really it means sharing everything with the Shepherd."

Once more we sat still for a long time. At last the clergyman spoke:

"I have to go to my church now," he said gently, "and you must go home, or your aunt will think you've run away somewhere else. But before you go I'm going to give you a copy of that picture for your very own. Take it with you and look at it often, and each time you look at it remember that you are that lost lamb and that the Good Shepherd is waiting to find you as soon as you ask Him. One other thing—have you a Bible of your own?"

I said I had a very nice Bible in my drawer at home.

"Then when you get home find the Gospel of St. Luke, and read a little bit every night. It will tell you all the story of the Shepherd and how He came to earth to look for lost sheep. And when you've finished it read the other Gospels."

He had opened a drawer and produced a postcard-size copy of the picture on the wall. I took it with shining eyes, and whispered my thanks.

I followed him out, holding my new treasure tightly in both hands; he came to the front gate and stood watching me as I set out along the road. When I had gone about a hundred yards I turned round and ran back. I stood on tip-toe and pulled his head down so that I could whisper in his ear.

"Shall I come back and tell you when it's happened?" I asked.

He nodded. "I was hoping you would," he admitted. "I shall always be glad to see you, so come whenever you like."

So I left him and turned the corner; the road ahead of me led back home, and at the thought of home my heart beat rather fast. What would my aunt and uncle say to me, and what should I say to them?

But I did not worry much, for I had more important things to think about. I would find some quiet place far away from everyone, and before I went back home I would ask the Good Shepherd to find me and make me one of His lambs.

I was very particular about the spot; the cornfields would not do, because I could be seen from the road, and I wanted to be quite alone; so I trotted on until I came to that part where the road ran between woods, and in late summer the boughs nearly met overhead; here I climbed the bank and slipped in and out among the trees till I had reached a little clearing right away from any path; here the moss grew thick on the ground and clematis hung in curtains round me; here I knelt down and felt as though I were in some secret chapel, far away from the world.

I looked again at my picture, but at first I dared not pray. I felt as if my whole life was going to depend on the next few moments. What if I spoke and nothing happened? What if the Shepherd had gone away and was not listening any more?

Then I spoke aloud to the Good Shepherd. I told Him about my naughtiness, and how I couldn't be good by myself; I told Him I was sorry because I'd kept Him waiting so long; and then I asked Him to forgive me and find me and pick me up in His arms, and never to let me run away from Him again.

Then I waited, perfectly still, for my answer, almost expecting to feel the gentle arms thrown round me: and what happened? I heard nothing, and I felt nothing, but I knew that my prayer was heard. I could not possibly have put it into words, but I knew that Love and Forgiveness were round about me as certainly as the sunlight and the quiet air—knew at that instant that I was sought and loved and found.

I was so happy that I stayed where I was for a long time, as though by moving I might break some spell; I was not only happy, I was grateful, too; I remembered how long He had waited, and I thought of Mr. Tandy's poor bleeding hands, and remembered how the hands of the Shepherd had been wounded when He died on the Cross for me. I did not understand it all, but the clergyman had said that the Bible made it very plain, and I believed him. So I folded my hands again and tried to thank Him.

Then it suddenly struck me that I was supposed to be going home; my aunt was waiting for me. So I left my little sanctuary, and went back to the road.

But I walked very slowly; would they be very angry with me? I wondered; and, worst of all, would I be naughty and rude again? My rudeness seemed to come out whether I wanted it to or not, and if I was naughty now everything would be spoilt.

Then I remembered something else; the Shepherd had picked me up in His arms, and I could tell Him everything if He was really as close to me as all that. So I told Him all about it as I trotted home, and somehow all my happiness came back to me. I was not alone any longer.

I swallowed hard as I opened the front door and slipped inside—a dirty, scared, untidy little figure clasping my hands tightly together in the hall. I had no idea what I was going to say to my aunt; only to myself I kept whispering the words, " Even if I'm punished, help me to be good."

Then my aunt suddenly appeared at the kitchen door, and we both stood looking at each other in silence.

But the loving Shepherd had found me, and when we first come to know His love He begins to make us more loving, too; as I stood stiffly in the hall something happened to my hard little heart that I had not expected. I suddenly ran forward and flung myself into my aunt's arms.

" I'm sorry, Auntie," I whispered, " I will try to be good. And please, please, don't send me to boarding school. I want to stay with you here, and I'll never, never run away or be naughty again."

My aunt, kneeling in the passage, pressed my tear-stained cheek against hers and held me close to her. Then she smoothed back my tangled hair and kissed me.

" Ruth," she whispered back, " I don't want to send you away if I can possibly help it; we'll try again."

Then she took my hand and led me to the table in the kitchen, where I sat down and ate a whole second breakfast to make up for my supper the night before.

9

MY SHEEP HEAR MY VOICE

I caught a bad cold from sleeping in the church, and had to go to bed for three days. Philip stayed with me most of the time, so we put in a lot of work on the bird book. When we were tired of drawing and writing we lay and talked. He was never tired of hearing about my night in the church, and I was enormously flattered to hear how much everybody had missed me.

"I don't think auntie or uncle went to bed all night," Philip informed me. "I couldn't go to sleep either. I thought you might be dead, and I was crying and crying in bed; then I went downstairs and I found auntie crying a little bit in the kitchen; we had a lovely drink of cocoa together, and she gave me a chocolate biscuit, and we sat by the fire and talked."

I felt rather hurt that Philip should have found such comfort in a chocolate biscuit when I might have been lying dead in a ditch.

"What did you talk about?" I said, hoping it had been about me.

"Oh, lots of things," answered my brother cheerfully. "I said perhaps you'd been drowned in Whippet brook. Auntie said she thought you were probably just hiding, and she might send you to boarding school as a punishment, and I said I thought it was a jolly bad idea."

"Why?" I enquired hopefully.

"Because I shouldn't have anyone to play with on Saturdays," he explained. "I said I thought it wouldn't be any use, because you would run away at once."

"And what did she say, then?"

"She said you wouldn't be able to. So I said it would be a pity to send you to boarding school, in any case, because I should probably have a nervous breakdown."

"Whatever's that?" I asked, with great interest.

"Oh, it's an illness you get when people do things you don't like. I heard auntie talking about someone who had a nervous breakdown because the cook went away. So I said I would have one if you went away."

"Like measles?" I asked; measles was the only illness I had ever had, and I thought it of great importance.

"Oh, I don't know," answered Philip. "I don't think it had spots, but it doesn't matter, anyhow; you're not going now, but you'll have to be awfully careful about being good, because once she's thought of it she may think of it again."

I was silent. I hadn't told anyone yet about what had happened to me in the wood, for somehow I did not know how to put it into words. How could I persuade Philip that something had really taken place? There was nothing to show for it, and sometimes, lying there with a sore throat and a stopped-up nose, I began to wonder how much of it was true, or whether perhaps I'd imagined it. And then I would take out my precious picture and look at it until my doubts disappeared, when I would bury my face in the pillow and ask the Shepherd to let me feel close to Him again, as I had felt that morning when we had walked home.

There was my Bible, too; directly I got home, I un-earthed it from the drawer and started to read it. After much searching I found the chapter Mr. Tandy had read to me about the sheep that was lost; I read it over to my-self again and again until I almost knew it by heart. I read the rest of the chapter, too, about the boy who ran away, just like me, and who came home again and said he was sorry, and was forgiven by his father. I thought it was exactly like me and Aunt Margaret; I liked it very much indeed.

I tried to pray, too; I had been taught to say my prayers, but somehow it was different now; before, it was just saying words because I thought I ought to, but now I was talking to Someone I knew and Who loved me.

It was on my second night in bed that I made a great dis-covery. Philip had gone down to supper, and I had pulled out my Bible from under my pillow, for I was rather shy of letting anyone see me read it. As I turned the pages of the Gospels, looking for stories, I came across the tenth chapter of St. John, and the word " Shepherd " caught my eye at once.

I had often heard the chapter read in church and at school, but I had forgotten whereabouts in the Bible it came. Now I read it eagerly, for it was the very thing I was hungering for. Here it was, all over again:

" I am the Good Shepherd: the Good Shepherd giveth His life for the sheep." That meant that the Shepherd had come to die on the Cross before He could find me.

I did not understand the verses about thieves and robbers, but I understood about the sheep following; that meant being good and doing what the Shepherd said—but what could it mean about ' hearing the Shepherd's voice '? The clergyman had said that Jesus would speak to me, and that I must obey, but although I had lain in bed with my eyes shut, listening hard, I could hear nothing. The room seemed perfectly silent, and I did so want the Good Shepherd to say something to me. How could I know His voice if He never spoke to me?

This question troubled me quite a lot that night and next day, until I suddenly had a good idea: I would go and see Mr. Tandy, take him my postcard and tell him all about what had happened; perhaps he would be able to tell me about the Shepherd's voice.

I was very impatient to get up after this, and was allowed to go down to tea on the fourth day. At last, on the fifth day, which to my relief was sunny, I was able to go to the woods again, with Philip. It seemed a special afternoon, with the end of the holidays so near; and I could have played for hours with the wriggling baby squirrel Philip extracted from the drey high up in the oak. But suddenly I thought of something.

"Philip," I said, "I'm going home now; you see, I specially want to visit somebody on the way back."

"All right," answered Philip contentedly. "We'll go; who do you want to visit?"

"Mr. Tandy, the shepherd," I replied.

"Good!" agreed Philip. "I like Mr. Tandy; I'll come with you."

I stopped dead, wondering how I could explain. Philip walked on, watching a magpie, unaware of any difficulty.

"Philip," I said, rather awkwardly, "you can't come with me; you see, it's a secret, and I want to see Mr. Tandy alone. It's something you don't know about, and I've got to go by myself."

It was Philip's turn to stop and stare now. He turned right round and looked as though he thought he had heard wrongly.

"But why?" he asked at last. "You always tell me your

secrets. You shouldn't tell Mr. Tandy before me; I'm your brother, and he's only an old man."

There was a sort of shadow in his clear blue eyes, and his face was rather pink. I could see he was hurt, and I felt dreadful.

" But you wouldn't understand," I explained desperately. " You see, it's not a make-up or a pretend; it's a real, true, very important secret; you might not believe me and you might laugh."

He looked not only hurt, but downright indignant.

" But I've never laughed before," he said, rather piti-fully, " and I always believe you. You're unkind, Ruth, to have real true secrets and not tell me. I always tell you mine."

There was a long pause, and I did not know what to say.

" Oh, all right," he said at last, trying to speak casually. " I'll go on home. You'll find me in the orchard when you come."

He turned and went on, and I followed rather miserably. We walked single file in silence as far as the stile where the path divided : one way led over the meadow towards home and one led up to the sheepfolds.

" Good-bye," said Philip without looking round. " See you later."

He took the downward path and I took the upward one, but I had not gone many steps before I turned to look back. Philip was walking slowly across the field with his hands in his pockets and his head rather bowed as though he were staring hard at the ground. He must have been very miserable indeed, for he was not even watching the sky for birds.

And as I stood staring after his lonely little figure, I saw all in a flash—perhaps for the first time—what sort of a brother Philip had been to me. I remembered how gravely he had listened when I used to snuggle my curly head against his shoulder and whisper my baby fancies into his ear. How patiently he had entered into my make-believes with my dolls; how swiftly he would run back from school in case I should be missing him; and how faithfully he had stood by me when I was cross and bad-tempered and punished! As I thought of all these things, I suddenly didn't want to have any secret at all that I could not share with Philip. Of course. I wanted to go on belonging to the Good Shepherd, but not by myself. Philip must belong, too, and then we could enjoy the secret together.

I flew down the hill after him as fast as my legs would carry me, shouting his name at the top of my voice. He turned round and waited for me, and even as I ran I could not help thinking how much nicer he was than I; I should have walked on in a huff and pretended not to hear.

I was quite breathless when I reached him, and sort of fell against him to stop myself.

" Philip " I gasped. " I didn't mean it at all. I don't want to have secrets without you, and I'll tell you everything always, only you see there's a bit I don't understand and I can't tell you properly until I've asked Mr. Tandy; but then I shall know all about it and I'll tell you in the wigwam tomorrow and then you can have it, too."

The shadow passed instantly from Philip's eyes, and his beautiful smile shone out again. There never was a boy so quick to forgive and forget a quarrel.

" It's all right," he assured me. " I don't mind you going to tell Mr. Tandy, as long as you tell me afterwards. But it will spoil everything if we don't tell each other *all* our secrets."

I was so pleased to see him happy again that I flung my

arms round his neck and kissed him. I had not done such a thing for a long time, and he looked a little breathless and astonished, and glanced round the field to see that no one was looking. Then he wiped off the kiss with his sleeve, because it was rather a wet one, gave me another radiant smile, and trotted off towards home.

I turned and ran back up the hill, but when I had gone half-way up I turned to look at Philip. He was still trotting, but his head was thrown far back; he had forgotten all about everything and was watching swifts.

I was very red in the face when I reached the sheepfolds, because I had climbed the hill so fast. To my great relief Mr. Tandy was there mending the gate, and I ran straight up to him.

"Mr. Tandy," I said, without waiting for any introductions, "I've come to tell you something. I've found out all about that story you read me, and I know now that it means me, and that the Good Shepherd means Jesus."

He stood there with his hammer in his hand, looking down at me, with a look of the most amazing joy on his face.

"I'm real glad to hear it, little maid," he said, rather huskily. "Maybe you'll tell me a bit more about it."

"Oh, yes," I replied, pulling him down beside me on the seat and I told him everything—about running away, and Mr. Robinson and the picture and me belonging to the Shepherd.

Mr. Tandy listened gravely, but his wrinkled old face was alight with happiness.

"Thank God for that, little maid!" he replied, "for if you belong to Him now, you'll belong to Him for ever. No man can pluck you out of His hand."

"Mr. Tandy," I asked, "are you one of His sheep?"

"Sure, little maid," he answered, "I've been one of His flock wellnigh fifty years."

"Then, Mr. Tandy," I went on eagerly, "have you ever heard His voice? It says His sheep hear His voice, but I've listened and listened, and He never says anything to me, and I do want to hear Him so badly."

He thought a long time before answering that question. Then he spoke very slowly.

"I'm going to call my sheep, lassie," he said. "And when I call, take a look at 'em all, but you specially mark them ones over by the hedge, and see the difference."

I watched fascinated while he gave a low, clear call; every sheep in the meadow lifted its head expectantly and drew a step or two nearer, except for the group by the hedge. They went on feeding quietly as though nothing had happened.

"Why don't they answer?" I asked. "Can't they hear you?"

"They hears me well enough," answered the old man, "but they don't know my voice from all the others because they belonged to another shepherd who was took sick; they only joined my flock two days gone. But let 'em walk to the pastures with me for a week or so, and let me fold 'em, and put my hands on their heads, and feed 'em, and they'll soon come to know my voice same as the rest. Now there's a-many voices speaking to your heart, little maid, and you've only belonged to the Shepherd these few days, so maybe you haven't learned to pick out His voice from all them others—for 'tis only a still, small voice."

"Then tell me how I can start," I pleaded.

"Well, 'tis like this," he said at last, after another long pause, "do you ever want to be a bad little lass?"

"Oh yes, often," I replied. "Before I ran away, I used to lose my temper and be rude to Aunt Margaret nearly every day."

" Well then," went on Mr. Tandy, " you mind this : next time you want to lose your temper, you remember there's two voices a-speaking to you. There's the voice of the enemy bidding you kick up a row and stamp your foot and all the rest of it, but if you hold back a minute and listen, maybe you'll hear another voice—a little quiet-like voice—bidding you be gentle and do as you're told, and that's the voice of the Shepherd. And if you learn to mind that voice, He'll speak again, and you'll find you're hearing Him all the time and everywhere. He talks to me out in these fields, and when I reads my Bible He comes to me, and I know it ain't just a book of black and white print for scholars, but 'tis the voice of my Saviour a-speaking to me."

Drawn by his gentle voice, the sheep had come quite close and were standing near his knees, their mild faces upturned; when he stopped speaking they moved away, cropping the grass.

" 'Twill soon be time for the shearing," observed the old man thoughtfully.

I rose to my feet and held out my hand. " Thank you very much, Mr. Tandy," I said. " I'm going home now to listen, and I hope I shall soon want to get into a temper."

He shook his head. " Don't you wish any such thing!" he warned me. " And don't you try it alone. Remember, it is only the Saviour Who can stop you from doing wrong."

He spoke very earnestly, and I thought about it a lot as I ran home across the fields. How queer it was that I couldn't ever stop myself from losing my own temper! Yet I knew I couldn't, because I'd tried.

Philip was not in the orchard, so I went to look for him indoors; rather to my dismay I heard voices in the dining-room. They had started high tea, and I was late; we were not allowed to be late for tea, so I stepped into the room rather guiltily and made for my seat with an anxious glance at Aunt Margaret. She was looking extremely grim.

"Ruth," she said sharply, "you're late again and I'm not going to have it. Sit down and eat your tea in silence—and you are not to have a chocolate biscuit."

Now this was a dreadful punishment, because I loved chocolate biscuits, and we hardly ever had them. I gave a little stamp with my foot and threw back my head. All my happiness disappeared and a great torrent of angry words seemed to come springing up out of my heart all ready to tumble out of my mouth. In fact, I had actually opened my mouth, when I suddenly remembered!

If I got in a rage now I shouldn't be able to listen to the little quiet voice of the Good Shepherd; and if I didn't listen now perhaps He wouldn't speak to me again.

It was so difficult to stop those angry words that I had to clap my hand in front of my mouth to keep them in. And so I stood in the middle of the room, listening, while my aunt and Philip stared at me in the greatest astonishment.

"What is the matter?" asked my aunt, coldly. "Have you bitten your tongue?"

I didn't answer, because it had suddenly come back to me —the verse that Mr. Tandy and I had been talking about— "My sheep hear My voice, and I know them, and they follow Me." Following the Shepherd meant being like Him: if I was going to be like Him I must stop stamping, shouting, answering back and sulking, because the Lord had never done any of these things. "Help me to follow You," I whispered in my heart; "stop me being angry, quick."

I drew a great big breath and put my hand back in my pocket; then I sat down in my chair without saying anything, for my anger was all going away. Auntie still continued to stare at me, as though she was rather scared as to what might happen next, but I went on munching my bread and butter in silence. I did not look at the chocolate biscuits, because I was afraid the sight of them might make me angry again.

We were all very quiet for the rest of tea, and when it was finished Aunt Margaret said that, as it was my first day up after my cold, I had better go straight to bed; I did not mind at all, for I had such a lot to think about that I wanted to be alone. I got in as soon as possible, and lay by my open window staring out at the summer dusk.

The sky was the colour of deep harebells, and when I'd stared at it a long time I suddenly discovered that there were stars hidden in its blue depths. I lay with my arms thrown above my head on the pillow, looking and listening, till I fell asleep. I was perfectly happy, because for the very first time, I had heard the voice of the Good Shepherd.

10

THE ACCIDENT

WE meant to go straight to the wigwam next day, and talk about the secret, but just as we climbed over the stile Terry popped up out of the ditch like a rabbit and said he'd come to spend the morning with us; he had hidden in the ditch to give us a surprise, so having been duly surprised we all settled down on the bank to make plans.

As a matter of fact Terry had already made all the plans, and we were merely meant to follow them. He had found a high ash tree with a wood-pigeon's nest at the top, and if Philip wanted to see a wood-pigeon's egg he'd better come along right now because there were two beauties. It was an ash tree with a fork; Terry's plan was to collect some branches and bits of wood and make a sort of platform opposite where we could sit and watch the eggs hatch.

We were thrilled with the idea, and went scuttling off single-file through the wood; the tree in question was quite a long way away, across the stream in the valley, and some way in among the larches that grew on the farther side. The larches were beautiful by now. studded all over with crimson baby cones, like jewels on a coronet, the sweeping boughs such a vivid green that other trees looked dull in comparison. When I was tiny I always imagined that the fairies swung on the larch boughs, but now I knew better; yet I still loved them and I lingered behind for a moment to finger the tassels while the boys went crashing on ahead. The tree was well off the beaten track, and the brambles and nettles grew thick hereabouts. I followed in their path as best I could, but even so my bare legs got dreadfully scratched, and were the colour of unripe blackberries when I finally caught up. I sat down on the tree root and began mopping up the scratches with my handkerchief.

"Sorry," said Philip, apologetically. "I fogot your legs were shorter than ours for jumping; you keep up on the way home and I'll tread the brambles down for you."

Terry stared at my damaged knees. "She's a game little kid, ain't she?" he observed, and I glowed with his praise. I would willingly have walked through brambles and nettles to have earned such praise.

Terry had no time to waste; he crouched like a small panther and then leaped for the nearest bough of the ash. He caught hold with one hand and dragged himself up, the muscles rippling all over his taut little body.

"Now," he yelled, lying astride the bough, "hoist up Ruth, and I'll catch hold!" Philip heaved me up on his shoulders and Terry seized my wrists and pulled until I was able to clutch the bough; I gave a convulsive wriggle, more or less turned myself inside out, and arrived panting beside Terry. Philip gave two mighty leaps, but fell backwards. On the third he caught hold of the branch and dragged himself up too. So we sat dangling our legs, like three happy monkeys, and we shared our elevenses with Terry, who always took it for granted that my aunt included him in the housekeeping, and always ate much more than his share; but we gave it ungrudgingly for we had long ago decided that Terry's mother must have starved him at home, as no one but a starving child could eat so wolfishly.

"Come on," said Terry, gulping down the last mouthful, "we'll nip up and take a look at her."

Off he went like a sailor on a rope, while Philip and I followed more slowly. The nest was on a sort of platform of interwoven twigs, and as we got nearer to it we could hear the nervous murmur of the pigeon deep in her throat; then suddenly there was a whirr of beautiful pearl-grey wings and the bird rose and settled on the very topmost twig of the opposite fork, where she sat looking down at us and her nest.

It was such a careless nest that I wondered how it was that the eggs escaped rolling out; just a few loosely-woven sticks with some moss stuffed in the holes. But the eggs were burning hot and well cared-for, and the mother was in a frenzy of anxiety. Terry leaned back and stared at her.

"Nice spot to watch them eggs from," he remarked cooly. "I'm a-going up there myself."

"You couldn't!" protested Philip. "The branches wouldn't bear you; why, they'll hardly bear the pigeon."

But Terry was rather a boastful little boy. If anyone ever said "you couldn't do" a thing, he immediately had to do it to show that he could. So now he merely said, "Garn, I'll show you," and swung himself across to the opposite fork.

Philip and I watched in fascinated silence, as the thin, agile little figure mounted higher and higher. The pigeon saw him coming, rose softly, and alighted back with half-spread wings on to her nest; we had no eye for anyone but Terry. We had seen him do such daring and almost impossible feats before, but this beat all; already the grey stems were bending outwards beneath his weight.

"Stop!" called Philip in a rather husky voice; but Terry

took no notice; instead, his gay laugh came ringing back to us through the leaves, and still he climbed—only he was climbing very cautiously now.

"He's got there!" breathed Philip, and indeed he had. He was standing out right against the sky, clinging to a frail branch. The wind that moved lazily over the tree-tops had caught his hair and blown it back from his face, and his dark starry eyes were alight with laughter and triumph.

As we watched, Terry, ignoring our frightened plead-ings, began to swing to and fro; twice the branch bowed with him, but the third time it snapped. Terry was flung outward into space.

He gave one shrill scream that shattered the silence of the summer woods, and haunted me in the night for many weeks to come. Then we heard his light body crashing through the leaves and twigs, which mercifully partly broke his fall; then came a sickening thud—and then silence.

I don't know to this day how Philip and I escaped falling after him and breaking our necks—we swung down that tree at such a speed. Even so, Philip reached the bottom long before I did, but I got there somehow, and dropped on to the ground gasping and sobbing, and lay in a trembling heap with my face hidden in the moss. I dared not look at Terry.

But Philip was down on his knees beside him, and had come to the conclusion that Terry was still breathing. He came over to me at last and put his arm around me.

"Ruth," he said, in a voice that was shaky and fearful, "I'm not quite sure, but I think he's alive. We can't pos-sibly carry him; we shall have to fetch some men and a doctor, and I think I'd better go, because I can run faster than you and I'm not crying so much. But, Ruth, we can't leave him alone, because he might wake up and be frightened and want someone; so would you mind staying with him, and I'll come back as quick as I can?"

I shuddered and shook my head violently; I couldn't be left alone—I was much too frightened; I clung to him sobbing, and begged him to let me go instead; but Philip wouldn't hear of it.

"You see, Ruth," he explained urgently, "he may die very soon, and if the doctor came in time he may be able to do something to make him better; I shall get there much quicker because of my legs being so much longer. You must let me go at once, and try and be brave and stop crying."

He freed himself from my grasp, gently enough, and made off like the wind. I lay and listened to his footsteps crackling over the dead leaves and twigs, until the sound died away and only the murmuring of the pigeons broke the silence of the woods.

Now that I was left alone it occurred to me that I must make myself look at Terry. So I clenched my teeth and my fists, and sat up.

What I actually saw was a great relief to me. I had never seen anyone badly hurt or unconscious before, and I had imagined that it would be a very horrid sight; but Terry, lying on his back with his arms spread wide, might have been asleep, except that his lips were unnaturally pale, and he breathed so lightly. He did not look hurt or frightened —only curiously peaceful, and as I sat there staring at him I began to feel curiously peaceful myself—as though he must soon wake up refreshed by such deep sleep and we should all be happy again.

The minutes seemed like hours and Terry did not stir; still I sat watching and wondering. Perhaps Terry was already dead—the thought made me feel cold and sick, and once again my eyes filled with frightened tears. If only

Philip would come back! What was death, in any case? And if Terry were dead, where had he gone? We should bury his quiet little body under the ground in the church-yard, but I knew that that was not really Terry—Terry, I supposed, had gone to Heaven, like we sang about in hymns in church; but would Terry be happy? One grubby, rather naughty little boy, amongst all those golden streets and white wings!

Then I suddenly remembered Jane Collins, who had gone 'to be with the Lord'—and the radiant face of the child in my dream. Perhaps dying just meant going to live with the Shepherd—hearing Him speak with our proper ears and seeing Him with real eyes, instead of just inside our hearts—that would be lovely, I thought; no wonder the little girl had looked so happy; and perhaps that was why Terry looked so peaceful.

But Terry did not know about the Good Shepherd, so perhaps he might not be so pleased to go and live with Him. I was sure Terry had never heard anything about it; if only I'd had a chance to tell him! If he didn't die I should tell him at once, and then Philip and he and I would all belong together. But anyhow, even if he were dead, I was sure that the Good Shepherd would see that he was happy. Because, after all, it wasn't Terry's fault that he had never asked to be found and forgiven—it was really mine, because I had kept the secret to myself instead of sharing it.

So I sat hugging my knees, with my eyes fixed on Terry's still face, torn between hope and fear; every few minutes I thought I heard Philip coming back, but each time it turned out to be only a rabbit, or a bird, or a gust of wind in the trees; the sunshine streamed through the thin vivid foliage of the larches and rested in a bright patch on Terry's hair; almost as though God were touching him, I thought to myself; and I remembered how in the Gospel of St. Luke, which I read every morning, the Saviour had touched men and women and children who were hurt and ill, and they always got well again at once.

" O God," I whispered, looking up through the branches, " please make Terry better—don't let him die— we want him here so much. Amen."

It was then that I heard Philip's voice through the trees and some men's voices talking too; a moment later a little procession came into sight with Philip leading the way; behind him came Uncle Peter, who was always at home on Saturdays, and kind Doctor Paterson who had come to see me when I had measles; behind them came two men in a dark uniform carrying a stretcher; I heard later that these were the ambulance men.

Dr. Paterson knelt down at once and put his fingers on Terry's brown wrist; he held it for a long time and then passed his hands over Terry's head, drew back his eyelids, and bent his legs and arms backwards and forwards very gently. Then he turned to me:

" Has the boy moved since he fell?" he asked.

" No," I answered, " he's been as though he was fast asleep all the time." Then, emboldened by the sound of my own voice, I gave his coat a little tug. " Is he dead?" I whispered.

Dr. Paterson put his arm round my shoulder. " No," he answered gently, " he's not dead, but he's very badly hurt; you were a good girl to stay here alone and look after him; now we'll take him along to the hospital as soon as we can, and I'm going to see what I can do for him."

Very gently and carefully Terry was lifted on to the stretcher, and the men set off through the brambles with the precious burden between them. Uncle Peter, seeing how white and scared I looked, stooped down and picked me up in his arms like a baby; I snuggled up against him, and laid my throbbing head on his shoulder, and felt greatly comforted. I had always been good friends with Uncle Peter.

But I noticed Philip's face only when he glanced towards me, for he had walked with his head turned sideways; he said nothing, but his lips were pressed tightly together and his eyes were desperate—they reminded me of the eyes of a rabbit I had once found caught in a trap—his cheeks high up were scarlet, but the rest of his face was quite white; in that moment I realized that all my uncertain fears were nothing to Philip's steady misery. I longed to run and comfort him, but knew that there was nothing I could say or do; nothing would comfort him except Terry getting well.

We all walked very slowly so as not to jolt the stretcher, for the ground was rough and uneven. We took a narrow, overgrown path which led on to the road, and the hazel bushes brushed my face as I lay in Uncle Peter's arms; the ambulance was waiting there, and Dr. Paterson climbed in with Terry while the men sat in front.

"When will you tell us if he's better?" I asked, just as he was about to shut the door.

"I shall be passing your house tomorrow," said the doctor "and I'll drop in and let you know."

The door was shut and the engine started up; the ambulance sped off in a cloud of white dust, and Uncle Peter, Philip and I were left to trudge home. Uncle asked us a few questions about Terry on the way, but otherwise we were very silent; nobody felt like talking.

It was a long, wretched day; we hung about the garden unable to settle down to anything, and with no appetite for our meals. Aunt Margaret felt sorry for us and read aloud to us after tea, but we were both glad when bedtime arrived. She came upstairs and kissed us Good night, but as soon as her footsteps had died away I hopped out of bed and ran over to Philip; he was lying huddled up in bed, and I think he had been crying, for his voice sounded sniffy and his pillow was damp. I got under the rug at the bottom and curled myself up in a ball like a kitten.

"Ruth," whispered Philip, rather shakily, "do you think he'll die?"

"No," I answered decidedly, "I don't."

"Why not?" enquired Philip, rather surprised at my being so sure of myself. "Did Dr. Paterson say anything to you when I wasn't listening?"

I wriggled my bare toes up and down under the rug, as I always did when I was shy. It was difficult to explain, but I thought now was the moment to try and tell.

"Well, you see," I answered, "when you'd gone to get the others, I prayed to God very hard that Terry would get better again, so I expect he will."

Philip stared at me over the top of the sheet.

"So did I," he admitted, slowly. "I said, 'O God, please don't let Terry die', all the way home, but I don't know whether it was much use; I'm not a very good boy and I usually forget to say my prayers altogether, and nothing much happens when I do."

"But Philip," I said, uncurling myself, and sitting up straight, because I was so very much in earnest, "you don't have to be a specially good person to say your prayers; you just have to belong to the Shepherd. That's what my secret was, that I was going to tell you about today. I didn't make it up; the clergyman told me when I ran away, and it's in the Bible too. When we're naughty we're like sheep that run away and get lost, and can't find the way back. But Jesus is the Shepherd; He comes to look for us, and when we ask Him He finds us—but He always waits till we ask. Then we belong to Him and He listens to everything we say, and He speaks to us back and tells us how to be good. Mr. Tandy told me that bit, and He spoke to me last night and stopped me from losing my temper with Aunt Margaret, when she wouldn't let me have a chocolate biscuit."

I could see Philip staring at me, his face pale in the moonlight. " Go on," he said.

" There's not much more to say," I continued, " except that when Terry was lying on the ground the sun suddenly shone through the trees right on to his hair, and I thought perhaps it was God's way of touching him and making him better, like Jesus touched people in the Bible. And after that I was almost sure he wasn't going to die."

There was a long silence, broken at last by Philip.

" Did you ask Him to find you?" he asked, curiously.

I nodded. " I did it on the way home," I said, " in the primrose woods, under a tree. I asked Him to forgive me for being naughty, and to find me and make me one of His lambs as the clergyman said—and oh, Philip, I wish you would come with me and see that clergyman, because he'd tell you about it much better than me, and I do so want you to belong to the Shepherd, too."

" I wish I did," said Philip in a small sober voice. " Do you think I could?"

" I'm sure you could," I answered, very decidedly. " I should think you'd be much easier to find than me because you're so much gooder—I don't think you'd take much finding at all."

But Philip shook his head. " You don't know," he said sadly. " You only see me outside. I'm not at all good inside."

" Well," I argued, " it doesn't matter. I'll show you my picture and you'll see; the sheep there is nearly falling over a precipice, he's got so lost, but the Shepherd is just going to find him all the same."

I tiptoed across the passage and returned with my precious picture in my hand. We both went over to the window, and could see it quite clearly because the full moon was shining right in at the window. Philip went on looking at it for a long time.

"Could I ask now, Ruth?" he said at last, rather anxiously.

I nodded.

"Then you must go away," he explained, "because I shall have to be alone—we'll talk more about it in the morning."

So I left him, with his elbows on the window-sill, looking at the hills. I snuggled into bed and stared up sleepily at the millions of stars, and thought of my story.

11

A VISIT TO THE VICARAGE

THE rest of the holidays passed all too quickly because there was so much to do. The doctor came to see us next day, and as soon as we heard his car stop we flung ourselves out of the gate, and nearly knocked him backwards in our eagerness to hear the news.

"Steady, steady!" exclaimed Dr. Paterson, collaring us both. "If you knock me out I shan't be able to tell you anything."

Terry was alive, he told us, but he had hurt his back and head very bady indeed, and would be in hospital many weeks; his mother was with him nearly all the time now, but as soon as he was a little better he should probably be moved to another hospital—a special hospital for people with broken bones. We could not go and visit him because it was too far away, but we should probably be able to write to him in a few weeks' time.

This was quite enough to calm our fears and make us happy again. Terry was alive and being looked after; he would certainly get better soon, we told ourselves, just as we had always got better in time from measles and colds and tummy-aches. So we stopped worrying, and settled down to enjoy the last few days of the holidays as much as we could.

We decided that we must pay one last visit to each of our friends, So Philip went to call on the birdman, and was taken down to see a moorhen's nest, and I paid a visit to Mr. Tandy in the sheepfolds. But there wasn't much time for conversation, because Mr. Tandy was busy shearing.

The last day of all we set apart for visiting the clergyman, and we set out about half-past three, because I'm afraid we thought it would be rather nice to arrive about tea-time.

The village lay at the bottom of the hill, and we marched in at the vicarage gate very sure of a welcome. We did not have to walk far, for my friend was in his shirt sleeves mowing the lawn, and recognized me at once. He seemed delighted to see us both. He did not even ask us if we would stay to tea; he simply said; "You've both arrived just at the right moment." It certainly seemed as though we had, for no sooner had I introduced Philip, than Mrs. Robinson, the clergyman's wife, appeared on the lawn with a tea-tray. From the way Mr. Robinson rushed indoors and fetched jam tarts and chocolate spread, you might almost have thought that we were expected!

We had a lovely tea. Mr. and Mrs. Robinson sat in deckchairs and we sat on a rug and ate a tremendous lot and then we both told Mr. Robinson all about our special secret. He was so pleased—his face just looked like Mr. Tandy's when I told him, and he began to talk to us about reading our Bible.

"We'll do it together," I said eagerly; "Shan't we, Philip?" but before he could answer Mrs. Robinson appeared at the window, wearing a flannel apron. "Twins' bedtime, Ruth," she called. "Do you want to come and watch?" I jumped up. "Will you excuse me, please, Mr.

Robinson?" I enquired, a little anxiously, for I did not wish him to think me rude.

"Certainly," he replied. "You go and help Mother: she'll be glad of a nursemaid; Philip and I will stay here a little longer, and do some more talking."

I sped across the lawn, and into the vicarage. The twins were crawling about on the carpet while their mother collected their night things; they were ten months old and very lively, and I, who had never had anything to do with babies, thought I had never seen anything to equal them.

I spent a glorious half-hour; once they were safely in the big bath, Mrs. Robinson let me soap their plump little bodies and then pour the water all over them; then we sailed a yellow sponge duck, and the twins screamed with laughter and beat the water with their fat hands. I was allowed to sprinkle sweet smelling powder into their folds and creases, and when they were safely in their nightgowns I was given a soft little hairbrush with which I brushed their hair up on end. It was not proper hair at all; it was more like yellow chicken-down that rolled itself into sausage-curls down the middle of their heads; and all the time I was doing it they wriggled, and chuckled, and tried to bite their ten toes.

It was not till their mother was tucking them firmly into their cots that I noticed the picture that hung on the wall behind them; it was another picture of the Good Shepherd —but it was different from mine. This Shepherd was standing by a lake, with His hand stretched out to bless the little lambs that stood beside Him and lay asleep at His feet.

It was an evening picture, and it reminded me of the lambs in Mr. Tandy's sheepfold, when the sun sank behind the bluebell woods and the shadows crept up the fields.

"Why," I cried joyfully, pointing up at it. "I've got a

Good Shepherd picture, too, but it's not like that—my sheep is on a precipice."

"I know your picture," answered Mrs. Robinson, " and I love it very much, and later I shall show it to the twins; but they are not old enough to understand anything about precipices yet. I like to think that all through the night, when I'm asleep, the Good Shepherd is looking after my babies for me; so I put that picture there to remind me, and whenever I look at it I remember they are perfectly safe."

I stared at the twins. They had both fallen asleep instantly; Janet had curled herself up and had stuffed two fingers into her mouth; Robin lay on his back with his arms thrown out on the pillow, his cheeks flushed with the warmth of sudden deep sleep.

I nestled up to Mrs. Robinson and looked up into her face. " Can I come again?" I whispered.

"Of course you can," she replied. " You can come on Saturday week if your aunt will let you—I'll write and ask her. I expect you have a holiday on Saturday; we'll take them out in the pram, and then you shall help me give them their supper and put them to bed. It's a great treat for me to have a nurse, and I can see that you're handy with babies."

I blushed with pride and slipped my hand into hers. I couldn't exactly have Mrs. Robinson for my mother, but perhaps in time I might become a sort of elder sister to the twins.

On returning to the garden I found Mr. Robinson and Philip deep in conversation. I was eager to get back and ask my aunt about Saturday week, and my delight was doubled when the Vicar said that Philip might come, too, and help him in the garden, and we'd all have tea together. Saturday

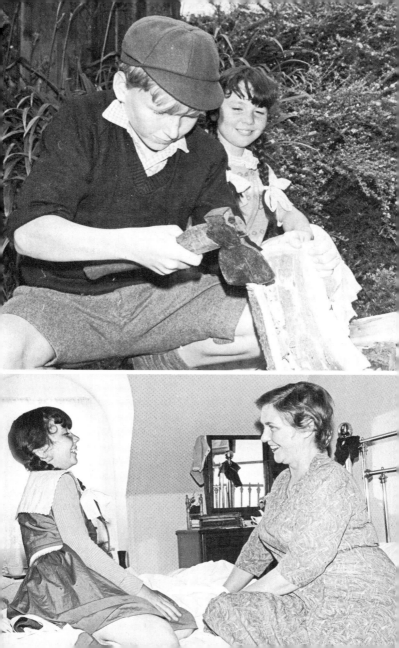

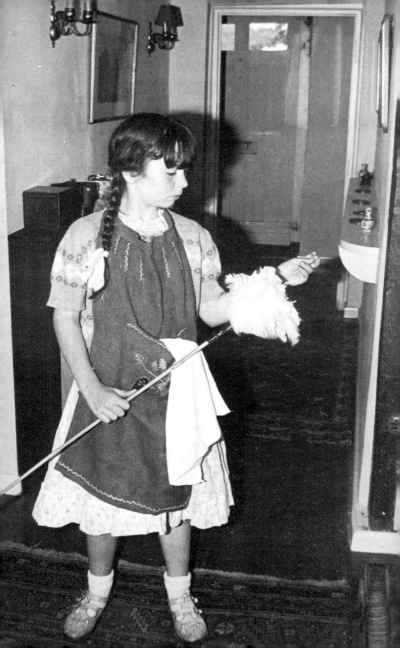

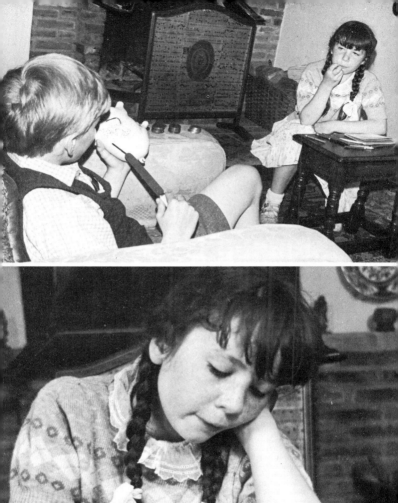

afternoon was Mr. Robinson's weekly holiday and we should always find him at home.

We got back in good time for supper, and I ran straight off to my aunt.

"Auntie," I cried, hopping about on one foot, "Mrs. Robinson has invited me to tea with her on Saturday week —her and the babies—and I can push the pram and put them to bed. I can go, can't I? Do say Yes!"

My aunt looked rather annoyed.

"Who is this Mrs. Robinson, Ruth?" she asked, rather coldly. "You are not to visit people without consulting me; I have never heard of the lady."

"Oh, she's quite all right, Auntie," I assured her, anxiously. "She's a very nice lady indeed, a clergyman's wife at Fairways; she's going to write to you."

"I should hope so," retorted my aunt, "but I'm afraid the answer will have to be No this time, because Miss Montgomery called this afternoon to say that her little niece was coming to stay, and I said that you would go and play with her that afternoon. I'm sorry you should be disappointed, but perhaps this Mrs. Robinson will invite you another day. If she is really the wife of the Vicar of Fairways, I have no objection to your accepting; I have heard they are very nice people."

I flew into a rage at once.

"But Auntie," I stormed, "you know that I *hate* going to tea with Miss Montgomery; and I *hate* Juliana Montgomery—she's like a little white mouse. She doesn't know how to play anything nice, and we have to sit indoors and play dominoes, and I *hate* dominoes. Oh, *please*, Auntie, say I needn't go—I told Mrs. Robinson I could come!"

"Then you had no business to tell Mrs. Robinson," replied my aunt, sharply. "I never heard such nonsense!

You are never to accept invitations without my permission —and stand still while you talk; you are making me quite dizzy."

But I had thoroughly lost my temper by this time, and was nearly crying with disappointment.

"I won't go!" I shouted, "I shall go where I like—I told Mrs. Robinson I'd come, and I shall jolly well go, and you shan't stop me!"

My aunt took hold of my arm.

"Go straight to bed," she said, firmly. "Don't let me hear any more of this rudeness; I thought you were going to try and improve, but this does not look like improvement at all—off you go!"

I shook myself free and marched off with my head in the air.

"I don't care," I muttered over my shoulder—and slammed the door behind me as hard as I could.

But I *did* care—very much indeed! Almost before I'd reached the top of the stairs, I'd realized what I'd done, and by the time I crept into bed I thought my heart was breaking. I curled up in a ball, buried my face in the pillow, and wept and wept.

I had forgotten to listen to the voice of the Good Shepherd. Perhaps He would never speak to me again; perhaps He would stop loving me. Perhaps I should even stop belonging to Him, and then there would be no one to help me to be good. Oh, why hadn't I waited and listened?

"Ruth, what *is* the matter? You mustn't cry like this!"

I had been sobbing so bitterly that I never heard my aunt come in; I turned around quickly and swallowed down my tears, for I did not really want her to see how sorry I was; she was sitting by my bed, and she had a glass of milk and a plate of biscuits in her hand.

"What is the matter, Ruth?" she asked again, and her

voice was rather anxious, for she had never seen me cry like that before.

I tried to answer in my ordinary voice, but could not manage it; I buried my head afresh in the pillow and began crying again.

I did not want to tell her, but it suddenly occurred to me that she might be able to answer my questions, and I wanted to know the answer so badly that I blurted it all out.

"It's the Shepherd," I sobbed. "I lost my temper and perhaps I shan't belong to Him any more. Oh, Auntie, do you think I shall be able to come back to Him, if I'm good next time?"

I lifted my face in my eagerness to hear her answer, but she was staring at me as if I had lost my senses.

"What *are* you talking about, Ruth?" she asked, helplessly.

I dived for the chair and found my picture in my Bible: I pulled it out, and held it in front of her with a great sniff and a gulp.

"That," I answered. "You see I was His sheep, but I forgot to listen, and perhaps He'll never speak to me again, because I lost my temper so badly. Do you think, Auntie, He'd forgive me just this once?"

My aunt was staring very hard at the picture, and she didn't speak for a long time.

"Who gave you this picture, Ruth?" she asked at last.

"Mr. Robinson," I replied, "and he told me all about it —you know the story, don't you, Auntie? Do you think He will, Auntie, if I never, never do it again?"

She was still staring at the picture and the answer was a long time in coming.

"Auntie," I whispered impatiently, giving her arm a little shake, "do you think He might?"

"If you are really sorry for being naughty, and are determined to try and be different, I am quite sure God will forgive you. You had better ask Him."

My aunt stayed with me while I ate, but we said very little. When I had finished, she kissed me Good night and left me very drowsy and quite comforted; but before I fell asleep I buried my face in the pillow again, and breathed out a prayer for forgiveness to the One who stood close beside me, and who cared equally for lost lambs, fallen sparrows, sleeping babies, and bad little girls.

12

WE GET A LETTER

THE summer term sped by. Philip went mad over cricket and we spent long happy evenings on the Common bowling overs to each other. Philip's school was a good way off and he had no friends from our part of the district—while I never wanted to have anything to do with other girls when Philip was about.

The baby birds we had watched and loved were all fledged and out in the world by now, and the nests deserted; but early in the mornings we often climbed the hills to watch the larks spring up from the bracken and soar singing up into the sunrise. Then we would race home to breakfast, leaping over the rocks and gorse bushes, shouting to each other as we ran, so that the mountain sheep fled away from in front of us and the ravine between the hills echoed with the sound of our voices.

The summer holidays had come round again before we heard from Terry. All the summer he had been in a children's hospital in Birmingham, and from time to time we got news of him from Dr. Paterson. We wrote to him quite a lot and told him all about the woods, what flowers were coming out, and what birds we had seen, but he never answered. So it was a great surprise when the postman, meeting us at the gate one morning, handed us a letter addressed to us.

Nobody but Father or Mother ever wrote to us, and this was certainly not their writing. It was larger, and shaky, and looked as though the writer was not very used to writing letters at all.

"Dear Filip and Ruth," it ran, I am come home but I has to stop in bed. Please come and see me from Terry my adress is Willow Cottage, The Hollow, Tanglewoods."

We were so impatient to start that we could scarcely eat our dinner, and we talked about it all the time. My aunt seemed slightly doubtful when we showed her the note, but said we could go all the same.

"I only hope it's a clean cottage, and that you won't catch anything. Don't stay too long, will you?"

Directly dinner was over we raced to our rooms to hunt in our drawers, for we wanted to take Terry a present. I found a bar of chocolate and Philip found a catapult, so we wrapped them up in separate parcels and put them in our pockets. Then we hurled ourselves out of the front door and set off for Tanglewoods. Tanglewoods was such a little village that it was really quite difficult to tell when you got there. There was a public house called the Goat and Compasses. A long way farther down the road was a shop which sold groceries and candles and cattle food and medicine and cough-mixtures, and had a Post Office in one corner. Farther on still was a tiny church with some old tombstones falling backwards. But none of these by themselves could be called the village, for the real Tanglewoods consisted of scattered farms and cottages resting on the flanks of the low hills, and of barns and outhouses hidden among the hop-yards. No one knew where Tanglewoods started, and no one knew where it ended, so Terry's address took us some time to trace.

We came through the woods, and down over the ridge where swathes of hay from the late second mowing lay in tidy rows up the meadows. The view in front reminded us of a patchwork quilt, with its dark green hop-yards, golden corn-fields ripe for the sickle, and its pink stretches where willowherb grew in a rosy harvest; everywhere we looked we saw risings and hollows and little hills and valleys, and we stood for a while trying to guess in which particular hollow Terry lived.

There was no one in sight, and we made for the nearest farm to ask the way. We found a woman churning in a cool stone dairy. She came to the door, and pointed farther down the valley.

"You'll be meaning that tumbledown place down Sheep's Hollow; there's a gipsy sort of woman lives there with a boy—she's been up begging a deal of times. Follow the track down through the gorse bushes, and then follow the brook—it leads right down into the hollow."

We thanked her and passed on, and she stood staring after us curiously as though she would have liked to know our business at Willow Cottage. But we did not want to be hindered, and we hurried down the hill as fast as we could until we could see the cottage in the hollow lying just below us, with its broken chimney-pot and the holes in the roof where slates had blown off.

It was a dark little hollow that had once been part of a quarry, although the clematis had covered up the bare rocks and made a green curtain round its sides; the stream trickled through it in a stagnant, slimy ooze, and we wondered why anyone should have chosen to build a cottage in such a damp, cheerless spot, when there was all the open hillside to choose from. But we learned later from Terry that it had been built as a hut for storing dynamite for the quarry, and only later made into a house.

It looked so desolate and deserted, with its broken windows stuffed with rag and the nettles growing round the door, that we hung back half-frightened. Surely Terry couldn't live here! But even as we stood hesitating at the entrance of the hollow, the door opened and a woman appeared and stood staring back at us.

She was a big, powerful woman with dark skin and black, untidy hair gathered back in her handkerchief; her face was hard and unhappy and she looked at us as if she disliked us.

Nobody spoke for a moment or two—then the woman broke the silence.

" Well," she asked, " What be you kids a-wanting here?"

We came forward slowly.

" Please," explained Philip, " Terry wrote us a letter to come and see him, so we came. Please, we're so glad that he's well enough to come home."

The woman's face did not clear.

" Be you the children as was with my Terry when he fell?" she asked, suspiciously.

" Yes," we answered, rather guiltily.

" You didn't ought to have let him done it," she muttered. " Still, he's been carrying on something awful about you two coming to see 'im, so you'd best come in."

She jerked the door back roughly and led the way inside; we followed, but I slipped my hand into Philip's and held it tight. The little room into which she entered was gloomy, hot, and airless, and there was a queer smell, too, that made me want to sneeze. There was only one little window, and it was too high to see through it.

But a moment later we had forgotten all this, and had both run forward with a cry of welcome. For on the bed in the corner lay Terry, and we had not seen him for three-and-a-half months.

He did not smile at us, for his face had grown so sullen
and unhappy that he looked as though he hardly knew how
to smile; but he held out his hand and remarked gravely
that he was real pleased to see us, and he'd been looking
out for us ever since morning.

We said equally gravely that we were very pleased to
see him, and then there was a long silence because none
of us could think of anything to say at all.

Philip broke it at last by enquiring how Terry had enjoyed hospital.

" 'Tweren't bad," Terry admitted, " but I got browned
off with lying so still like, and nothing to look at but them
streets. And here 'tis just as bad—nothing to look at but
that there wall; the window be too high up to see out of,
and if I could, there'd be nothing to see 'cept the side of
the hollow."

" But couldn't we carry your bed outside?" I asked,
looking doubtfully at the heavy iron bedstead on which he
lay.

He shook his head.

" Couldn't get it through the door without taking it to
pieces," he replied gloomily, " and yer can't move me off
it—me back hurts too bad."

" Haven't you any books?" we asked.

" I ain't much hand at reading," he answered, although
maybe I'd enjoy 'em if they'd pictures in. What I wants
to see is them hills and birds and animals, and things."

His voice shook a little, and his big eyes filled with tears.
Poor, tired, cross little Terry! We both felt dreadfully
sorry for him, and didn't know how to comfort him.

" I'll bring you all my bird books," said Philip, who was
looking most upset. " We'll come ever so often and tell you
what things are looking like, and then when we're gone
you can shut your eyes and pretend you're seeing them.

I'll tell you what Tanglewoods looks like now, when we came over the hills this afternoon. They haven't got in the second mowings yet, so the hay is still lying out in the fields, and the willowherb patches are just beginning to turn woolly; the hops will soon be ripe and are beginning to smell when you go past the yards, and the apples in the orchard are beginning to turn rosy and weigh down the branches. Oh, and I think they will cut the harvests very soon because the wheat is ripe and the wind makes nice noises in it, and I saw Mr. Lake getting out his tractor, and there are lots of flowers—scabious, and poppies, and knapweeds, and bedstraws and things; we'll bring you some round next time, and some apples."

Terry seemed pleased; a faint pink tinge crept into his almost colourless cheeks.

" You goin' to the hop fields?" he asked wistfully.

" We might," I answered, " if Auntie will let us—we could earn some money then, couldn't we, Philip?—to help with the camera."

" I used to earn a heap of money down at the hop-yards," said Terry. " 'Nuff to buy me a pair of winter boots. Mum'll have to try and go this year, but she can't leave me long, and she's had to give up her work to stop and mind me."

" The gipsies are arriving already," I went on eagerly. " I saw them putting up camp outside a lovely little yellow caravan, with lots of little children with black hair tumbling up and down the steps. They're camping in Mr. Lane's field. I'd love to be a gipsy, wouldn't you?"

But Terry, who knew much more than I did about gipsies, shook his head darkly.

" You be thankful fer what yer are," he advised, wisely.

We found no further difficulty in thinking of things to say—indeed we talked so much that we stayed much longer than we meant to, and were interrupted by Terry's mother coming in with his tea.

Terry's meal consisted of a cup of very strong tea and a crust thinly spread with margarine, on a chipped old plate; it did not look at all appetizing to me, but it reminded me of the chocolate I'd brought. It had begun to melt rather, in my pocket, but it was still very nice, and Terry's eyes absolutely gleamed when he saw it. We did not give him the catapult because it did not seem as though it would be any use—his arms looked too thin and white to aim with it.

" Terry," asked Philip just as we were leaving, " when are you going to be able to get up and play with us again?"

He did not answer for a minute, but the frightened, unhappy look came back into his eyes.

" Maybe never," he whispered. " They thinks I don't know, but down at the 'ospital I 'eard the doctor talking to the nurse, and 'e said ' It's all up with 'im, poor little chap —I can't do nuffing more for 'im.' And I think maybe that's why they let my mum take me 'ome. They can't do nuffing more to make me better."

We were horrified to hear this, and once again we could think of nothing to say to comfort poor Terry. So we left him rather sadly; but just as we were going out of the door he called after us:

" When 'yer comin' again?"

" We can't come tomorrow," answered Philip, " because we've got to go to the dentist. But we'll come the day after and bring the bird books."

" For certain sure?" called Terry.

" For certain sure," we called back.

Terry's mother was out in the hollow hanging up a torn little nightshirt on the clothes line; she gave us a surly glance, but did not speak. When we said good afternoon she only grunted.

" What a cross woman!" I remarked, as we climbed the hollow. " I'm glad she's not my mother."

But on the whole we were very silent on the way home, because we were both feeling so sorry for Terry and we were both wondering what we could do to make his life happier. Nothing we could think of seemed much good, because nothing could make up for having to lie all day in a dark, stuffy room, staring at the wall, while the apples ripened and the harvest fields rustled outside.

13

A MOONLIGHT EXPEDITION

WE went to see Terry very often during the next few weeks, and I believe now that it was only our visits that kept him alive through those long dark days when he lay flat on his aching back, staring at the wall. Philip lent him all his most previous Nature books, and we took him all the chocolate we had, and baskets of fruit from the orchard. We felt well rewarded every time by the faint flush of pleasure on his white cheeks and the flicker of happiness that would light up his eyes. He never thanked us in words, and his mother still stared at us as though she hated us, but we knew nevertheless that Terry's waking hours were spent wondering if we would come, and that he lay from dinner-time onwards with his eyes fastened on the door and his ears straining for the sound of our footsteps.

We had told Aunt Margaret about him, and once or twice she had sent him little presents; Aunt Margaret and I were slowly getting to understand each other, and I no longer tried to wriggle out of helping her in the mornings. At first I had done my jobs because I thought I ought to, but after a few days I found that housework was really quite fun, as long as I was doing my best and not trying to get out of it all the time. My aunt said nothing, but I knew she was pleased at the change, and gradually we grew fond of each other and I began to talk to her more freely, instead of keeping everything a secret from her.

Uncle Peter was interested in Terry, too, and once or twice he had taken the step-ladder to the orchard and picked the enormous rosy apples that grew right at the top of the tree against the sky, for us to take to him. They were the size of big grape-fruit; when they were polished up we could see our faces in their shiny skins. Terry loved them, and even his mother looked interested.

"Did yer pick those there in your garden?" she asked suddenly one afternoon, as we placed one of them between his small white hands.

We quite jumped, for except for her first greeting it was the first time she had ever spoken to us. We turned smiling towards her, for we wanted her to come to like us as much as Terry did.

"Yes," I answered, "we've lots of trees full of big, shiny apples like these. We shall be picking them in about a week, and then we'll bring some more; but we picked these early because we thought Terry would like them."

She only grunted and turned away, but I could not help feeling pleased she had spoken to us and admired our apples. I thought I would try and talk to her again another day.

The nights just then were very hot, and owing to the extra 'Summer Time' it did not get dark until very late. Philip and I used to kick our bedclothes on to the floor and lie in our night things by the open windows trying to get cool; and often I got tired of lying alone, and would go and sit on his bed. We would talk until the cool darkness gathered round us and we felt ready for sleep.

It was on one of these hot, still nights, when the sky was still red with the last glow of sunset, that I tiptoed across the passage and found Philip with his head out of the window. I pushed him up a little and stuck my head out beside him; a breath of air seemed to move towards us from the hills, bringing with it the cry of a sheep somewhere up among the rocks.

"I don't think I shall be able to go to sleep all night, Phil," I remarked. "It's such a beautiful night I seem to want to look out of the window all the time. It's full moon, too—look, I can see it coming up behind that fir tree."

We watched it climb above the horizon, almost blood-red in colour; it seemed all tangled up in the black boughs of the fir, but soon it would steer clear and all the world would be flooded with soft silver light. I turned suddenly on Philip, my head full of moonlight.

"Phil!" I whispered excitedly. "Have you ever been out on the hills at night?"

"No," answered Philip, "I haven't—not proper night. Why?"

"Oh, Philip," I breathed, giving his arm a little squeeze, "let's go now, just out through the hedge and up above the quarry. It would be so beautiful—just you and me, and the big yellow moon. Come on, Phil!"

Philip hesitated. "Do you think it would be very naughty?" he asked. "After all, you know, we were going to try to be good these holidays."

"I know," I urged. "And we really have been rather good, too—at least I've been cross with Aunt Margaret once or twice, but last holidays I was cross nearly every day. And it isn't really a bit naughty either—after all, what's naughty in wanting to see the moon? It's not hurting anyone and it's not even being disobedient, because Aunt Margaret has never actually told us not to go out at night and look at the moon."

Philip thought this over for a minute or two. It seemed to strike him as sensible, for all he said was, "Are you going to dress properly?"

"Oh, no," I said, "I shan't bother—I shall tuck my nightie up and put on my mack. You put on your Sunday trousers, those long ones, over your pyjamas, and put on your mack, too."

This was no sooner said than done, and, looking rather lumpy about the lower quarters, with our handkerchiefs stuffed in our mouths because we wanted to giggle, Philip and I tiptoed down to the front door and turned the key. It creaked and grated alarmingly, but my uncle and aunt must have been very soundly asleep, for although we stood rooted to the spot for several moments nothing happened.

We shut the door noiselessly behind us and stepped out into the open. Then we both stopped and looked round, because the world seemed so strange and different, and the sky with its millions of stars looked so far away. I slipped my hand into Philip's as I always did when things seemed strange, and together we tiptoed through the shadowed orchard towards our gap: the shadows of the apple boughs looked so fierce and frightening that I almost ran back— only Philip, having made up his mind, kept going.

Out through the gap and up the stony track that led to the hills we went without a word—up the steps behind the clock tower, over the first group of grey rocks—and we were there, standing on the lower slopes by moonlight, with the silver world lying at our feet.

"Come on!" whispered Philip, and seizing my hand again he began to climb.

We climbed in silence until we reached the very top of

the North Hill and stood by the little cairn of stones that marked the summit. The wind came sweeping up the valleys, clean and pure, and laden with the scents of gorse and bracken; a sheep lifted its head at the sound of our footsteps and bleated a warning to the stars—otherwise all was silent and we sat down on the cairn to look.

There was such a tremendous lot to see in spite of the darkness. Behind, there were the black shapes of the beacon and the camp rising up into the night, and dark ranges of wooded hills massed beyond them; while in front of us stretched the plains dotted with points of light, and every river and pond gleaming in the moonlight like some silver fairy lake.

But mostly we looked up because we both loved stars, and tonight they all shone clearly, right over the vast panorama of the sky.

We stayed quite a long time, until Philip remarked that he thought we'd better get back, as it would soon be morning and we should be so tired next day. Actually it was not quite as bad as that, for when we reached the bottom of the hill, the clock on the tower struck one—and nearly made us jump out of our skins.

We sang all the way down because we knew there was no one to hear us, and it was a relief to make a noise after that tremendous solitude. We sang all the songs we could remember, mostly about seas and ships and one about a mermaid who lured mariners to their death, and while we sang we jumped over the gorse bushes, or leaped from one rock to the other like two mountain goats.

But when we got back to the stony track we suddenly felt tired and thought how nice it would be to cuddle down into bed and go to sleep.

" Now," said Philip, " in through the gap and very, very

quietly across the orchard. How awful if auntie's noticed! We must absolutely creep."

We were right through the gap, and well into the orchard when Philip suddenly stopped dead and dug his finger-nails into my arm. With the other hand he pointed, and as I followed his finger my heart seemed to turn right over, and I only just stopped myself from screaming.

14

A MIDNIGHT ADVENTURE

A TALL figure in a dark cloak was moving towards us through the trees, bowed under the weight of a sack.

She had not seen us, for we had come very quietly, and we stood hidden in the deep shadows of the apple trees; but the figure was making for the gap, and in a few minutes must pass right by where we stood. I think I should have fainted outright if it had not been for Philip, who seemed less frightened than I was.

"It's a woman stealing apples," he breathed. "We ought to try and stop her. They're auntie's apples and she's got a great big sackful."

I could not argue or tell him to stop, because I was much too scared to speak. But I clung tightly to Philip and was sort of dragged with him when he suddenly stepped out into the open to confront the figure, who was nearly upon us. The moonlight shone full on her face, and we recognized her in a flash. It was Terry's mother!

She gave a short, terrified shriek and dropped the sack, so that the apples rolled out and scattered in all directions. Then she cowered down in the grass, and covered her face with her cloak and began mumbling words very fast, almost as though she was saying her prayers. Neither

Philip nor I knew what to do, until she suddenly flung back her fierce, proud head and spoke to us.

"So ye'd be a-spying on me by night even, would ye?" she hissed, shaking her fist at us. "And now ye'll be sending the police after me tomorrer and they'll take me from my poor dyin' boy. You, with yer fine food, and yer grand clothing, yer can't spare the price of a few apples for my laddie what's starvin' and cold—and him a-dyin' before my very eyes, and me with nothing ter give him—oh! Terry, Terry, they'll take me from you. . . ." She hid her face in her cloak again and burst into bitter, passionate weeping.

I looked at Philip, feeling more troubled than I had ever felt before. Philip was frowning, too, as though he was wondering what to do next. Presently, however, he made up his mind, for he suddenly squatted down in the grass beside the poor huddled-up figure, and tried to draw her hands from her face.

"We weren't spying on you," he said, gently, "we were only here by accident, 'cos we wanted to see the moon.

The woman had stopped sobbing, and was looking intently at him, with a gleam of hope in her wild eyes.

"Little gentleman," she answered in a trembling voice, taking hold of him in her eagerness, "listen to me! I swear before God I'll never come again. I know I'm a wicked woman and I didn't oughter have come, but my Terry's a-dyin' and the doctor he says to me, you get 'im extra milk and a warm blanket for the winter, and you feed 'im up proper if you wants to keep him a little longer. And my Terry, he's all that I've got."

She was kneeling in the grass, clasping her hands almost as though she was praying to us.

I wanted to assure her that of course we wouldn't tell, and she could have all the apples she wanted, because I felt so sorry for her, but Philip stopped me.

"We won't tell" he said slowly, "but if you really stop stealing, as you say, I can't see how you are going to get any money. And yet, of course, it is awfully wicked to steal. Won't anybody give you any money?"

She shook her head.

"If I applied for relief they'd only put Terry back in 'ospital where I couldn't get at 'im. They'd say our house weren't fit for a sick child, and no more 'tis—but we're together. That's wot we wants."

She looked at us hungrily, as though pleading with us to understand. Philip still seemed wrapped in thought.

"Listen!" he said at last, in his most earnest voice, "I think I've got a sort of an idea; but I can't tell you about it now. You go back to Terry, and we'll come and see you tomorrow when we've talked about it—but we've promised not to tell, haven't we, Ruth?"

"Oh, yes," I agreed, "we won't say anything and we'll come tomorrow."

"God bless you, little lady and gentleman," whispered Terry's mother.

She picked up her empty sack and was gone through the gap in the hedge before we had time to bid her good-night. We were left alone gazing down at the scattered fruit.

"I wish we'd let her have them," I remarked.

"No," said Philip. "It's Uncle Peter's fruit and it would have been as bad as stealing ourselves if we'd given it her. I've thought of something else, Ruth, but I'll tell you in the morning. I'm so tired, and I want to go back to bed."

I was very tired, too, so I pressed him with no further questions. We crept upstairs and tumbled into bed; I was just falling asleep when Philip's head came round the door.

"How much is there in the money-box?" he whispered.

"One pound seventy two and a half," I murmured back drowsily, and the next moment I was deep in the land of dreams.

15

ABOUT GIVING

Of course we both overslept next morning and were wakened only by the ringing of the breakfast gong and the sound of my aunt's footsteps coming up to see what had happened to us. She was rather suspicious at the sight of us only just waking up.

"It's my belief you don't settle off properly at night," she remarked severely, "or you'd be awake at the proper time; I believe there's a lot of running about when you should be tucked up, and I won't have it. Once in bed, you're to stay in bed, or I shall have to start locking you in."

Philip and I looked at each other guiltily out of the corners of our eyes, and hoped our aunt would not say any more on the subject; fortunately it was washing day, and she was very busy lighting the copper, so no more questions were asked.

I was simply longing for a good talk with Philip, but felt that I had really been so naughty the night before, in spite of all my excuses, that I had better try to be extra good to-day to make up. So I presented myself in the kitchen and offered to turn the mangle and stir the copper, and my aunt was only too pleased to accept. We chatted together in a friendly way while we worked, and I couldn't help thinking how nice it was to have Aunt Margaret talking to me almost as though I was grown up; she never used to do it, and I began to wonder how it was that things were different.

"I think it's all to do with the Good Shepherd," I thought to myself as I pegged out the handkerchiefs. "It really has been different since Philip and I began to know about Him. I do believe He really is beginning to make me less cross and less lazy, and I do believe Aunt Margaret is getting nicer, too. Perhaps after we've been to see Terry this afternoon we might tell Aunt Margaret more about him, and ask her if she has a blanket to spare so he wouldn't be cold in the winter."

"Come along, Ruth!" she called. "Think what you're doing; you've been standing there doing nothing the last three or four minutes."

I turned very pink and went on with my work in a great hurry. But I was longing to finish and get to Philip and tell him about my plan, and, fortunately for me, the wash was nearly over.

"You can go now," said Aunt Margaret, taking off her apron. "You've been a great help this morning, so you must have a good game before dinner."

I scuttled upstairs two steps at a time, and found Philip lying flat on his bed with all the contents of his money-box spread out in front of him. I knelt down and we counted it together.

"One pound seventy two and a half," observed Philip thoughtfully, "and I saw a camera for four pounds seventy pence. If we both saved our pocket-money for the rest of the holidays, we could get it by the beginning of term."

There was a pause, and I watched him anxiously.

"On the other hand," went on Philip, "if we gave Terry fifty pence for extra milk, we could get it round about Christmas."

He gave a little sigh, and I knew he was thinking of the squirrels' dreys and the dormouse nests that we should find when autumn came, and the nests of harvest mice that turned up when the corn was cut. I felt I could not bear it for him.

"Oh, but I don't think we need give fifty pence," I cried. "Surely twenty five would buy an awful lot of extra milk, and I vote we ask auntie for a rug. She's sure to have an old one."

Philip fingered his coins.

"Well," he said, "I don't think we need really decide now. We can think it out on the way. I'll take the whole money box, and then if I want to give her our twenty five pence, I can, and if I feel more like fifty pence, I can too!"

I agreed that it was too important a matter to decide in a hurry, and we packed the money back.

We set off after dinner along the well-trodden way that led to Terry's house. I carried a Bible and my picture tucked inside; Philip carried the money box, which was most satisfyingly heavy and jingled as we walked; but he was rather depressed, and I thought he must be hankering after the camera, so I longed to comfort him.

"Philip," I said "I think thirty pence might buy quite a lot of extra milk. Let's ask how much extra milk costs."

Philip only grunted; he didn't seem to want to talk about it at all, so we walked on in silence.

We were half-way down the hill towards the hollow when Terry's mother suddenly appeared from behind a tree, where she seemed to have been waiting for us. She looked at us very anxiously, as though we might have forgotten our promise.

"Thought we might have our bit of a talk out here," she began nervously, "before you goes on down to Terry.

You won't be telling my Terry nothing about them apples, will you now? I did it for his sake, but he'd take on something terrible if he knowed; he's a good straight lad, is Terry."

"Of course we won't tell Terry," Philip assured her. "We promised we wouldn't tell anyone."

We sat down among the thyme and harebells, and were silent for a little while. Philip looked at me because he was expecting me to begin. I looked at the ground because I was shy, and Terry's mother looked very hard at the money box.

I gave Philip a little kick, but he still wouldn't start talking. What if he took me at my word and gave only five shillings, when the Good Shepherd had given His life? If only I could make him understand!

Philip moved nearer to Terry's mother.

"We've brought you some money to buy milk and bedclothes for Terry," he said simply. "It's not very much, but it's all we've got," and so saying, he tipped up the money box and emptied the whole contents into Terry's mother's apron.

"It's one pound seventy two and a half," he said distinctly, so that there might be no mistake about it, "and we hope it will do Terry a lot of good. Now we will go down to the cottage and see him for a little bit."

He stood up and started off down the hill, but I stayed behind for a moment. The Good Shepherd had given His life; Philip had given all the money for his camera—I wanted to give something, too. I suddenly remembered that my most precious possession was in my hands. So I opened the Bible and pulled it out, and laid it with the coins on the black apron.

"It's my picture," I said softly. "And you can have it too. It's the Good Shepherd."

"Thank you, little lady," she replied, and I left her sitting there counting her coins on the hillside, while I ran after Philip.

"I hope you didn't mind that I gave all the money," said Philip apologetically, as we were walking home an hour later. "After all, a lot of it was yours really, but somehow I felt we couldn't keep it—I mean the camera doesn't seem to matter much compared with Terry, when you come to think of it, does it?"

"No," I agreed. "and the funny part is; I was thinking the same thing. When I thought of the Good Shepherd giving His life, it seemed awful to be giving such a little, and I was trying to make you look at me—to tell you to give more."

"Funny," said Philip, "I thought I should feel miserable without my money, but actually I feel awfully happy."

"Funny!" I agreed. "I thought it would be terrible giving away my picture, but I sort of feel glad she's got it now. Isn't it queer?"

"Yes," said Philip. "We never guessed it would be so nice, but when you come to think of it, Ruth, I believe it's the first time we've given away anything that we really wanted to keep badly, so we couldn't have known."

And we walked on in silence thinking about it.

16

HOPS AND MUSHROOMS

THE summer holidays were specially exciting that year, because my aunt gave us permission for the first time to spend certain afternoons in the hop fields, where we earned quite a lot of money; we had given up saving for the camera for the present, and our idea was to earn the price of a warm blanket for Terry. We had told Aunt Margaret about it, and this was her suggestion, as she hadn't actually got one to spare herself. But she gave us other little things for him, and mended up Philip's old pyjamas, which were flannel and warm and would be much more comfortable than his thin little cotton nightshirts.

Mr. Robinson had also promised to go and see Terry. On one of our many Saturday visits, Philip and I had told him about Terry and had begged him to call.

"You see," I explained, "I've tried to tell him about the Good Shepherd, but he doesn't want to listen. He says if God loved him He'd make his back better and let him run about again, and when he said that, I didn't know what to say—but if you came, you could explain it all nicely, I expect, couldn't you?"

Mr. Robinson had smiled.

"No," he answered, "I couldn't explain it at all, because when God sends sad things into our lives He often doesn't tell us why. He just tells us that it is the best thing for us, and if we really love Him we believe what He says even if we don't understand. That is what 'trusting' means. In any case, Terry would probably listen to you more than he would to me, because you are a child like himself and I'm only a grown-up."

"But he doesn't listen," I had insisted. "He doesn't take any notice of me at all; he just tells me to talk about something else."

"Well, then," Mr. Robinson had replied, "you must start praying every day that he will listen. God doesn't always answer our prayers at once, but He hears them, and if they are right prayers He always answers them in the end —and I will come and visit the little boy when I come home again, and see what I can do for him."

So Mr. and Mrs. Robinson and the twins had gone off on their holiday and would not be back for three weeks, and in the meantime Philip and I earned what we could in the hop fields, We loved the hop fields with the noisy pickers and the strange smell that clung to our clothes and fingers; we sat round a bale with a family from Birmingham to whom we had attached ourselves, and listened to their friendly chatter while we picked; at six o'clock we would line up for our pay and feel wonderfully important and grown-up when all our wages were handed out to us.

Once the family from Birmingham invited us to stay to supper with them, and we sat round a glowing brazier. They cooked a queer sort of pancake in a big frying pan. It smelt delicious, and when it was tossed on a tin plate and handed to us we thought we had never tasted anything so good. But Aunt Margaret was cross with us because we got home so late, and when we explained she was crosser still, and said goodness knows what we might catch if we went sitting around braziers and eating off tin plates with gipsies. So that delight had to be given up.

We found another way of earning money, too, which Aunt Margaret thought a better way than hop-picking—she was always a little nervous of our catching things or hearing bad language in the hop-yards. But one misty September morning we got up early and ran out into the silver fields where the spiders were festooning the grasses with their webs. We took off our shoes and stockings because we liked the feel of cold dew between our toes, and were skipping up and down the field, when Philip suddenly stopped; he had caught sight of a little white button mushroom and stooped down to look underneath and make sure it wasn't a puff ball.

" Mushrooms, Ruth!" he called. " Let's see if we can find some more!"

We found lots more—in fact, the field was full of them—tight buttons and big umbrellas—and we heaped them up until we could have filled a whole basket full, only we had no basket.

" There's only one thing to be done," Philip remarked. " You must take off your vest and tie the sleeves in a knot so that it makes a bag. We must get these mushrooms home somehow."

So I retired behind a willow tree in case any neighbouring farmers might appear, or in case, as Philip said, I might shock the cows; and when my vest had been filled up with mushrooms it began to stretch, and by the time we reached home it had grown so long that it almost touched the ground. We were going to give some to Aunt Margaret to cook and we were going to ask whether we might sell the rest to the greengrocer up the road.

Aunt Margaret was pleased with the mushrooms, but she was not at all pleased with my vest. She said it was enough to give me a bad chill, and in any case it was the ruination of good underwear. So I was given a dose of cold mixture and made to wash the vest, and was rather sulky all breakfast in consequence.

But I cheered up later, because when we asked Aunt Margaret if we might sell the rest of our mushrooms to Mr. Daniels the greengrocer, she said she did not mind at all, provided we took them in a proper basket. So we set out, highly excited, presented ourselves at the counter, and asked to see Mr. Daniels personally.

Mr. Daniels was fat and bald, and wore horn-rimmed spectacles on the end of a large red nose. He liked Philip and me, and beamed at us over the counter. When he saw our mushrooms he threw up his hands in admiration.

"Dearie me!" said Mr. Daniels. "Now I'll weigh 'em out and pay you same as I pay the farmers, and if you find any more you bring 'em along to Mr. Daniels!"

We did find lots more, and what with mushrooms and hops, the money-box began to get really heavy again, and we were beginning to talk about the colour of the blanket we would buy, when a wonderful thing happened.

We had wandered over the hills in the heat to take Terry some of the Victoria plums, and we found him alone; the cabin was particularly stuffy, and Terry looked hot and flushed; his dark hair lay in damp locks on his forehead, and he had thrown all his bedclothes back. He did not notice us come in because he was staring so hard at the wall opposite, where his mother had hung the picture I had given her.

"Hullo, Terry!" we greeted him, sitting ourselves down on the bed. "Is you mother out?"

"Mm," answered Terry, wearily. Poor Terry! He seemed so exhausted that even our arrival had failed to cheer him up. "Her's been gone a long time."

" Where to?" we asked.

" Dunno," replied Terry. " Her wouldn't say."

There was a pause, then Terry spoke again in a fretful voice.

" Take that there picture away with you!" he commanded. " It bothers my mum awful. Last few days she's kinder cried when she's looked at it; she was happier before you brought it, and we don't want it."

" But I can't take it away," I objected. " It's your mother's—I gave it her; it would be sort of stealing to take it away."

Terry passed his hand wearily over his forehead and turned his face to the wall.

" Wish I was dead," he muttered.

We had never seen Terry quite so discouraged before, and we longed to comfort him; but what could we say to comfort a boy who had to lie in this hot, cheerless gloom all day long? Even when we offered him a plum he pushed it away.

" I'm feelin' sick," he explained. " Maybe I'll eat it later."

We left very soon, because he seemed too tired to want us. His mother had not returned, and we felt very depressed as we climbed the hill.

" Philip," I said, " do you still pray every day that Terry will get better?"

" Not *every* day," answered Philip, " because sometimes I feel sure he won't—I mean perhaps God thinks he'd better not get better. The doctor said he wouldn't, you know, and doctors are usually right."

" But God could do a miracle," I insisted, " like He did in the Bible—it seems too awful, doesn't it? Terry seems sadder every time we go."

" It isn't really being ill that's the worst part," Philip observed thoughtfully; " it's that awful little house. It's so hot and dark, and there's a sort of not very nice smell about it and it must be so dull. If he could be ill somewhere nice it would be different."

But I could see no way out of this difficulty at all, unless we prayed that someone with a nice house would adopt Terry—and, on further thought, we decided not to pray for that after all, as Terry would hate to leave his mother and his mother would hate to lose him.

We were talking so earnestly about it all when we reached the gate that we did not look where we were going and nearly bumped into my aunt, who was coming down the path talking to a tall woman in a dark cloak. We looked up quickly into the visitor's face, and to our utter astonishment we saw that the tall woman was Terry's mother, and her dark eyes were red with weeping. And, stranger still, my aunt, who was generally extremely severe with beggars and gipsies, was talking gently to her and had laid her hand on her arm.

They neither of them took any notice of us, and we went indoors quickly because we somehow felt that Terry's mother hadn't really wanted to meet us at all; but once inside we looked at each other in astonishment. What could my aunt and Terry's mother have been saying to each other? "Perhaps she's asking for things for Terry," I suggested.

Philip shook his head.

"I don't think it's that," he said, "because auntie was being so nice to her, and usually she's rather cross with beggars."

If we had hopes that my aunt would explain things, we were disappointed. She came back into the house a few minutes later and went upstairs to her bedroom. When she came down she was very quiet and took no notice of us at all. I thought her face was sadder than usual, and although she started cooking the supper she looked as though she was thinking of something that wasn't supper at all!

Next day at breakfast another surprise awaited us. My aunt laid down her knife and fork and looked at her watch.

" Ruth," she announced, " I am going out for the morning; it is very important and I shall probably not be back for some hours, so I am going to let you get the dinner. The potatoes are peeled, and there is cold meat, so you will only have to wash the lettuce, and peel and stew the apples and make some custard. I showed you how to make custard the other day, so it will be a good chance to try."

Philip and I stared at her in astonishment. Never before, that we could remember, had our aunt gone out for the morning, or missed cooking the dinner; it must have been dreadfully important business that called her, and we were extremely curious to know what it could be. However, of course, we didn't ask, and I felt so proud at being allowed to cook the dinner all by myself that I soon forgot to wonder.

Aunt Margaret was as good as her word. She got up from the breakfast table, put on her hat, and walked straight out of the front door—and that was the last we saw of her until dinner-time.

Philip and I, left to ourselves, went to work with a will. Being mistress of the house for the morning rather appealed to me, and we carried the breakfast things out and started to wash up feeling tremendously important. I began by tipping nearly a whole jar of soap flakes into the bowl and whisking until the foam stood up nearly as high as the taps —and after that, of course, we had to spend ten minutes or so scooping it up with our hands and blowing soap bubbles all over the kitchen, squealing with delight as they landed on the top shelves. Then I suddenly remembered that I was not behaving in a housewifely way, so I turned to the sink in a great hurry and plunged my elbows into the soapy flakes and began fishing for the silver.

The morning passed very pleasantly. Philip and I peeled enough apples to feed a regiment, and although I burnt our saucepan badly while making the custard, it didn't taste much. We caught three little slugs in the lettuce and carried them carefully back to the lettuce patch in case their mothers should be missing them; then when dinner was ready to our satisfaction we started on the housework. We took all the rugs into the garden and danced up and down with them, smothering ourselves with dust. Yes, it was certainly great fun being left in charge of the house. The morning sped past, and it seemed only a very short time before my aunt walked in at the gate. It was dinner-time.

I made a dive for the potatoes, which were boiling merrily, and the dinner was served up by a very flushed untidy little cook, who had to be sent away from the table to brush her hair the minute Grace had been said.

However, my aunt seemed pleased with my efforts; she praised the potatoes and salad and said nothing about the burnt flavour of the custard. She looked happy, too; much happier than she had looked at breakfast, and now and then we noticed her smiling to herself as though she had some very nice secret.

"I hope you enjoyed yourself this morning, Auntie," said Philip politely.

Aunt Margaret's eyes twinkled, and the little smile played round the corners of her mouth again.

"I've enjoyed myself very much indeed, thank you, Philip," she replied solemnly; then after a moment she added:

"Tonight, when Uncle Peter comes home, and I've

talked to him, I'm going to tell you about it; but till then it's a secret."

Philip and I were enormously interested. When evening came we kept running out into the road to see if Uncle was coming. When at last we saw him approaching we tore madly into the kitchen.

"He's coming, Auntie," we shouted; "now, the secret, the secret!"

She shooed us both out of the kitchen with a wooden spoon.

"Get along with you," she said. "I can't make fish cakes and talk secrets at the same time. You tell your uncle to come here, and then you run out into the garden."

So Uncle Peter went in and shut the door.

17

THE SECRET

" Now for the secret!" we exclaimed, and settled ourselves really comfortably on the stools at my aunt's feet.

We were sitting in the summer dusk just outside the French windows, and the air was sweet with the scent of late roses, while bats fluttered past on restless wings. My aunt leaned forward in her chair while she talked, and as the story went on, we crept closer and closer until our heads were resting against her knees.

" Well," she said, " before we start talking about secrets, I want to know what you were doing in the orchard at one o'clock in the morning a few weeks ago?"

We both jumped and went very red; this was most unexpected. But strange to say, auntie did not sound particularly cross; in fact, there was a tiny shake in her voice that might have meant that she was trying not to laugh.

After a very uncomfortable silence, Philip answered in rather a small voice.

" We couldn't go to sleep that night," he explained, " and we wanted to see the stars close up. So we put some clothes on and went up to the top of the Hill and then. . . ."

" You went up to the top of the North Hill, alone in the dark?" interrupted my aunt, aghast.

" You've never actually told us not to," I chimed in quickly.

" Ruth," said my aunt solemnly, " there are a great many things I have never actually told you not to do, but which you know in your heart I shouldn't like, so don't make silly excuses. Now before we go any further I want you to promise me that you will never go out alone again at night as long as you live with me."

We both promised most earnestly.

" Very well, then," continued my aunt. " As long as you understand that, we will say no more about it. Now perhaps you are wondering how I came to know about it."

As a matter of fact, we thought we could guess, but we did not say so.

" Yesterday," said my aunt, " just after you had gone out, Terry's mother came to see me. She had a long story to tell me. She told me that some weeks ago she was in despair about earning some extra money to buy a blanket for her little boy, and when she saw those big rosy apples you took to Terry she decided to come at night and help herself. She did this once or twice, taking a few pounds from each tree so that your uncle wouldn't notice, and earned quite a little sum by selling them to the greengrocers in the villages round Tanglewoods. Then one night she met you in the orchard."

We looked guiltily at each other and wondered whether my aunt would be very cross with us for not telling. We weren't enjoying this secret much!

" You promised not to tell," went on my aunt, " which wasn't very sensible of you, because if you had told me all about it sooner I might have been able to help her sooner, but still, I know you meant it kindly. And then she tells me that you went to see her and took her all your money. And you, Ruth, gave her your picture."

I blushed again; I was rather shy about my picture.

There was a long silence. The moon was rising behind the black pines, and the garden was full of little whispering breezes and rustles; but we sat quite still with upturned faces waiting for Aunt Margaret to go on.

" She came to see me and brought me the money because she said she felt as though Jesus the Shepherd in your picture was calling her, and she could get no rest until she answered Him. And then we had a long talk and she told me all about that little boy of hers, who seems to be dying in that dark hovel of a home; I went to see him this morning and it's all true. She can't leave him to go to work, and she won't be parted from him to let him go back to hospital, and they are as near starving as one can be nowadays."

My aunt stared out into the twilight. She seemed to have almost forgotten us.

" And when she had gone last night, Philip and Ruth, I think the Shepherd spoke to me, too. I have not thought about Him much for a long time, but last night He showed me a lot of things."

My eyes were fixed on my aunt's face, and I had drawn so close that she put her arm around me.

" He showed me a great many things I can't tell you about now, but I will tell you about two of them. He showed me a lot of money lying doing nothing in the Bank, and He showed me an empty room all covered up with dust sheets, but with a beautiful window looking out over the plain with the sun shining in through it every morning, and the beech tree just outside."

I gave a little jump. "The best spare bedroom," I whispered.

My aunt nodded. "Yes," she agreed. "The best spare bedroom that's been empty for such a long time. But it's not going to be empty any longer, because we want to use it for the Good Shepherd. So the day after tomorrow Terry and his mother are coming to live here with us for a time. Terry's mother is going to help me in the house, and Terry is going to lie by the window in the spare room and get some colour into his cheeks. It will be his very own room, and you and Philip shall help arrange it, and get it ready tomorrow. Would you like that?"

Should we like it? We were both so glad that we could not speak one word, but I think we must have looked our joy, for Aunt Margaret laughed a little and seemed to understand. Philip's eyes at any rate were quite starry with happiness.

So we sat and talked until the moon swung clear of the pines and the last glimmer of light had faded in the West; then Uncle Peter came and stood in the doorway and we flung ourselves upon him.

"Do you know?" we shouted joyfully. "Do you know?"

"Of course he knows," said my aunt, laughing. "You don't think I'd turn the house into a hospital without asking him?"

So we were hustled off to bed, and were told we needn't even wash, except for faces and hands, because it was so late—which was certainly a perfect end to a perfect day.

We spent most of next day getting the room ready for Terry; we spring-cleaned it ourselves and made up the beds—one in the corner for Terry's mother and one by the window for Terry. We collected our nicest books and toys and arranged them where he could see them, and then hung up our brightest pictures on the walls. We picked the rosiest apples and the yellowest pears and put them in a dish by his bed; then we stood and looked round, and decided that it was quite perfect.

18

TERRY AT HOME

TERRY arrived in an ambulance, at teatime, and his mother came with him, carrying their few little belongings in an old tin box. My aunt had arranged for the ambulance, and Terry had been lifted and carried as gently as possible, but even so he was tired out. And when they laid him in his bed by the open window and his dark eyes turned wistfully to the beech tree, his small face looked as white as the pillow on which he rested.

The rest of the summer holidays passed quietly. Terry seemed perfectly happy, and would lie for hours looking out of his window with his arms thrown around his head.

Philip was supposed to be working for a scholarship, so most of his evenings were spent at the dining-room table with his school-books spread out in front of him; at these times I would slip upstairs and sit with Terry. Sometimes I would put the light on and read aloud to him, but sometimes I would perch on the bed, and leaning my elbows on the sill, I would stare out into the dusk and talk.

We talked about a great many things, for Terry, now that he was too ill to do much else, thought a good deal. We often went back to those happy days in the wigwam, and talked about nests and animals. Sometimes we talked about the accident and about the hospital and the long, dreary days in the dark hut; sometimes about my mother and father, and how pleased they would be to see Terry when they came home. Sometimes we just compared our thoughts—the queer thoughts that grown-ups forget about, and that children only tell each other.

"Ruth," said Terry suddenly, as we sat in the twilight one evening, "what's dying like?"

I shuffled my feet uneasily. "Oh, I don't know," I answered, "but I think it's very nice. At least, I think it's just like going to a beautiful place where Jesus is, and where everyone is happy. Why, Terry?"

"'Cos I 'eard the doctor in the 'ospital say it," said Terry, looking round to see that no one else was going to come in at the door. "I told you once. He said, 'It's all up with 'im, poor little chap!'—and that means dyin'."

"But that was a long time ago," I objected.

He shrugged his thin shoulders.

"I ain't got no better," he replied. "Ruth, do everyone go there?"

"I'm not sure," I answered, slowly. "I think perhaps you have to ask the Shepherd to find you. I think you have to belong to Him. But that is quite easy, Terry. You only have to ask to be found, like the sheep in the picture."

He frowned.

"I were a bad boy," he admitted, doubtfully. "I pinched ever such a lot of things whenever I could lay hands on 'em. The cops nearly got me once."

"I think it would be all right, all the same," I assured him. "But, Terry, I'll ask Mr. Robinson to come and see you. He could tell you about it ever so much better than me."

There was a pause; Terry didn't seem particularly cheered by the prospect of Mr. Robinson.

"Ruth," he said at last, "where's the picture—the one you gived us?"

"Oh, you mean my picture?" I answered. "I don't know, Terry; I suppose your mother's got it."

"I'd like ter look at it again," he said. "I told Mum to take it away 'cos it kind of fretted me to see that sheep stuck on the rocks and wondering whether maybe the Shepherd couldn't reach it; but seein' as 'ow it's Jesus, I specs He could reach anywhere, couldn't He?"

"Oh, yes," I answered, with perfect confidence, "Jesus can reach anywhere; nobody could stray away so far that Jesus couldn't bring him back. Mr. Robinson told me so, so you needn't worry about the sheep. It's quite all right."

"What I'd like," went on Terry rather dreamily, "would be a picture of that there sheep after the Shepherd had took him up—when he was safe like, in the Shepherd's arms and being carried home; I'd like that fine."

"Would you, Terry?" I enquired eagerly. "I'll try to get you one. I'll look everywhere and see what I can find."

Terry gave a wan little smile and seemed too tired to talk any more; so we sat in silence until his mother came up to settle him for the night, and I slipped downstairs to see whether Philip had finished his lessons.

I did not forget my promise, and on the first Saturday of the autumn term I set out to ask Mr. Robinson's advice about the picture. Philip had stayed at school to play in a football match, so I had to go alone.

Mrs. Robinson was sitting at the window sewing, so I stopped and had a chat and a chocolate biscuit with her. The twins were rolling about in the pen, and I couldn't leave without a game with them—so by the time I eventually reached the church where Mr. Robinson was arranging the table for the Sunday services, the afternoon was drawing on, and I felt that I must waste no time in unnecessary explanations.

"Mr. Robinson," I started, walking up the aisle, very fast, "do you remember that picture you gave me?"

He stopped what he was doing and sat down on the steps; I sat down beside him. It was a rather nice thing about Mr. Robinson—he always gave you his whole attention.

"Indeed I remember it very well," he replied. "Because, as you know, I have the same one hanging in my room."

"Oh, yes," I answered, "of course you have. But, Mr. Robinson, I want to get the next picture to that one. Do you think it would be possible? Do you think there *is* such a picture?"

Mr. Robinson looked very puzzled.

"I'm afraid I don't understand what you mean by the *next* picture," he said, gently. "Do you mean another picture by the same artist?"

"Oh, no," I answered. "I don't mind who's painted it—I mean a picture of what happens next, after the Shepherd has picked up the sheep, and when it's safe in His arms. You see, Terry doesn't like my picture. It makes him feel unhappy because he says he can never feel sure when he looks at it that the Shepherd will really be able to save that sheep. You see, the Shepherd's arms don't look very long and the sheep is a long way down the precipice, and sometimes it bothers Terry, so I thought I'd try and get him the next picture, where the sheep is safe, and where there's nothing more to bother about."

Mr. Robinson's eyes had never left my face while I was speaking, and when he answered his voice was very earnest.

"I will try my very hardest to get Terry the next picture," he said. "But, Ruth, you mustn't let Terry think that about the sheep. Do you think you could teach him a text, if I taught it you first?"

"Oh, yes," I answered, "I'm sure I could. I've taught him lots already. Is it a Shepherd text?"

"Not exactly," said Mr. Robinson. "At least, it doesn't actually mention the Shepherd, but it's about Him all the same. It's this: 'He is able to save to the uttermost.' Do you know what 'the uttermost' means, Ruth?"

No, I didn't.

"It means as far as anybody could go. It means that however far the sheep had strayed, however high it had climbed, however low it had fallen, the Shepherd could still reach it. It means that there are no people in the world, however naughty or however far away from God, whom the Lord Jesus cannot save as soon as they ask Him."

I looked up quite satisfied. "To the uttermost," I repeated carefully. "Yes, I'll remember that and tell Terry, and then he needn't worry about that sheep any longer. Thank you, Mr. Robinson."

"And on Monday," my friend promised, as we left the church hand in hand, "I am going over to Hereford and I will see if I can find in the shops the picture you want."

I told Terry all about the new text and we said it over together that night; he was glad to learn it, and promised to feel quite certain about the poor sheep getting safe home, because "to the uttermost" meant that even the worst precipices couldn't stop the Shepherd finding that sheep.

But poor Terry was very tired that night—so tired that I stayed only a few minutes. His face looked even whiter than usual, and he kept screwing it up as though the pain was very bad. His mother had hardly left him all day, and my aunt had been cooking wonderful little dishes to try to tempt his appetite, but it was all no good. Terry turned his face to the window and lay silent and uninterested.

Several days passed and the beech leaves outside began to fall rapidly; Terry seldom spoke, but he liked watching them whirling about, and although his mother sat beside him most of the time, he usually lay looking out. The doctor came two or three times during the week, but each time he looked so grave and sad that I dared not ask him how Terry was getting on, and when he would be able to play again.

It was one afternoon about tea-time that I came bounding in from school to find that Philip was late. So, flinging down my satchel, I clattered upstairs and then stopped short at Terry's door and opened it softly, for during the past few days even I had come to realize that I ought to be quiet here.

But I stopped in amazement at the threshold, for beside the bed sat Mr. Robinson, and Terry's drawn face was turned towards him with something like a smile on it, while he listened to a story about a tiger.

I drew up a stool and listened, too, until the tiger was dead and buried under a palm tree; then Mr. Robinson drew a flat parcel from under his coat. " We waited till you came to open this, Ruth," he said.

With eager hands I tore off the paper and string while Terry watched, and when it was unwrapped and the picture lay before us in all its beauty we were so pleased that we did not say anything at all; we both just gave a little gasp and sat staring at it.

It was a framed picture of a meadow full of clean white sheep all walking one way and nibbling the grass as they went; in front of them walked a Shepherd with a crook, and in His arms lay a little lamb peacefully asleep.

It was Terry who broke the silence.

" Where's 'e carryin' 'im to? " he asked suddenly, in his fretful voice.

"Home, Terry," answered Mr. Robinson, with a look on his face that I did not then understand. "Safely through each day until they get home."

"Where's home?" went on Terry.

"It's the place where the Shepherd lives and where we see Him face to face," Mr. Robinson replied. "Shall I read you something about home, Terry?"

The boy nodded, and Mr. Robinson took his New Testament out of his pocket and read in his slow, clear voice about a city where God lived.

"And God shall wipe away all tears from their eyes; and there shall be no more death, neither sorrow nor crying, neither shall there be any more pain."

There was another long silence, broken again by Terry.

"Coo!" he whispered thoughtfully, "No more pain! that won't 'alf be smashin'!"—then, after a minute's thought, he added,

"May everyone go, or only the good 'uns?"

"Why, yes," answered Mr. Robinson. "The gate is open for everyone who wishes to go in, and who belongs to the Good Shepherd, whether he's been good or bad; you see, the Good Shepherd died to make every one of us fit to go in. Do you remember the hymn? I'll say it, in case you've forgotten:

> ' He died that we might be forgiven,
>   He died to make us good,
> That we might go at last to Heaven,
>   Saved by His precious blood.
>
> ' There was no other good enough
>   To pay the price of sin,
> He only could unlock the gate
>   Of Heaven, and let us in.'"

Another silence, and then Terry whispered, "Tell me some more about them tigers."

And while he lay listening to the tiger story, Terry fell asleep with his hand on his picture, and Mr. Robinson and I tiptoed out of the room.

Philip and I made a shopping expedition the following Saturday; we bought two daffodil bulbs for Terry, and some fibre to plant them in. We thought we would put them in a bowl on the window-sill so that he could watch the green shoots and the golden flower blossoms next spring. We sat on the floor burying them in the pots, and Terry lay watching us listlessly.

"Funny," said Philip suddenly. "You wouldn't think there was a daffodil hidden down inside this dead-looking old thing, would you?"

"No," I replied, "you wouldn't; there hardly seems room to pack it all inside; I'm going to bury mine near the top, and then it will come up quicker."

"It won't make any difference," said Philip. "It won't come until its proper time, and when that comes, however far under the earth it's lying, it will shoot up at once."

I was about to argue this, when I caught sight of Terry's face. It was even whiter than usual and all twisted up with pain. I wriggled nearer the bed and took hold of his hand.

"Oh, poor Terry!" I cried. "Is it very, very bad? Shall I fetch your mother?"

He shook his head.

"No," he whispered. "She takes on so when the pain's real bad." Then with a little sob, he added. "Wish I could go to the place where there ain't no more pain."

"I think," said Philip softly, after an uneasy silence, "that we'll ask God to take away your pain and help you go to sleep—like in the Gospels when people came to

Him and He stopped their pains. Kneel down, Ruth, and let's try."

Philip had never prayed aloud before, and the words came very haltingly.

"Dear God—please take away Terry's pain—please make him well soon—please let him go to sleep—Amen."

Then we opened our eyes and looked hopefully at Terry, for we almost expected to see the shadow of pain pass at once. Terry's eyes were open already and fixed on his picture which hung just above his bed.

There were many footsteps up and down in the house that night while we lay asleep, for my aunt and Terry's mother did not go to bed at all, and the doctor arrived just before midnight. But no one heard the feet of the Good Shepherd when He drew near and picked Terry up in His arms.

So Philip's prayer was answered in a way we had never dreamed of. For before the sun had risen again, while the stars were still high in the sky, Terry had left his twisted, suffering body, and all his pain, behind him for ever. The Shepherd had carried him home.

19

MR. TANDY EXPLAINS

THE path to the wood was almost overgrown with yellow bracken and completely arched by golden beeches, but I pressed on because I wanted to get right into the heart of it, far away from everybody, where I could sit and think about the strange things that had happened since Terry died.

I walked a long way, because I was not thinking where I was going; I just wandered, kicking at the damp leaves and brushing aside the yellow bracken and trying to forget that we had left Terry alone in the earth. But I could not forget; and when at last I came to a clearing where a great chestnut tree spread out its branches, I lay down on the roots, and resting my head against the trunk I gave way to my sorrow, and my tears fell thick and fast on to the moss.

I was so tired and so miserable that I never heard slow, heavy steps rustling through the leaves, and I quite jumped when a well-known voice above me spoke to me.

" Why, little maid, little maid," said the voice, " what be all this about? Ye'll catch your death of cold a-lying there on the ground."

It was Mr. Tandy. He stooped down and wrapped his

big rough coat about me just as though I had been one of his own stray lambs. Then he sat down on the root, and I snuggled up against him in my enormous wrap and gave a very big sniff.

I had not seen Mr. Tandy for several months because he had left our district to go and work at the Cradley folds. I was very pleased, but very surprised to see him.

Very glad to have someone to talk to after my lonely walk, I told the old man my whole story: all about Terry and his pain, and his picture, and how he had come to live with us and hadn't got better.

"I prayed so hard he would get better," I said despondently, "but it didn't do any good. God didn't listen, and Terry died."

"Little maid," replied Mr. Tandy rather hesitatingly, "if you come to me and says, 'There's a little lame lamb down yonder what can't run about'—on account of the pasture being steep like, and the stones sharp—and s'posin' I comed down and picked up that there little lamb and carried him in my arms to another pasture where the grass was sweet and the ground easy-like, you wouldn't come and tell me as I hadn't heeded you, would you now?"

I gazed at him dumbly; I was beginning to understand.

"Little maid," he went on, "the Shepherd took His lamb home, that's all. Ye've no cause to fret."

"But," I cried, my eyes once more filling with tears, "it didn't seem like that at all. They buried Terry in the earth and we left him there, and it seemed so sad and lonely. How can Terry be with the Shepherd when we left him lying in the earth?"

The old man did not answer for a moment, and then he started scraping about with his hands in the leaf-fall as though he were looking for something. His search was rewarded and he held out a shiny brown conker in one hand, and an empty seed box in the other—a withered old thing with green prickles turning brown.

" Now tell me," he said, in his slow, thoughtful voice, " what's a-goin' to happen to the conker, and what's a-goin' to happen to the covering?"

" Oh," I answered, " the case will get buried in the leaves and then I suppose it will just wither away. It isn't needed any more; but the conker will grow roots and leaves and turn into a chestnut tree."

" That's right," said Mr. Tandy, encouragingly. " Ye couldn't have said it better; now, tell me this, little maid; when you see the young chestnut tree a-waving its little new leaves in the sunshine next spring, with the birds a-singing round it, and the rain a-watering of it, you ain't goin' to fret any more for that old case what's crumbled under the leaves, be you?"

" No-o," I answered, with my eyes fixed on his face. Once more I thought I understood.

" Well, then," said the old man, triumphantly, . " you cease fretting for what you laid below ground—t'weren't nothing but the case. The laddie's a-growing strong in the sunshine up yonder, along of his Saviour."

His kind old eyes lit up with joy as he spoke; he threw down the conker and case, shouldered his axe and rose stiffly to his feet, because his knees were " full of rheumatics " as he had once told me. Then he unwrapped me and bade me go home.

" For if I don't get along," he said, " I shan't get that there gap mended up, and my sheep'll be strayin' out again. Goodbye, little maid, and God bless you."

I watched him as he moved off into the golden shadows

of the wood, and then I stooped down and picked up the conker and its case. Clutching them tightly in my hands, I set off home rather fast, for I was cold and tired and the dusk was falling. When I reached our fields again the sky was aglow with orange light, and against the sunset stood a little black figure scanning the landscape. It was Philip, and he had come to look for me.

I ran to him and slipped my hand into his, and we walked along in comfortable silence. As we climbed the stile, he glanced at my other hand.

" What are you holding so tight?" he asked curiously.

I unlocked my fist and held out my new treasure.

" It's a conker and its case," I said shyly, " and it's like Terry—Mr. Tandy told me so."

" Why?" asked Philip.

" Because," I answered, finding it difficult to explain, " what we put in the earth was like the case; it doesn't matter because Terry didn't need it any more. The inside part that's alive has gone with the Shepherd, so I'm not really sad about it now. Mr. Tandy said it was like a lamb being taken to another field where the grass is nicer.

Philip nodded understandingly. " I see," he said, " and I'm glad you're not sad any more."

When we got home, we found that my aunt had lighted a fire in the nursery, and she, Terry's mother, Philip and myself were going to have supper. It was a lovely, picnicky sort of supper with hard-boiled eggs and treacle, gingerbread, rosy apples and pears, and hot cocoa. I had been for a long walk and Philip had been playing football, so we were both starving! We wriggled nearer the blaze and rubbed our shoulders together to show how much we were enjoying it. Even Terry's mother smiled faintly.

It was when we had eaten all we possibly could that my

aunt, holding out her hands to the blaze, said softly, "Terry's mother and I have been making plans."

"Have you?" we asked, much interested. "Will you tell us?"

"Yes," said my aunt, "because it's a plan that you can both help in—in fact, I shall need your help a great deal. You see, now that little Terry has gone, we want to do something in memory of him. Terry was weak and ill, and we couldn't help him get better—but there are other weak, ill children whom perhaps we could help to get better—and now that I have Terry's mother to help me in the house, and Ruth is getting so handy, I was thinking we'd try to find some of these children and have them here in the holidays. I used to know someone who worked in a prison in London, and I think he could help us. I thought I would write to him and ask him to find two or three children who needed good food and country air, and invite them here for Christmas; we would give them as lovely a time as possible. Would you like it, Philip and Ruth?"

We thought it a wonderful idea, and both began to talk at once, eagerly planning what we would do to make it a happy Christmas for them. It was a great relief, for somehow, since Terry died, we had almost felt as though we ought not to talk about other things but now we could talk freely and happily about this, for it was all because of Terry and somehow part of Terry.

So we planned about Christmas stockings and Christmas carols and Christmas dinners and Christmas trees, and our cheeks got redder and redder in the firelight and our eyes grew brighter and brighter.

"Auntie," I cried at last, cuddling up against her, "it *is* a good idea; how *did* you think of it?"

" Well," replied my aunt, "you are fond of 'Shepherd' texts, so I'll tell you how I thought of it. It was the morning I went to visit Terry for the first time; as I walked through the woods I remembered a verse I had forgotten for years. It is what the Lord Jesus said to one of His disciples just before He went back to Heaven. He said, ' Feed My lambs '—and that's why I wanted Terry to come to us so badly. Then when he died, three mornings ago, I said to myself, ' This lamb doesn't need me any more; but there are plenty of others. . . .' "

She stopped and stared into the fire. I held my hands out to the blaze, and we all sat thinking our own thoughts —sad thoughts about Terry, but all mixed up with happy thoughts about Christmas and the future.

The 'phone bell startled us all, and my aunt went out to answer it. She was gone some time, and when she returned she was laughing, and her face looked most mysterious.

" Another piece of news," she announced " and this is the very nicest piece of news we've had for years."

We both stared at her in astonishment. Then suddenly Philip jumped to his feet and made a dash at her.

" I know!" he shouted. " I can guess! Mummy and Daddy are coming home!"

Auntie nodded. " Yes," she answered " you've guessed right first time. They will be here in time for Christmas."

Philip's face, flushed with the firelight, was radiant with joy; but I stayed perfectly still with my hands clasped on my knees. I suddenly felt miserable and obstinate, and all my old fears came back to me; I remembered Aunt Margaret's words of long ago, and how she had said that I should be such a disappointment to my mother, and I didn't want to meet her. She would like

Philip better and I should be cross and unhappy and jealous again—and things were just beginning to get comfortable. I turned my head away and looked gloomily at the coal scuttle.

Philip gave me an impatient little shake.

"Aren't you pleased?" he almost screamed. "Why don't you say so?"

I gave a little shrug of my shoulders.

"Yes," I replied, because that was what everyone expected me to say. . . . Then I got up, because I wanted to get away from them. "It's bedtime," I said, coldly. "Good-night, Aunt Margaret."

But it wasn't really Good-night, for half-an-hour later Aunt Margaret came softly to where I lay in the dark, and knelt by my bed.

"Ruth," she whispered, and her voice sounded all troubled, "why aren't you glad like Philip?"

I wriggled uncomfortably and buried my hot face in the pillows; but my aunt did not go away; she waited patiently, and seeing that she really expected an answer, I whispered back.

"You said she wouldn't like me, and I don't suppose she will."

"Oh, Ruth!" cried my aunt, "I never said that; I said she would be disappointed when you behaved rudely and selfishly, but that was a long time ago. I know you have been trying hard to be good, and something has certainly made a difference to you. I have felt much happier about you lately, and of course your mother will love you dearly."

I stopped wriggling and lay quite still. I had suddenly stopped feeling shy.

"I know what it is," I answered quietly. "It's my

picture; it's knowing the Shepherd that's made the difference."

"Yes," agreed my aunt, "you're right. Your picture, and learning about the Shepherd, has made a tremendous difference to all of us."

20

A PERFECT CHRISTMAS

IT was Christmas evening. We had had such a happy day that I kept having to stop and tell myself that it was all really true.

Mother and Father had arrived just a fortnight before, and Philip and I had missed school and gone to Liverpool with Uncle Peter to meet the boat. We had been on a moving staircase, and we had stayed in an hotel where we had chicken and coffee-ices for supper, and we had gone up to bed in a lift and the lift man had let Philip work it. Then we had been wakened early, and gone down to the Merseyside in a wet, windy dawn; we had watched the passengers streaming down the gangway of the great liner, until Uncle Peter had suddenly said, in quite a quiet voice, "Here they come," and there were Mother and Father showing their passports at the barrier.

Philip, absolutely trustful and joyful, had flung himself straight into Father's arms, and had then turned to Mother and hugged the hat right off her head. But I stood still, because I wanted to be quite sure of everything first; and when Mother ran towards me I looked up into her face and suddenly knew that I had found something I'd been wanting all these years without knowing it. I was so overcome with this discovery that I just went on staring up at her, and she didn't hurry me. She waited, looking down at me, until I was ready and held up my arms to kiss her. Then she stooped and drew me to her, and there on the quayside, with the rain falling, and the crowds jostling, and the fog-horns wailing, she told me in a whisper how much she loved me, and I made up my mind, then and there, that I was never going to be parted from her again.

Then, with one hand in Mother's and one in Father's, and with Philip prancing round us like an excited puppy, we made our way back to the hotel, had kippers and toast and marmalade for breakfast, and nearly missed the train home.

And now it was Christmas evening and the great moment of the day was approaching. We had opened our stockings, and been to church, and eaten turkey and Christmas pudding until we all felt as tight as drums. We had been for a walk on the hills in the afternoon with Father and Uncle Peter, and had come back as hungry as though the dinner had all been a dream. We had had tea by rosy candlelight, Father had cut the cake with his Indian dagger and we had all pulled crackers but little Minnie, one of the London children, didn't like the bangs and had been carried out screaming, and fed with choco-late biscuits in the kitchen by Terry's mother. Now Auntie was saying, " Run away for five minutes, children," and Mother was saying, " Go into the kitchen and see how Minnie is getting on," and Father was saying, " Any-one who comes into the drawing-room will be eaten by a big brown bear," and Philip was pinching us all in turns and saying, " Come on everybody, now's our chance."

So when the drawing-room door was safely shut on the grown-ups, we slipped on our coats and tiptoed out of the front door. The world was quite silent and the starlight lay silver on the snow. Philip looked at us intently and hummed the note, and then we all threw back our heads and started singing:

> " *The shepherds had an angel,*
>   *The wise men had a star,*
> *But what have I, a little child,*
>   *To guide me home from far,*
> *Where glad stars sing together*
>   *And singing angels are?"*

We sang the carol right through, and I kept on thinking that the Baby Jesus was now *my* Shepherd. The Shepherd who was going to look after me day and night and carry me home some day to where Terry was. I looked out into the wide white world with its snow, and smiled—I knew that I was perfectly safe for ever and ever.

But the carol was over and Alfie was hammering excitedly on the door. It was flung open, and there in the hall, under the mistletoe and holly, were Mother and Auntie in paper caps, and Father and Uncle pretending they didn't know it was us, and Terry's mother with tears in her eyes and little Minnie clasped tightly in her arms. We flung ourselves wildly upon them.

" Did you like it?" we shouted. " Did you really think it wasn't us?"

But at that moment a piercing shriek from Lizzie made everybody jump. She had caught sight of something through the open drawing-room door and was making for it. With one accord we fled up the passage behind her and crowded in. The candles on the beautifully decked Christmas tree were alight and shedding a rosy glow over the dark room.

It was so pretty that we stopped screaming, and sat down

quietly, cross-legged on the floor while Father started giving out the presents.

Soon it was our turn. Father took a square parcel from the pile at the bottom of the tree, and handed it to Philip.

"Open it carefully, Phil!" he warned. "It's very fragile."

Philip annoyed me by taking a long time over the unwrapping, but he always like to spin out his pleasures as long as possible. However, at last it came to light, and Philip made a funny noise in his throat like something trying not to explode. It was a black Kodak camera, just like the one we had so often gazed at in the chemist's shop.

"Philip!" I squealed, "you've got it!" Then I stopped short, for of course it was my turn now. Father had selected a flat, hard parcel and was holding it out to me.

Everyone crowded round to watch as I, unlike Philip, tore the wrappings off as quickly as possible and gave a little gasp of delight and went pink all over.

It was my own picture, but not a crumpled, torn postcard one. It was a big, beautiful copy in a carved wooden frame for me to hang over my bed and keep for ever. In fact, it was just like the one in Mr. Robinson's study.

The grown-ups opened their presents after that, and seemed as pleased as we were; they were mostly homemade things and we were very proud of them: fret-work book ends for Uncle Peter, a purse for Aunt Margaret, a blotter for Father and a hot-water cover for Mother; Terry's mother was presented with a highly-coloured embroidered hanky sachet, which she admired very much indeed.

Of course there were other presents, too, but these were the main ones.

Philip and I helped clear up, and then Philip and Father sat down on the sofa together and looked at the bird book together for about the tenth time. But it was different now, because the camera lay in Philip's lap and they were planning the photos.

I wandered off by myself with my picture in my arms, and climbed the stairs. I wanted to curl up behind the curtain on the landing window-sill and look at the Christmas stars and snow, and listen to the bells that were ringing from the church nearby. But when I reached my hiding place, I found that Mother had got there first, and that was even better than being alone, so I climbed on to her lap and held up my picture, because I wanted us to look at it together.

"Isn't it beautiful?" I asked.

"Yes," replied my mother, "but what made you love it so specially, Ruth? Tell me about it."

So I told her rather shyly, and she listened, looking out over the snow, until I had finished.

"And it's not only me," I ended up; "He found me first but after that He found Philip and Terry's mother, and He found Terry, too, and carried him right home; and, Mummy, sometimes I think perhaps He found Aunt Margaret, too. At least, I think she had forgotten about Him a bit, and when she saw the picture it reminded her of Him again."

"Yes, I think it did," answered Mother, "and do you know, Ruth, I also want to learn so much more about Him; won't it be lovely all learning together? Sometimes, far away in India, I used to kneel down and pray that somehow you would get to know about Him, but I never felt I knew enough to teach you myself."

I looked up quickly.

"Did you really?" I exclaimed. "Then I suppose that's why it all happened. I suppose you sort of sent Him to us. I'm glad it's like that, because it makes it even nicer than it was before."

I laid my head against her shoulder, and we sat quite quietly looking out. I think I nearly fell asleep, and in a half-dreaming way I saw us all sought and found, and following through the green fields in Terry's picture: Mother and Father, Auntie and Uncle; Mr. and Mrs. Robinson and the twins; their tiny feet stumbling through the daisies; old Mr. Tandy with his flock behind him; Terry's mother; Philip and me; Alfie and Lizzie and Minnie—because I had promised to tell them all about my picture in the morning; and, in front of us all, the Good Shepherd with the wounded hands leading us on to a Land far away, where Terry was, perfectly strong and happy.

PIRATES!
In an Adventure with
SCIENTISTS

GIDEON DEFOE was born in 1975 and lives in London. He is also the author of *The Pirates! In An Adventure with Moby Dick, The Pirates! In An Adventure with Communists*, and *The Pirates! In An Adventure with Napoleon*. You could be forgiven for thinking he is a bit of a one-trick pony.

PIRATES!
In an Adventure with
SCIENTISTS

Gideon Defoe

B L O O M S B U R Y
LONDON · BERLIN · NEW YORK · SYDNEY

First published in Great Britain in 2004 by Weidenfeld & Nicholson
This paperback edition published 2011

Copyright © Gideon Defoe 2004
Map copyright © 2004 by Dave Senior

The moral right of the author has been asserted

Bloomsbury Publishing, London, Berlin, New York and Sydney

50 Bedford Square, London WC1B 3DP

A CIP catalogue record for this book is
available from the British Library

ISBN 9781408824955
10 9 8 7 6 5 4 3 2 1

Typeset by Hewer Text UK Ltd, Edinburgh

Printed in Great Britain by Clays Ltd, St Ives Plc

MIX
Paper from
responsible sources
FSC® C018072
FSC
www.fsc.org

www.bloomsbury.com/gideondefoe

To Sophie,
who has a quarter of a million pounds.

CONTENTS

CHAPTER ONE
A pirate brawl – The Pirate Captain – A decision is made – Cooking the ham – Setting sail

CHAPTER TWO
A pirate feast – A letter arrives – The *Barbary Hen* – Meeting Black Bellamy – Another pirate feast – A game of cards – Setting sail again

CHAPTER THREE
Piratical entertainments – A delicate question – Making ready for attack

CHAPTER FOUR
A reluctant duel – Under attack! – Looking for gold – In conversation – Darwin's dangerous idea – Another decision is made

COMPREHENSION EXERCISE

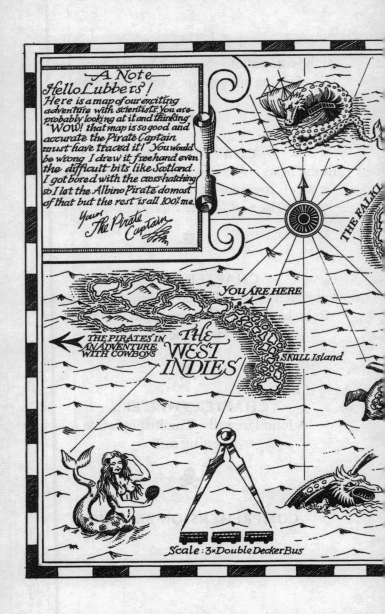

The HIGH SEAS

Chesterfield

LONDON

LITTLEHAMPTON

THE
GALAPAGOS
ISLANDS

DS '03

Royal Society
Gentlemen's
Club

CARNABY ST

SOHO

NATURAL
HISTORY
MUSEUM

BIG BEN

HOTEL
METROPOLITAN

FORK CONVENTION

RIVER

AN
OUT OF
CONTROL
FIRE

THE LADY
WITH A
PHOBIA of TINFOIL

THE MER-MAID

THE
ELEPHANT
MAN

A M
WITH

A SPECIAL
EXHIBIT
FOR
LADIES

LONDON ZOO

ST JAMES' PARK

THAMES

STENDERS

SOOTY ORPHANS

FOG

P. T. BARNUM
(in association with
the Bishop of Oxford)
is Proud to Present
His WORLD FAMOUS

CIRCUS
~ OF ~
# FREAKS

FEATURING
THE ELEPHANT MAN
THE MER-MAID
A BEARD OF BEES
Tuesday, Wednesday, Thursday, Friday, & Sat

LADIES NIGHT
FREE ENTRY ALL DAY TO LADIES

D·S '03

One

INTO ACTION UNDER
THE PIRATE FLAG!

'The best bit about being a pirate,' said the pirate with gout, 'is the looting.'

'That's rubbish!' said the albino pirate. 'It's the doubloons. Doubloons are easily the best bit about pirating.'

The rest of the pirates, sunning themselves on the deck of the pirate boat, soon joined in. It had been several weeks since the Pirates' Adventure with Cowboys, and they had a lot of time on their hands.

'It's the pirate grog!'

'Marooning! That's what I like best!'

'Cutlasses!'

'The Spanish Main!'

'The ship's biscuits!'

One of the pirates pulled a special face to show exactly what he thought of this last comment, and soon all the pirates were fighting. With a sound like a bat hitting a watermelon, pirate fist connected with pirate jaw and a gold tooth bounced across the deck. The pirate with gout found himself run through in a grisly manner, and one of the cabin boys accidentally got a shiny pirate hook in the side of the head. It would probably have gone on for hours in this fashion, but both of the heavy wooden doors that led to the downstairs of the boat crashed open, and out onto the deck strode the Pirate Captain himself.

The Pirate Captain cut an impressive figure. If you were to compare him to a type of tree – and working out what sort of tree they would be if they were trees instead of pirates was easily one of the crew's favourite pastimes – he would undoubtedly be an oak, or maybe a horse chestnut. He was all teeth and curls, but with a pleasant open face; his coat was of a better cut than everybody else's, and his beard was fantastic and glossy, and the ends of it were twisted with expensive-looking ribbons. Living at sea tended to leave you with ratty, matted hair, but the Pirate Captain somehow kept his beard silky and in good condition, and though nobody knew his secret, they all respected him for it. They also respected him because it was said he was wedded to the sea. A lot of pirates claimed that they were wedded to the sea, but usually this was an excuse because they couldn't get a girlfriend or they were a gay pirate, but in the Pirate Captain's case none of his crew doubted he was actually wedded to the sea for a minute. Any of his men would have gladly taken a bullet for him, or even the pointy end of a cutlass. The Pirate Captain didn't need to do much more than clear his throat and roll his eyes a bit to stop the fighting dead in its tracks.

'What's going on, you scurvy knaves!' he bellowed. Pirates were often rude to each other, but without really meaning it, so none of the brawling pirates took being called a 'scurvy knave' too much to heart.

'We were just discussing what the best bit about being a pirate is,' answered the pirate dressed in green, after a bit of an awkward pause.

'The best bit about being a pirate?'

'Yes sir. We couldn't quite decide. I mean, it's all good . . .'

'The best bit about being a pirate is the shanties.'

And, with the argument settled, the Pirate Captain strode back into the galley, indicating for the pirate with a scarf to follow. The rest of the crew were left on their own.

'He's right. It's the shanties,' said the albino pirate thoughtfully. One of the other pirates nodded.

'They are really good. Shall we sing a pirate shanty?'

The Pirate Captain was secretly relieved when he heard the strains of a rowdy shanty coming through the roof of the galley. Just recently he had been worrying about discipline on board the pirate boat, and there was an old pirate motto: if the men are singing a shanty then they can't be up to mischief.[1]

'Come into my office for a moment,' he told the pirate with a scarf, who was his trusty second in

---

1 'Shanty' probably derives from the French word 'chanter' meaning to sing. Most shanties tended to be about frisky mermaids who loved putting out for sailors more than anyone.

command. The Pirate Captain's office was full of mementoes from the previous pirate adventures. There was a ten-gallon hat from the Pirates' Adventure with the Cowboys, and some old bits of tentacle from the Pirates' Adventure with Squid, as well as several Post-It notes reminding the Pirate Captain to say things like 'Splice the mainsail!' or 'Hard about, lads!'. On the walls there hung several fantastic paintings of the Pirate Captain himself – one of them showed him looking anguished and cradling a dead swan: this painting was titled WHY? Another was of the Pirate Captain reclining naked except for a small piece of gauze. And a third pictured the Pirate Captain sharing a strange futuristic-looking drink with a lady who seemed to be made from metal. There were also quite a lot of nautical maps and charts about the place, and even an astrolabe. The Pirate Captain wasn't 100 per cent sure what the astrolabe did, or whether it was actually an astrolabe rather than a sextant, but he enjoyed fiddling with it when he got bored nonetheless. Right at the moment boredom was an issue that weighed heavily on the Pirate Captain's mind.

7

'Care for some grog?' he asked politely. The scarf-wearing pirate wasn't very thirsty, but he said yes anyway, because if you start turning down grog when you're a pirate it doesn't help your reputation much.

'Ship's biscuits? I've got ship's custard creams, and ship's bourbons,' said the Pirate Captain. He held out a tin that had a boat painted on it and the pirate with a scarf took a bourbon, because he knew custard creams were the Pirate Captain's favourites.

'What do you think all that brawling was about, number two?' asked the Pirate Captain, absent-mindedly seeing how fast he could spin the astrolabe using just one finger.

'Like the men said . . . it was just a friendly discussion that got a bit out of hand,' replied the scarf-wearing pirate, not entirely sure where the Pirate Captain was going with this, but amazed as always that he could carry on a conversation whilst doing complex calculations with an astrolabe. That sort of thing was why the Pirate Captain was the Pirate Captain, the pirate with a scarf reflected.

'I'll tell you what it was about,' said the Pirate Captain. 'It was about bored pirates! I've made a mistake. We've been moored here in . . . in the . . .' The Pirate Captain rubbed his nose, which he liked to think of as a stentorian nose, even though stentorian is actually a tone of voice, and squinted at one of the charts.

'The West Indies, sir,' said the scarf-wearing pirate, helpfully.

'Mmmm. Well, we've been here too long. I thought that after our exciting adventure with those cowboys, we could all do with a break, but I guess us pirates are only really happy when we're pirating.'

'I think you're right, sir,' the scarf-wearing pirate said. 'It's nice enough here, but I keep on finding sand in my grog, from all that lying about on the beach. And those native women, wandering about with no tops on . . . it's a bit much.'

'Exactly. It's time we had another pirate adventure!'

'I'll let the other pirates know. Where will we be heading for? Skull Island? The Spanish Main?'

'Oh, Lord, no! If we plunder the Spanish Main² one more time, I think I'll tear out my own beard,' said the Pirate Captain, trying on the ten-gallon hat and narrowing his eyes like a cowboy as he studied his reflection in the mirror.

'So what were you thinking?'

'Something will come up. It usually does. Just make sure we've got plenty of hams on board. I didn't really enjoy our last adventure much, because we ran out of hams about halfway through. And what's my motto? "I like ham!"'

'It's a good motto, sir.'

Back on deck, the other pirates had finished their shanty – which had been about how a beautiful sea-nymph had left her rich but stupid Royal Navy boyfriend for a pirate boyfriend

---

2   It was Francis Drake who had first made the Spanish Main a popular target, back in 1571. A replica of his boat, the *Golden Hind*, can be found today next to London Bridge.

because he was much more interesting to talk to and could make her laugh – and now they were roaring. This was another common pastime amongst the pirates.

'Rah!'

'Oooh-Arg!'

'Aaaarrrr, me hearties!'

It didn't mean much, but it filled a few hours. They all stopped when they saw the pirate with a scarf had come back from his meeting with the Pirate Captain. He almost slipped in a pool of the cabin boy's blood that was left over from the fight.

'Can somebody swab these decks?' he said, a little tetchily. Left to their own devices the pirates tended towards the bone idle.

'It's Tuesday! Sunday is boat cleaning day!'

'I know, but somebody could get hurt.'

The diffident pirate gave a shrug and went off to find a swabbing cloth, whilst the remaining crew looked up expectantly from where they were sprawled. The scarf-wearing pirate gazed out across the sparkling water, and at the tropical beach with its alabaster sands, and the forest of coconut palms behind that, and then he noticed one of the pretty native ladies and so he quickly looked back down at his pirate shoes.

'Listen up, pirates,' he said. 'I know all this endless wandering up and down the beach . . . and our interminable attempts at trying to choose which sort of mouth-watering exotic fruit to eat . . . and all these wanton tropical girls knocking around . . . I know it's been getting you down.'

A couple of the pirates muttered something to each other, but the scarf-wearing pirate didn't quite catch what they said.

'So you'll be happy to know,' he went on, 'that the Pirate Captain has ordered us to put to sea, just as soon as we've collected some hams for the journey.'

A buzz of excitement ran around the deck.

'Perhaps we should cook the hams first, before setting off?' asked the pirate dressed in green.

'That sounds like a good idea,' said the albino pirate.

'Do you think roasting is best?' asked the pirate with a nut allergy.

The scarf-wearing pirate sighed, because he knew how seriously the pirates took their ham, and he could predict how this was going to end up. He tried to look hard-nosed, which involved tensing all the muscles in his nostrils, and with as much authority as he could manage he said, 'Yes, roasting is good. It allows the free escape of watery particles that's necessary for a full flavour. But we've got to make sure it's regulated by frequent basting with the fat that has exuded from the meat, combined with a little salt and water – otherwise the hams will burn, and become hard and tasteless.'

'Roasting?[3] Are you sure?' asked the surly pirate who was dressed in red, barely concealing his contempt. 'What about boiling? I always find a boiled ham becomes more savoury in taste and smell, and more firm and digestible.'

'Ah, but if you continue the process too long,

---

3 In those days, roasting would have meant spit-roasting. A popular craze in the early part of the nineteenth century was to use a small dog fastened to a treadmill to turn the spit, freeing up the cook to prepare other dishes.

you risk the hams becoming tough and less succulent,' said the pirate in green.

'But the loss from roasting is upwards of 22 per cent of the ham! The loss from boiling is only about 16 per cent. More ham for us! That can only be a good thing.'

'We need to dust the hams with bread raspings if we're going to boil them. And we should dress the knuckle bone with a frill of white paper.'

'A frill of white paper? What kind of a pirate are you? Rah!'

The pirates started to fight again, and it wasn't until one of them noticed that the Pirate Captain had come back from his cabin and was now leaning against the mast, drumming his fingers on a barrel, that they shuffled to attention.

'That's enough of that, my beauties!' he roared. 'Let's set a course . . .' at this point the Pirate Captain paused in what he hoped would be a dramatic and exciting fashion, '. . . for adventure!'

The crew just gave him a bit of a collective blank look. The Pirate Captain sighed.

'All right,' he said with a pout, 'south.'

Two

RETURN TO
SKULL ISLAND!

'That was some hurricane!' said the pirate who was prone to exaggeration, emptying the sea- water that had collected in his pirate boots over the side of the boat. 'I don't think I've ever seen one like it! I thought the mast was going to crack for sure! And we must have lost half a dozen men, just washed away into the deep.'[4]

'That wasn't a hurricane. It wasn't even a storm,' said the pirate in red.

'Well, gale then. That was some gale.'

'Pfft!' said the pirate in red. He was fed up, because a whole day had gone by and they didn't seem to be any closer to actually starting an adventure.

---

4   The Caribbean and the Gulf of Mexico were, and are, subject to devastating hurricanes. In 1712 Governor Hamilton reported that a storm had destroyed thirty-eight ships in the harbour at Port Royal and nine ships at Kingston.

'According to my Beaufort Scale,' said the albino pirate, waving a nautical pamphlet at the rest of the crew, 'a hurricane is number twelve, or "that which no canvas could withstand". As you can see, our canvases are fine, so it obviously wasn't a hurricane. I should say it was somewhere between number six, a Strong Breeze – or "that which will send a pirate's hat flying and muss up his luxuriant beard" and number eight, a Fresh Gale – or "that which will make a pirate's trousers billow about so that it looks like he has fat legs".'

'Are you sure that's an actual Beaufort Scale you've got there?' asked the scarf-wearing pirate.

'Of course I'm sure,' snapped the albino pirate. 'The Pirate Captain wrote it out for me himself.'

All the pirates were too tired even to roar at each other, let alone sing a shanty, after their strenuous efforts in bringing the boat through the previous night's fantastic storm or fresh gale or strong breeze or whatever it happened to be. So they just sprawled on the deck, looking up at the last few seagulls to have made it this far out from land, circling above in what was now a clear blue sky. It wasn't until the smell of fresh ham wafted from the boat's kitchen that the pirates stirred and went below to the pirate dining room.

The Pirate Captain was already sitting at the table, tapping his knife and fork expectantly. Of all the pirates it was true that nobody loved his ham more than the Pirate Captain. The hams were brought to the table, and they had been roasted, which annoyed the pirate who had argued they should have been boiled, but he was so hungry he didn't bother to complain, and he had to admit that they tasted delicious. The pirates tore into their food and grog with the relish that comes from a hard night's pirating.

'Honestly, pirates! Have you forgotten that you are provided with teeth? Small wonder you complain about indigestion when you forget to chew!' admonished the Pirate Captain.

'I thought it was cold feet that gave you indigestion,' said the pirate with a hook where his hand should have been. 'And that wrapping your feet in a hot towel would prevent such belly pains.'

'That's headaches, idiot!' said the pirate in green.

'No. Headaches are most commonly caused from reading by candlelight, when the candle is positioned incorrectly. It should be placed behind you, so the rays can pass directly over your shoulder to the book.'

The pirates almost started fighting again over this, but the Pirate Captain held up an imperious hand, and started to speak.

'I got a letter this morning,' he said, 'from our old enemy, Black Bellamy.'

The pirates muttered a few oaths. Black Bellamy was the roguish rival pirate who the pirates had encountered during the Pirates' Adventure with Buried Treasure, and the Pirates' Adventure with the Princess of Cadiz. Somehow they weren't surprised that they had not heard the last of him.

'Black Bellamy has invited us to a feast onboard his schooner, the *Barbary Hen*, which is sailing just a few leagues from here.'

'It's Black Bellamy, Captain! You can't mean to trust him!' said the albino pirate. The other pirates nodded.

'Perhaps he's changed,' said the Pirate Captain. 'He says in his letter that he's changed, and that he wants to hold this feast to make up for all the trouble he and his villainous crew have caused us in the past.'

'Oh, well. You can't really argue with that sort of sentiment,' agreed the pirate in green.

'Yes, that seems really nice of him,' said the albino pirate, feeling a bit guilty for being so harsh on Black Bellamy just a few seconds ago.

'And it would be good to see how they prepare their hams on board the *Barbary Hen*,' added the pirate in red.

'So it's settled, we'll accept the invitation and set sail for Black Bellamy's feast at once!' said the Pirate Captain, picking a piece of ham from his immaculate beard.

The moonlit waters were clear and calm as the pirate boat moored up alongside the *Barbary Hen*. The pirate crew piled into a launch – 'Shotgun!' shouted the sassy pirate who liked to sit up front with the Captain – and paddled across to where a rope-ladder had been hung over the other ship's side. There were around forty head of hog wandering about the darkened decks, which was clearly Black Bellamy's way of impressing his guests. Black Bellamy politely took the pirates' coats and cutlasses. This showed he really *had* changed, because the Black Bellamy of old was famous for his lack of manners. But he was still a fearsome sight, with a beard that came up to his eyes, two pairs of pistols hanging at the end of a silk sling, and a big knife held between his teeth.

'Herro. Relcon ahord ha *harrarry hen*,' said Black Bellamy.

'What did he say?' whispered the pirate in green.

'I think he said "Welcome aboard the *Barbary Hen*". It's a bit hard to tell, because of that knife clenched between his teeth,' said the scarf-wearing pirate.

Black Bellamy made a few incomprehensible introductions, and then led the pirates into his feasting hall. Their old rival had certainly pulled out all the stops – there was roast veal, which had half a pint of melted butter poured over it, fillets of beef garnished with slices of lemon, a sumptuous pork broth, potato scones, stewed mushrooms . . . several of the pirates had to use their pirate neckerchiefs to wipe saliva from their mouths. It didn't matter that they had already eaten a sumptuous feast earlier that day, because they often had adventures comprised of nothing but sumptuous feasts. Initially, because there was so much history between them, the two sets of pirates were a bit hostile, and conversation was understandably awkward, but after some pirate grog they were soon carousing with each other. Piratical conversation buzzed about the boat.

'Diving. Have you ever tried it? It's fantastic! We went and dived at the wreck of an actual pirate ship!'

'My friend here thinks you should boil hams, but he's an idiot.'

'. . . 'twas the unmistakable tang of human flesh . . .'

'. . . and I'm not making this up – he had a wooden leg!'

Both Black Bellamy and the Pirate Captain were pleased it was going so well.

'Why don't we adjourn to my drawing room, for a spot of cards?⁵ Hmmm?' said Black Bellamy to the Pirate Captain. The Pirate Captain could have gone on eating mutton necks all night, but his host had been so gracious he thought it rude to refuse.

The pirates were a bit annoyed by how nice the drawing room was, especially when Black

---

5   Captain Johnson's General *History of the Pyrates* tells us that most pirate ships had a set of Articles, by which the crew had to adhere. Article 3 states 'No person to game at cards or dice for money', so Black Bellamy is showing his maverick colours here.

Bellamy flipped open the top of a huge mahogany globe to reveal a little drinks cabinet. The Pirate Captain's globe back onboard the pirate boat was made out of tin and about the size of a football, and he wasn't even sure it had Africa on it, so it was difficult not to feel a pang of jealousy. Black Bellamy poured out some rum from a crystal decanter and suggested a game of Cincinnati High Low.

'Oh, that's a lucky man's game,' said the Pirate Captain, because he had heard someone say this before.

'Well, what would you suggest?' asked Black Bellamy amiably. 'Crossfire? Seven Card Flip? Mexican Seven Card Stud?'

He was just showing off, thought the Pirate Captain, but he was no slouch at cards himself.

'How about,' said the Pirate Captain, 'Cat's Cradle? Or Round the World? Or Walking the Dog?'

'Those are yo-yo tricks.'

'Ha! Of course they are. Well then, that one with the Mexicans.'

They settled down to the card game. Pretty

soon the Pirate Captain was down several doubloons, and pretty soon after that he had lost all the boat's precious supply of hams. The trouble was that Black Bellamy's beard, coming up all the way to his eyes as it did, gave him a perfect poker face. The Pirate Captain's crew were starting to get worried, but then the Pirate Captain had a fantastic idea. He found himself with another useless hand but this time, instead of thumping the table and looking miserable, he gave a big grin, and whispered loudly to the pirate who wore a scarf, 'We'll be feasting on that forty head of hog, with this brilliant hand!'

Black Bellamy heard this, and decided to fold. The Pirate Captain shuffled the pile of doubloons into his pockets. Black Bellamy saw his cards and gasped.

'But . . . you had a terrible hand! Garbage!'

'Yes. But I knew that if I looked pleased with it, you would think it was a flush or something like that!'

'You're confounded clever!' roared Black Bellamy. 'But listen. Give me back all those doubloons I've just lost, and in return I'll tell you where you can find ten times that sort of loot.'

The Pirate Captain thought about Black Bellamy's offer for a second or two. Mathematics wasn't his strong point – obviously pirating was his strong point – but you didn't need to be Archimedes to realise that ten times the amount of doubloons he had just won was a good deal of cash.

'Very well, Black Bellamy,' said the Pirate Captain, taking the coins back out of his pockets. 'Where can we find this treasure?'

'I'll need to show you on the nautical charts,' sighed Black Bellamy, doing a sad face. 'Me and my men had been planning to sail to the south seas, near the Galapagos Islands, where a ship belonging to the – uh – Bank of England is right this moment transporting . . . ooh, at least a hundredweight in gold bullion, back from the colonies. I'd been really looking forward to a spot of plundering, but I guess I'll just have to let you set about the raid yourself!'

'You're sure about this?' said the Pirate Captain, his eyes narrowing. 'That's eight hundred leagues from here. It's a little out of our way.'

'I swear by the Pirate Code.'

'Do you know the name of this ship?'

'It's called the *Beagle*. And it's chock full of gold, mark my words. Can I have those doubloons back now?'

As the pirates crossed back to their boat they could hear laughter coming from the *Barbary Hen* – it was good, thought the Pirate Captain, that they had left their hosts in such high spirits, even though he had got the better of Black Bellamy. And now he was pretty confident that they really *were* setting course . . . for adventure!

Though he didn't bother saying it out loud this time.

Three

PIRATE ISLANDS AND
BLACKHEARTED MEN!

'So, there's two pirate boats sailing towards each other,' said the short pirate with thick black spectacles, 'and one of the boats is carrying all this blue paint. And the other pirate boat is carrying all this red paint. They crash, and you know what happened?'

'What happened?'

'They were marooned! Ha-ha! You see?'

The pirates had started telling each other jokes in an attempt to ward off the inevitable boredom between feasts, because there wasn't much else to do on board a pirate boat. They had been at sea for a couple of days now, searching high and low for the *Beagle*. When the boat had first reached the tropical waters surrounding the Galapagos Islands the pirates kept themselves amused by capturing a couple of the giant turtles that frequented this part of the world, and then racing them about the deck.[6] You could fit two whole pirates on each shell. They constructed an obstacle course from bits of old rope and rigging, but the turtles proved a lot less resilient than they had hoped. A few of the pirates then had the bright idea that if they caught enough of the huge diaphanous jellyfish that circled about the boat, they could construct a kind of bouncy castle. This kept them occupied for a few more hours, but it didn't really work, and eventually they got tired of it, and found that they had jellyfish guts stuck all over their pirate boots.

The pirate dressed in green went downstairs to get a glass of water because he was nervous and his throat was dry. There was a note stuck next to the ship's sink, written in the Pirate Captain's familiar bubble writing. It read:

---

6 Nowadays Galapagos Giant Turtles often accidentally eat plastic bags left as litter by unthinking tourists, mistaking them for tasty jellyfish.

Will whoever keeps taking my mug STOP IT. It is very annoying. Have a little respect for other people's property. The Pirate Captain.

Life at sea was tough and unforgiving, and tensions could run quite high on board a pirate boat, especially when crockery was limited and people didn't always do their washing-up, but generally the pirates all got along fine. The pirate dressed in green gulped down the tap water – it was much nicer than seawater – and tried to pluck up courage for the task ahead. He'd been putting it off for ages, but now seemed as good a time as any.

There was a knock at the Pirate Captain's door, and then the pirate in green came in.

'Sorry to be bothering you, Captain,' he said. The Pirate Captain looked up. He had a lot to sort out in preparation for their imminent and audacious attack, but he made a point of always having time for the men.

33

'What can I do for you . . . uh . . . my fellow?' said the Pirate Captain, who often found it difficult to tell his crew apart from one another. 'Grog? Ham?'

'No thanks, sir. I was wondering if I could ask you something?'

'It's what I'm here for. You don't mind if I help myself?' said the Pirate Captain, indicating the slices of ham. 'Now, what is it?'

'Well, I was thinking of getting a tattoo.'

'They're quite popular.'

'Yes, Captain.'

'But they don't come off, you know.'

'Yes, Captain. I've thought about that.'

'Well then.'

'I thought it might be good to get a Skull and Crossbones, like we have on our flag, but it turns out a couple of the men have already got that. So . . . I was wondering . . . that's to say . . . would you have any objections . . .'

'Spit it out man!'

'. . . if I got your face done instead? I was thinking of adding a little speech bubble, with – ha – you saying "Scurvy knaves!" like you

34

always do. It would be on my arm, if that's all right.' He indicated the patch on his upper arm where he was going to have the tattoo.

For a moment, the Pirate Captain was speechless. The ham on his fork just hung in mid air.

'Of course . . . I . . . ah . . . I don't know what to say,' he said.

'Are you okay, Captain?'

'Yes . . . it's just this, um, ham. It's very spicy, and it's making my eyes water.'

In all their many adventures, even the one where they had battled zombie pirates, the Pirate Captain had never been so touched by a gesture from any of his loyal pirate crew. His lip began to tremble, and the pirate in green was mightily relieved when at that point the pirate with an accordion, breathless with excitement, hurried into the Captain's office.

'Sorry to interrupt, Captain, but we've caught sight of a ship, and we think it's the *Beagle*, because it has a funny-looking dog painted on the side. Should I get the men ready for boarding?'

The Pirate Captain swiftly regained his

composure, and started to bark out orders. 'Get the cannons ready first, and remind the pirates not to stand right behind them this time,' he bellowed. The Pirate Captain had explained basic Newtonian physics and the principles of recoil to his men more times than he could remember, but it just didn't seem to go in.

'And I want to hear plenty of roaring until we've secured the enemy vessel,' he said, picking up a telescope and marching onto the deck, where several of the pirates were already gathered.

'It's just a ten-gun brig,' said the scarf-wearing pirate, scratching thoughtfully at a livid scar that ran the length of his cheek. On most people a scar can be quite disfiguring, but several of the pirates thought that in the pirate with a scarf's case it actually added to his rather rugged appeal.

'A ten-gun brig? Really?' said the Pirate Captain, frowning at the news.

'I was expecting something bigger. Seeing as it's carrying all this gold for the Bank of England,' said his number two.

'Perhaps they're trying to keep a low profile,'

said the Pirate Captain, with some misgivings. 'Are those cannons ready?'

'This sort of makes us bank robbers, doesn't it?'

'Aaarrr. But you knew you'd be bending a few laws when you became a pirate. I'm not sure the ivory smuggling we were doing the other week was entirely respectable. Or all that trawling for cod, come to think about it.'

'Cannons ready, Captain.'

An eerie silence suddenly becalmed the pirate chatter, as the crew waited for the Pirate Captain to give his order to make good the attack.

'Fire a cannonball at that boat!' said the Pirate Captain.

Four

WHAT EVIL
LURKS IN THE
UNFORGIVING DEEP?

'Confound it, man!' said Robert FitzRoy, captain of the boat about to be attacked by the pirates. 'I told you women and the sea were a mighty bad combination.'

FitzRoy was young for a ship's captain, just twenty-seven, but the man he stood back to back with was younger still, a full five years his junior. Yet neither bore the frisky demeanour that you would expect to find in people under thirty.

'I can't help myself, Robert,' said his companion, Charles Darwin, cradling his big round head in his hands. 'I love her, and I mean to marry her!'

'But I love her too!' said FitzRoy. 'She drives me to distraction! You already knew that.'

'Damn women, with . . . with their hair . . . and their faces . . .' muttered Darwin.

'I must demand satisfaction,' said Captain FitzRoy. 'You don't leave me any choice.'

The cabin was a little small for a duel, neither

man quite being able to stand up properly without grazing his head, but needs must at sea.

'Three years' voyage . . . and it should come to this,' said Darwin, shakily pouring powder into his pistol. 'May the best man win.'

'You're a botanist.[7] I'm a trained naval officer. I don't fancy your chances much,' said FitzRoy.

The door was flung open with a crash that made Darwin wince, and in ran the breathless cause of the two men's argument, the lovely Lady Mara. 'Please stop!' she said with her lovely mouth.

'There's—'

But before Lady Mara could say any more, a cannonball splintered through the cabin wall at tremendous speed, and buried itself in the side of her pretty head, knocking her off her feet, and leaving her quite dead on the floor. Darwin and FitzRoy stood, dumbfounded.

---

7   Darwin was serving as an unpaid naturalist onboard the HMS *Beagle*. The *Beagle* was unimpressive for its day – just ninety feet long and of a notoriously unseaworthy design. In his notes Darwin described the voyage as 'one continual puke'.

'Well. I . . .'

'Should we . . . ?' Darwin gestured at his gun.

'Hardly seems much point.'

'What a damned fool I've been!' laughed Darwin.

'Oh, I'm just as much to blame,' said FitzRoy with a grin, pocketing his pistol, and slapping his friend on the back. They would have hugged right there and then, but were interrupted by a further crash as first another cannonball and then a pirate screamed in through the window. The two men stood stock-still.

'Don't make any sudden movements,' whispered FitzRoy to his companion. 'Remember – he's more scared of us than we are of him.'

'That's bears, you idiot,' hissed Darwin out of the side of his mouth. 'I don't think it applies to pirates.'

At the doorway, a second pirate appeared, with a luxuriant beard and a pleasant, open face, all teeth and curls.

'I'm the Pirate Captain. And I'm here for the gold!' he said.

Everybody froze. For a moment the only sound was the gentle roar of the ocean, and some wheezing from the pirate with asthma.

'Well, uh, help yourself,' said FitzRoy eventually, slightly perplexed. Darwin was too terrified to speak.

'Not that there's a great deal,' continued the young captain. 'I think some of the portholes might be made of gold, but then again they could be made of brass. Same sort of colour, so it's difficult to tell.'

'Rah!' said the Pirate Captain, with a frightful bellow. 'I know you're carrying a hundredweight in gold bullion!'

'Really?' said FitzRoy, genuinely surprised. 'I haven't seen anything of the sort.'

'Perhaps the bit of boat that's under the water is made of gold,' ventured Darwin, finding his voice at last. 'I mean, it could be made of anything for all we know. You never get to see it.'

The Pirate Captain's icy blade against his throat struck him silent.

'Search the hold, men, and bring me back some gold,' said the Pirate Captain, with a sneer reminiscent of Elvis.

The pirates were pretty slick by this stage of their piratical careers, and they had managed to overrun the entire ship in a matter of minutes. The only casualty on the pirate side had been the pirate dressed in red, who had twisted his ankle trying to do that trick where you slide down the face of the mainsail, cutting it as you go with your cutlass – which worked fine up to a point but still left a twenty-foot drop once he reached the bottom of the canvas.

'Ouch! My ankle!' he cried, but none of the other pirates had much sympathy for his reckless showboating. A group of them headed into the hold – but instead of the clinking you would associate with gold, all they could hear was the chatter of creatures. One of the pirates tore at a tarpaulin, only to discover row upon row of cages, each containing some sort of monkey.

* * *

'The gold must be hidden inside these monkeys!' shouted a pirate. Several of the pirates put down their flickering lamps, picked up monkeys of various different types, and slit them end to end, but all that spilt out was monkey guts.

'Gold!' said the pirate with an accordion, holding something yellowish up hopefully.

'That's not gold. It's a kidney,' said the pirate with a hook for his hand.

Covered in bits of creature, and thoroughly dejected, the pirate crew tramped back to FitzRoy's cabin.

'Pieces of ape! Pieces of ape!' squawked Gary, the ship's parrot.

'Will somebody shut him up?' scowled the pirate in green.

'There's no treasure here, Captain. Just a lot of stupid creatures,' said the pirate with a scarf.

'Just like I told you,' said FitzRoy.

The Pirate Captain sat down and rubbed his eyes with a weary hand. It suddenly felt like it had been a very long day.

'But Black Bellamy . . . he said you were carrying gold for the Bank of England.'

'The Bank of England?' said FitzRoy, grabbing at a table as the *Beagle* started to list alarmingly. 'I believe I've heard there is such a boat. But it's sailing in the vicinity of the West Indies, from what I remember.'

'The West Indies? But that's where we've just come from!'

'That Black Bellamy!' said the pirate with a hook instead of a hand. 'He was just trying to get us out of the way, so that he could plunder it for himself! Why, he hasn't changed at all! We've been bamboozled!'

The pirates were all very disappointed with the way Black Bellamy had behaved.

'So, then. Um. What are you doing in these parts?' said the Pirate Captain to Darwin, trying to make a bit of light-hearted conversation, and feeling more than a little awkward now.

'We're on a scientific expedition.'

'Searching for creatures?'

'I have a theory,' said Darwin, looking serious.

'I'm afraid it's proved to be rather controversial. We came here looking for proof.'

'What is this theory? In terms a pirate might understand.'

'It is not something to be taken lightly. It will make you look at the world with fresh eyes. Things may never seem the same again,' said Darwin, in a spooky voice.

'Go on,' said the Pirate Captain, his curiosity bitten.

Darwin gave a dramatic pause.

'In short, I believe that a monkey, properly trained, given the correct dietary regime, and dressed in fancy clothes, can be made indistinguishable from a human gentleman. I believe he would cease to be a monkey, and become more a . . . a Man-panzee, if you will.'

A silence held the room. One of the pirates whistled.

'I . . . see. A Man-panzee?' said the Pirate Captain.

'But because of my outlandish theories I have made some powerful enemies – primarily, the Bishop of Oxford,' said Darwin, unable to keep the bitterness out of his voice.

'He finds it offensive?'

'He most certainly does!'

'Because it contravenes his religious beliefs?'

'Oh no! Nothing to do with that, my dear Pirate Captain. The Bishop of Oxford recently became the largest shareholder in P.T. Barnum's world-famous Circus of Freaks.' Darwin leant forward with a conspiratorial air. 'The circus has been making a killing of late, because all of London Town is entranced by its latest exhibit . . . the fantastical Elephant Man. Have you heard of him?'

'Aarrr. He was on show last time we were in England,' said the Pirate Captain. 'A real disappointment as I remember. Doesn't even have a trunk. The trick is not to treat him like a gentleman, because he always starts crying if you do that.'

'Anyhow, the Bishop of Oxford is clearly alarmed that my Man-panzee might steal his Elephant Man's thunder. So he denounced my ideas as blasphemous – he even said there was a bit in the Bible about how it was a sin to dress a monkey up in a waistcoat, but when

49

asked for the page reference he claimed to have forgotten.'

Darwin was clearly on the verge of an angry rage.

'So I joined this expedition in an attempt to find a suitable specimen. Only now I have received word from England that my brother Erasmus has gone missing! I believe he has been kidnapped by the Bishop of Oxford as a means of safeguarding against my successful return. I fear the Bishop intends to do him some great harm unless I abandon my research.'

'Does that mean you've had some success?' asked one of the pirates.

'Come, let me show you.'

Darwin and FitzRoy led the pirates to an adjoining cabin. The pirates gasped, for though the room was dark and cramped, they could still make out its sole occupant. Sitting in a leather-backed armchair was a monkey with the best posture any of the pirates had ever seen. Dressed in an expensive-looking silk suit, with a pipe in his mouth, the creature peered at the pirates through a gold-rimmed monocle. He appeared to be sipping on some sort of cocktail – the Pirate Captain thought he could smell gin. The monkey looked as if he had been freshly shaved, but he was still recognisably a monkey, though if you squinted he might have passed for a wizened old man, or a gigantic walnut.

'Obviously he cannot talk,' said Darwin, turning on a few gaslights. 'But he is able to carry on a conversation by use of flash cards. Though I expect that sometime in the future, technology will move on, so that rather than having to rely on the cards he'll be able to use . . . oh, I don't know, refrigerator magnets, something like that.'

The monkey straightened his cravat, and held up a series of cards in quick succession.

'Hello. There. Pirates. Pleased. To. Meet. You,' he spelt out. 'My. Name. Is. Mister. Bobo.'

'Erm, pleased to meet you too,' said the Pirate Captain who, truth be told, felt like an idiot talking to a monkey, even one as finely dressed as this.[8] He turned to Darwin. 'It's a fantastic achievement.'

'Yes, Mister Bobo is by far my most promising specimen. I'm glad you didn't hit him with a cannonball. Please, let me give you a demonstration.' Darwin turned to the dapper little creature. 'Mister Bobo, would you tell us how one goes about being a proper gentleman?'

The monkey appeared deep in thought, and then shuffled through his pack of flash cards.

'Moderation. decorum. and. neatness. distinguish. the. .gentleman; he. is. at. all. times. affable,. diffident. and. studious. to. please. Intelligent. and. polite,. his. behaviour. is. pleasant. and. graceful. When. he. enters. the. dwelling. of. an. inferior,. he. endeavours. to. hide,. if. possible,. the. difference. between. their. ranks. of. life;. ever. willing. to. assist. those. around. him,. he. is. neither. unkind,. haughty,. nor. overbearing. In. the. mansions. of. the. rich,. the. correctness. of. his. mind. induces. him. to. bend.

---

8 You share about 98.6 per cent of your DNA with a common chimpanzee. And upwards of 99 per cent of your DNA with a pirate!

to. etiquette,. but. not. to. stoop. to. adulation;. correct. principle. cautions. him. to. avoid. the. gaming-table,. inebriety,. or. any. other. foible. that. could. occasion. him. self-reproach,' said Mister Bobo with his cards.

'You see? Not exactly perfect, but he makes a good stab at it. For a monkey,' said Darwin.

Flash cards were hardly the fastest way of communicating, and by now the pirates' bellies were rumbling. Also their pirate boots were getting wet as the *Beagle* started to sink, so they'd been hoping that the young scientist might have finished his speech, but Darwin, obviously proud of his discovery, went on.

'Naturally, I intended to find a better class of tailor back in England, one who might be able to do something to conceal his huge unsightly ass.'

'It *is* a big ass,' agreed a pirate.

'How have you been able to train him so well?' asked the Pirate Captain.

'Mostly fire,' Darwin nodded at some hot tongs hanging on the wall, and Mister Bobo looked a bit frightened. 'But it's all been a waste. I'll never be able to show him off to high society, for fear of some terrible retribution suffered by Erasmus. And even if I did intend to confront the black-hearted Bishop of Oxford, now I don't even have a means of returning home to England. I am lost.'

And with that Darwin started to bawl like a baby. The pirates stared at the floor, and shifted from foot to foot. They couldn't help but feel a little responsible for the scientist's predicament, on account of their scuppering his boat with all those cannonballs. The pirates had a bit of a discussion amongst themselves. Then the Pirate Captain turned to Darwin.

'I don't much care to be hung in irons.[9] And that's what we've been promised if we ever set foot in England again. But we don't want to see you and your Man-panzee bested by this scoundrel bishop you've told us about. So just as soon as we've eaten, us pirates will help you rescue

---

9 As a warning to seafarers it was common practice in Britain and her overseas colonies to put the bodies of notorious pirates on display near the entrance to a port. Several pirates were hanged at Execution Dock on the banks of the Thames in London.

your brother, and get Mister Bobo accepted by Victorian high society and everything.'

Darwin went to plant a big kiss on the Pirate Captain's salty face, but then thought better of it and shook him by the hand. Everybody cheered, even Mister Bobo.

Five

TRAPPED IN
QUICKSAND!

'The pirates helped Darwin, FitzRoy and the crew of the *Beagle* shift their luggage from the slowly sinking boat.

'You'll have to sleep in a hammock, I'm afraid,' said the Pirate Captain. 'They're quite comfortable, but they can leave a criss-cross pattern on your buttocks.'

'Are you sure there's room?' asked Darwin, anxious not to be too much trouble.

'Don't worry about that. We'll make room,' said the Pirate Captain, adding with a merry wink, 'Truth is I've been meaning to have some of my pirates walk the plank for ages, I just haven't got round to it.'[10]

'Walk the plank? That's barbaric!' blurted out

---

10 Plank-walking as a punishment was nothing like as common as TV and films would suggest, but there is one report from *The Times* of 23 July 1829 of Dutch sailors being compelled to walk the plank by pirates from Buenos Aires.

Darwin, before remembering that pirate ways are not necessarily the ways of other men. 'I'm sorry, it's just . . . there's really no need to go to those lengths. We'll sleep standing up, like bats.'

The Pirate Captain swatted his objections away.

'Honestly, it's been far too long since we did this. Lately, if a pirate has been annoying us, we've just shaved off an eyebrow or drawn a little moustache on his face whilst he sleeps, but it's no real substitute.'

He rummaged about in a large pine box that one of the crew had fetched from the hold.

'Oh, I haven't seen those for a while!' said the Captain, pulling out a garish pair of old pirate trousers. 'What was I thinking?! Ah, here it is.'

He blew the dust off a big plank of wood. Seeing that Darwin and FitzRoy were still looking a bit concerned, the Pirate Captain shot them a reassuring grin.

'Listen,' he said. 'It's not like I make any old pirate take the terrible walk. Strictly fools and lubbers. It's for the good of the species.'

* * *

As soon as the pirate boat reached shark-infested waters, the Pirate Captain, with a steely glint in his eye, gave the order to drop anchor. There was a carnival atmosphere onboard once the pirates realised that there was going to be some plank-walking. Darwin and FitzRoy looked on aghast as the Pirate Captain called out the first name.

The ratty-haired pirate called Marcus was the first to go. He begged and pleaded and cried like a little girl, but a few cutlass prods from some of the other pirates soon had him edging along the narrow piece of wood. He stopped at the end, and began to blubber again, so the pirate with a scarf crept up behind him, and quickly pushed him into the sea. The remaining pirates crowded round the edge of the deck, craning their necks to see ratty-haired Marcus desperately splashing about. For a bit, nothing much happened, but all of a sudden the water around him seemed to churn and crash in on itself, there was a scream, a cracking sound, and then a cloud of red spread out like a flower over the blue sea. The cloud of red wasn't a flower – it was blood coming out of Marcus. The pirates all gave a mighty cheer.[11]

The other pirates singled out by the harsh but undeniably fair Pirate Captain were dispatched in similar fashion. They included: the balding archaeologist pirate called Stan; the rich pirate who tried to pass himself off as a hippy, whose name the Pirate Captain had forgotten; the pirate who had taught the Pirate Captain geography at Pirate Academy; a boring pirate from Oxford called Adam; and the stupid pirate who had got in the Pirate Captain's way when he was trying to eat pancakes. A late addition was a male model pirate whom the Pirate Captain hadn't even met.

As soon as the plank-walking was finished, the Pirate Captain pointed the boat towards England, and all the remaining pirates and

---

11 Despite the fearsome reputation of sharks, more people are actually killed each year by pigs. Also, sharks have no bones – their skeletons are made entirely from cartilage.

their guests went below decks for a feast. For a change the pirates had lamb instead of ham, with the usual accompaniment of green mint sauce and a salad. As a nice added touch the roast lamb was sprinkled with a little minced parsley. A few of Darwin's monkeys had also been served up as an appetiser. There had been some debate as to the best way to cook a monkey, but eventually the pirates had decided to treat the monkeys as if they were turkeys, so after the sinews had been drawn from the legs and thighs, and the monkeys carefully trussed, they were stuffed with sausagemeat and veal. It was all served with gravy and bread sauce. Too late the Pirate Captain realised that he had invited Mister Bobo to the feast, but if the creature was put out at being offered a slice of his chimpanzee brethren he was far too polite to say anything.

'So . . . have you been a pirate captain long?' asked Darwin, gulping down a mug of grog.

'Goodness me! Long as I can remember,' said the Pirate Captain.

'You've never considered a career as something a little more orthodox?'

'I dare say I've considered it, but the fact is I'm a slave to pirating! I love it! The salty sea air, the exotic locations, the shiny gold. Especially the shiny gold.'

'I can see you're pretty good at it,' said Darwin graciously. Pirates seemed a lot more civilised than he had expected. He was unaware of the tremendous effort most of the crew were making in an attempt to eat in a respectable manner because they didn't want to look sloppy in front of visitors. Several of them were wearing their most jaunty sashes, and they had spent all day cleaning the boat from top to bottom.

'I have to say,' said Darwin, looking misty eyed, 'a part of me is quite jealous of your villainous lifestyle. Free from the tyranny of what society deems acceptable! Masters of your own fate! Living beyond the law! Us scientific types must seem rather dull to your piratical eyes.'

'Not at all,' said the Pirate Captain to his guest. 'I've always been interested in science. Perhaps, as a scientist, you'll be able to answer a question that has perplexed me for many years.'

'I'll certainly do my best.'

'Tell me – scientifically speaking – who do you think the tallest pirate in the world is?'

'Erm. It's a bit outside my field of expertise,' replied Darwin apologetically.

'Ah well. Perhaps I'm destined never to know!' said the Pirate Captain with a wistful air.

'Darwin's not the only one with a scientific theory,' said FitzRoy. 'I've been doing some fascinating work to do with weather prediction. I hope to found a meteorological office when I return to London.'

Nobody at the table was at all interested in what FitzRoy was talking about, so he trailed off and stared miserably at his soup.[12]

Darwin chewed on a monkey's paw. 'How long do you expect it will take us to reach England?'

'There's plenty of hams onboard, if that's

12   In 1865 FitzRoy committed suicide at his home in Upper Norwood. In 1862 he had published *The Weather Book*.

what you're worried about,' replied the Pirate Captain reassuringly. 'But let's see now . . .' The Captain gazed into the middle distance and furrowed his brow to make it look like he was doing some difficult calculations in his head. In fact he was wondering if anybody had noticed how shiny his boots were, because he'd had the pirate with a scarf spend the whole morning polishing them. 'I should say we'd reach England by Tuesday or thereabouts, with a decent wind behind us. It would be a lot quicker than that if we could just sail straight there, but I was looking at the nautical charts, and it's a good job I did, because it turns out there's a dirty great sea-serpent right in the middle of the ocean! It has a horrible gaping maw and one of those scaly tails that looks like it could snap a boat clean in two. So I thought it best to sail around that.'

FitzRoy frowned. 'I think they just draw those on maps to add a bit of decoration. It doesn't actually mean there's a sea-serpent there.'

The galley went rather quiet. A few of the pirate crew stared intently out of the portholes, embarrassed at their Captain's mistake. But to everyone's relief, instead of running somebody through, the Pirate Captain just narrowed his eyes thoughtfully.

'That explains a lot,' he said. 'I suppose it's also why we've never glimpsed that giant compass in the corner of the Atlantic. I have to say, I'm a little disappointed.'

Six

PIRATES AHOY!

After a brief encounter with some lovely but black-hearted lady pirates[13] the pirate boat finally arrived in the sleepy seaside town of Littlehampton, on the south coast of England. Houses were still cheap there, compared to London prices, but of course there was always the risk of flooding. The beach was pretty good, and there was a lot of that seaweed which looks a bit like brains lying about. A couple of the pirates did impressions of the zombie pirates and said, 'Brains! Feed me brains!' and pretended to stuff the seaweed into their mouths.

'We must make haste to London,' said Darwin, fetching his suitcase up onto the beach, 'to meet my fellow scientists at the Royal Society.'

---

13 Lady pirates were rare but not unheard of. A famous example was Anne Bonny, who became the lover of Calico Jack and was tried for piracy in Spanish Town, Jamaica.

'Yes, quite right. Not a moment to lose!' agreed the Pirate Captain. 'Except a few of the men noticed an amusement arcade just along from here, and I promised them they could go. It has a gigantic slide and everything.'

'But Erasmus! He could be in all sorts of danger!'

The Pirate Captain's eyes flashed red like hot cannonballs.

'I'm sure your brother wouldn't begrudge my crew a little entertainment after such a hard voyage,' he said, a hint of steel in his voice.

'Oh, very well,' replied Darwin, sulkily.

The pirate crew were excited to be visiting an arcade, but it proved to be a dilapidated affair. The only halfway decent machines consisted of an ingenious mechanical series of shelves, which all shunted backwards and forwards, each shelf laden with piles of silvery doubloons. By putting a doubloon into a little slot the hope was to knock several doubloons over the edge of a precipice, where they could be collected. The pirates spent ages on one of the machines, because there was an actual pocket-watch resting on the doubloons near the edge, but no matter how much of their treasure they fed into the gas-powered beast the loot wouldn't fall down – it was almost as if the doubloons were stuck there with glue. A couple of the pirates got into trouble for trying to shake the machine, and they had to run outside and hide behind a man selling ice creams.

'This is rubbish,' said the pirate who was eating some candy floss, and the other pirates agreed, so they walked back down the beach to where Darwin and FitzRoy were waiting. Seeing them, Darwin leapt to his feet and gathered up his luggage once more.

'So, are we ready? There is a locomotive to London that leaves in half an hour,' said Darwin, eager to be off.

'Yes,' said the Pirate Captain. 'We must hurry! Oh look – a nautical-themed crazy golf! Let's have a go!'

'But the train . . .' said Darwin, with a touch of resignation.

'Nautical-themed! Do you think that's a genuine ship's anchor? It's very realistic. You and FitzRoy can play as a team if you want,' said the Pirate Captain, handing him a putter.

Darwin could see there was no point arguing with the Pirate Captain once he had made up his mind.

The Pirate Captain swung his golf club, and the ball pinged away, only to hit the side of a big metal anchor and roll back to where it had started.

'That's lucky, it's a free drop,' said the Pirate Captain, picking up his ball and placing it about a foot from the hole. 'Because I hit the anchor.'

'Eh? Are you sure about that?' asked Darwin, instantly wishing he had kept quiet.

'Yes. Because I hit the anchor,' repeated the Pirate Captain, this time in a menacing tone that spoke of rum and murder.

The pirate with a scarf hit his ball, which

bounced off a barrel, hit the anchor and rolled back again. He went to pick it up.

'What do you think you're doing?' roared the Pirate Captain incredulously.

'My free drop. Because I hit the anchor.'

'But you hit the barrel first!'

'Erm . . . yes.'

'So that invalidates any effect the anchor might have.'

'Oh.'

'And by hitting the barrel and then the anchor, you've put the anchor permanently out of play for everybody else. So no more free drops, I'm afraid.'

In all, they played three rounds of crazy golf and the Pirate Captain won all three, but everyone had a good time. As they ambled back along the sea front, the Pirate Captain told them all an exciting story about the time he lost a leg in a fight with a Great White Shark. FitzRoy remarked that the Pirate Captain seemed to have two perfectly good legs, at which point the Pirate Captain went a bit quiet and pretended to be very interested in a shell he had picked up.

'We'd better be off to rescue my brother,' said Darwin.

'Yes,' said the Pirate Captain. 'We shall. Just as soon as we've paid a visit to that sweet factory to find out how they get the words inside sticks of rock. Aargh! I'm just pulling your leg. Don't look so worried. I've sailed the seven seas, and I've never had an unsuccessful adventure yet!'

'Really? You've sailed all seven seas?' asked Darwin admiringly.

'Every last one!'

'What are the seven seas? I've always wondered.'

'Aaarrr. Well, let's see . . .' said the Pirate Captain, scratching his craggy forehead. 'There's the North Sea. And that other one, the one near Mozambique. And . . . what's that one in Hyde Park?'

'The Serpentine?'

'That's the one. How many's that then? Three. Um. There's the sea with all the rocks in it . . . I think they call it Sea Number Four. Then that would leave . . . uh . . . Grumpy and Sneezy . . .'

Darwin was starting to look a little less impressed.

'Would you look at that big seagull!' said the Pirate Captain, quickly ducking into a beach hut.

Seven

TARGET: PIRATES!

And so the pirates and their companions arrived in Victorian London. It was not the London you would recognise from nowadays – there was no Millennium Wheel or Tate Modern or Eurostar or Starbucks or Millennium Dome or Jubilee Line Extension or any of the other things you probably assume have always existed. There was soot and orphans everywhere, and gas-lit cobbled streets full of fog and sinister gentlemen out for a night of illicit murder. It was a strict and unforgiving society – looking at a piano, eating too much butter, dancing with elan – the sour-faced Queen Victoria forbade all these things. Also, it was always raining in the London of themadays – dirty grey slabs of rain that left everywhere shining and slippery.

To Darwin's continued dismay the Pirate Captain insisted they visit London Zoo before doing anything else. All the pirates agreed that it wasn't as good as Berlin Zoo, which they had visited on a previous adventure to Germany, and that it had far too large a hoofed-animals section. 'Who cares about hoofed animals? They never get up to anything!' said the pirate in green, wisely. The chimps were an especially sorry bunch – the chimps in Berlin Zoo had put on quite a display when the pirates had visited, shouting and weeing right in front of shocked tourists, but the London chimps just rocked back and forth, obviously suffering from zoo-psychosis. Mister Bobo stared sadly at them through the glass, a bit embarrassed on their behalf. The albino pirate noticed a sign which pointed to an exhibit of 'The Most Destructive Animal in the World!'. Some of the pirates had bets on whether it would be a bear or a shark, but it turned out to be a big mirror. The most destructive animal in the world was mankind itself! Especially pirates! But to show they weren't all bad, two of the pirates decided to sponsor a polar bear.[14]

---

14 London Zoo is still going today, and this year's baby bear naming competition was won by Sandokan Soloman for his name 'Ursula'.

After that, even though Darwin kept on looking pointedly at his watch and rolling his eyes, the pirates went shopping in the West End. Several of them got themselves the latest pirate stylings from Carnaby Street. Apparently that year's fashion could be summed up as 'the more buckles the better!', and the pirates now made a loud clanking noise as they walked along. They also all bought a few postcards and union jacks. The pirate in green who wanted to have the Pirate Captain drawn on his arm had managed to find a tattoo parlour in the Soho district, and now carried a bundle of pamphlets with titles like 'Inky Skin', which he said he'd picked up because he was now very interested in tattoos, and not because of the pictures of ladies wearing next to nothing, but the other pirates weren't sure they believed him.

As they trailed down Charing Cross Road, finally exhausted from their exciting day out in the Big Smoke, the Pirate Captain noticed a poster stuck to a pillar box. It said in oldendays writing:

P.T. Barnum

(in association with the Bishop of Oxford)
is proud to present his
WORLD – FAMOUS

Circus of Freaks

featuring the Elephant Man! The Mer-maid! A Beard of Bees!
Tuesday, Wednesday, Thursday, Friday and Saturday
are
'Ladies' Nights!' <u>Free entry all day to ladies.</u>

'That's a lot of ladies' nights,' said the Pirate Captain thoughtfully.

'Yes,' said Darwin. 'It's a peculiar thing. I heard from my cousin that ever since the Bishop of Oxford became the major shareholder in the circus – about seven or eight months ago – the number of ladies nights has risen dramatically, to at least five a week.'

'I wonder if that foreshadows anything sinister?' said the Pirate Captain.

'We shouldn't leap to conclusions, just because the unspeakable Bishop is our enemy,' said Darwin reasonably. 'After all, it may be that he feels sorry for ladies, and thinks they could do with some free entertainment.'

'Why would he feel sorry for ladies?' asked the albino pirate.

'Well, what with so many of them going missing lately, and then being found washed up in the River Thames, all shrivelled and lifeless.'

'How long has *that* been going on?'

'Oooh, about seven or eight months, I should say.'

The conversation was interrupted when the pirate with a scarf spotted a policeman coming along the street towards them. The pirates and their companions quickly ducked into Leicester Square.

'It's not safe on the streets for you pirates,' said Darwin, still pushing Mister Bobo along in a pram so as not to draw any unwanted attention. 'Upstairs in the Natural History Museum there is the Royal Society Gentlemen's Club, where we might plan our course of action.'

'Will they have grog there?' asked the sassy pirate.

'Yes. And cigars. But I don't think they'll let pirates in. And lord knows what my colleagues would think if they saw me associating with sea-dogs like you.'

The pirates were a bit hurt by this, and Darwin was quick to try to save their feelings.

'I mean, obviously, FitzRoy and I know that you're stand-up fellows, it's just the other members . . . they may be rather quick to judge.'

'There's only one thing for it then,' said the Pirate Captain, a gleam in his eye. 'We'll have to disguise ourselves as scientists!'

Holding pens and rulers, and with white lab coats covering their piratical paraphernalia, the pirates followed Darwin into the Royal Society Gentlemen's Club.[15] There were several famous

15　The Royal Society was set up in 1660, and many famous scientists have been members, including Robert Boyle, Robert Hooke and John Venn. Why not try drawing a Venn Diagram of 'pirates' (A) and 'ham' (B) and 'barrels of tar' (C). How large is the intersection (X)?

scientists present, some sitting around smoking, some engaged in animated discussion about the latest scientific topic, and some just watching the dancing girls. The smell of opium hung heavily in the air.

'Anyhow,' one of the scientists was saying to another, 'there simply isn't room in the museum's Fishes Hall, so we've decided to pretend to the public that a whale is actually a mammal without any legs. It's patently ridiculous – I mean to say, just look at the thing, it's a gigantic fish if ever you saw one – but mum's the word! In my experience the public will believe just about anything, so long as you write it down on a little piece of card.'

The Pirate Captain coughed.

'Goodness! Look, everybody, it's Darwin! Darwin's back!' exclaimed one of the scientists with bushy sideburns, and everybody crowded round Darwin and FitzRoy, slapping them on the shoulders and asking questions. It was a couple of minutes before Darwin could get a word in edgeways.

'Uh, these here are some scientists I met on

my travels,' he said, indicating the disguised pirates. 'I hope you'll make them feel welcome.'

'Sorry. We're forgetting our manners. It's just so good to see Charles back, alive and well. One hears such stories about life on the high seas. Giant squids and pirates and the like,' said a genuine scientist, shaking the Pirate Captain's hand. 'What sort of science do you do?'

'What sort of science? Well . . . it's mainly . . . chemicals,' said the Pirate Captain, thinking on his feet. 'There's a lot of stirring things together. And then writing things down, of course.'

'Fascinating,' said the scientist. 'And what about you? What's your field?' he added, turning to the pirate with a hook for his hand.

The pirate with a hook for his hand didn't know what to say, but the quick-witted Pirate Captain cut in deftly. 'My modest colleague does a lot of work with minerals. He likes gold best. He heats it up, with matches.'

'Surely, as a man of science, you'd use a Bunsen burner?'

'Did I say matches? Yes, I meant Bunsen

burner. It's been a long day,' the Pirate Captain shrugged apologetically.

The pirates managed to do a pretty decent job of mingling with the scientists, nodding politely and saying 'Really?' a lot as they listened to them drone on about their latest inventions and discoveries, but the Pirate Captain soon found himself involved in a particularly awkward conversation about molecules, so he was relieved when FitzRoy interrupted him before it got to the stage where he had to say if he was for or against them.

'As a fellow nautical man, there's somebody I'd like you to meet,' said FitzRoy, grabbing the Pirate Captain by the sleeve of his lab coat and dragging him over to shake hands with a fresh-faced young scientist.

'This is James Glaisher, the famous meteorologist,' said FitzRoy. The Pirate Captain wasn't sure what a meteorologist did, but he suspected it was something boring.

'James and I have long held the belief that the weather does not operate in some capricious manner, and that with sufficient information, it should be possible to give advance warning of storms at sea. Our voyage has only served to further convince me.'

The Pirate Captain made sure he was doing his best interested-face whilst he wondered what time scientists tended to eat dinner.

'So tell me, James,' continued FitzRoy, 'how have the experiments been going? Did you get a chance to make the modifications I suggested for your ship?'

'What's this?' said the Pirate Captain, his ears pricking up, eager to find a topic he could make head or tail of. 'You have a ship? Why, I have a boat myself!'

'I'm afraid it's not that kind of a ship,' explained the scientist.[16] 'For some time now, FitzRoy and I have pursued the idea of a motor-ised weather balloon. I believe it to be the world's first lighter-than-air-ship. A dirigible, if you will.'

---

16 James Glaisher of the Magnetic and Meteorological Department at the Greenwich Observatory made a series of twenty-nine balloon ascents in the nineteenth century to investigate barometric pressure at altitude.

'A lighter-than-air-ship?' said the Pirate Captain, rubbing his hairy chin. 'How many cannons does it have? My boat has twelve cannons.'

'Cannons? It doesn't have any cannons.'

'You're not going to be much cop when it comes to plundering if you haven't got any cannons!' the Pirate Captain snorted imperiously.

'Plundering? I'm not sure you understand. We've not invented the airship to go plundering.'

'So what on earth *is* it for?' asked the Pirate Captain.

'For? What is all science "for"!' exclaimed the scientist. 'Pushing back frontiers! The thrill of discovery! Advancing the sum total of human knowledge and endeavour! And looking down ladies' tops.'

Over dinner Darwin told the story of his voyage, missing out the bit with the pirates, then he showed off Mister Bobo, who performed impeccably and proved excellent when it came to the after-dinner charades, making everybody laugh as he acted out Daniel Defoe's *Journal of the Plague Year*. All of the scientists agreed that Mister Bobo was a breakthrough, but none of them knew what was to be done about the predicament of Erasmus. A glum gloom settled over the table, and even Darwin's pet bulldog, Huxley, whimpered as it ate the scraps of ham surreptitiously fed to it under the table by the pirate with a scarf.

It was time for action. The Pirate Captain slammed down his After Eight mint with a mighty crash.

'It's clear to me what must be done,' he told the assembled scientists and pirates-dressed-as-scientists. 'Darwin must go ahead and announce a lecture tour with Mister Bobo as if nothing were wrong. I'll get my crew – my scientist crew, that is – to put up posters, and we'll hold the first lecture in this very museum, tomorrow night.'

'But what about the repercussions? Until I know Erasmus is safe, how can I dare?' said Darwin, aghast.

'If my years of experience solving crimes has taught me anything,' said the Pirate Captain, looking reassuringly nonchalant by tipping his chair back dangerously, 'it's that you can't catch a mouse without cheese!'

'Your years of experience solving crimes? But you're a pirate,' whispered Darwin. 'Surely that doesn't involve much detective work?'

'Aarrrr,' roared the Pirate Captain, because it seemed a good way to end the conversation.

Eight

BATTLING
THE OCTOPUS!

The next morning, waking up for the first time in three years in a proper bed with fresh linen that didn't stink of fish and monkeys, Darwin felt a great deal better about things. Before he had retired for the night the Pirate Captain had taken him aside and gone on to explain his piratical plan. He reasoned that they had no means of ascertaining the whereabouts of Erasmus until the evil Bishop of Oxford showed his face. By announcing the lecture tour with Mister Bobo they would force the Bishop's hand, and he would be sure to turn up in order to try threatening Darwin into backing down. The Bishop would be expecting scientists. What the Bishop wouldn't be expecting were pirates! At this point the plan got a bit hazy, but Darwin felt confident in the Pirate Captain's abilities nonetheless. He propped himself up on his pillows and flicked through that morning's edition of *The Times*, pretending not to look at the more salacious pictures of table legs. There was another big headline about a mysteriously shrivelled lady being found bobbing about in the Thames, and an article in the Style section where he saw that for the fifth year running, 'sinister and macabre' was still very much in vogue when it came to the Victorian gentleman's interior design choices. He sighed. With sunlight streaming in through the window, and a plate of toast already brought to him by the Royal Society's butler, Darwin was tempted to spend the whole morning in bed, but he had a lot to sort out, so he shook Mister Bobo awake and started preparing for the evening's lecture. A lecture, he pondered, that could make his name as a scientist – and, by that token, hopefully lead to a good deal more success with women.

In one of the Royal Society's bathrooms just down the hall the Pirate Captain was busy flossing.

'Are you going to be in there much longer?' asked an unfamiliar voice with an impatient knock. The Pirate Captain flung open the door, ready to run through with his shiny cutlass whosoever it happened to be, but then he remembered he was supposed to be a mild-mannered scientist, not a bloodthirsty Terror of the High Seas. So instead he fixed the knave who had the cheek to interrupt his toiletries with a steely stare. He recognised one of the scientists from dinner.

'Yes,' growled the Pirate Captain. 'I am going to be in here much longer. Beards like this don't look after themselves, you know.'

'Right, sorry,' said the scientist, backing away meekly. 'Gosh. You've got a lot of scars.'

The Pirate Captain was wearing only a risqué towel, and he did indeed have a number of scars from previous adventures.

'That's from bumping against scientific apparatus in my laboratory,' explained the Pirate Captain, a murderous gleam in his eyes.

'And is that . . . a treasure map tattooed on your belly?'

'No. It's the periodic table.'

'It doesn't look like the periodic table. X isn't an element.'

The Pirate Captain decided to run the scientist through with his cutlass after all. He washed it off in the sink, attended to his beard and then went back to the room he was sharing with some of the other pirates.

'They may know how to make a mechanical pig,' said the Pirate Captain, 'but these scientists have got a lot to learn about manners.'

The other pirates all nodded at this.

'Now, does everybody know what they're doing today? You two,' the Pirate Captain pointed to the albino pirate and the pirate with a hook where his hand should have been, 'will help Mr Darwin with anything he needs for his lecture. And you two,' this time he indicated the scarf-wearing pirate and the pirate with an accordion, 'will check out P.T. Barnum's Circus. Why is a Bishop involved in running a circus, that's what I want to know. I'm not sure how it fits in with his diabolical plans, but I have my suspicions about the place. It's ladies' night, so you'll have to disguise yourselves as women.'

'It's going to be quite difficult fitting a lady

disguise on top of our scientist disguises, which we're already wearing on top of our pirate outfits,' said the scarf-wearing pirate.

'You'll just have to do your best,' said the Pirate Captain. 'I'd go myself, but obviously my luxuriant beard would make it difficult for me to pass as a lady. And don't forget that ladies speak in squeaky voices. Like this – "Hello, I'm a lady!"'

Everybody laughed at the Pirate Captain's brilliant impression of what a lady sounded like.[17]

'The rest of you pirates go round town and paste up these posters advertising tonight's lecture.'

The Pirate Captain handed out a stack of A4 posters. They were illustrated with a picture of Darwin and Mister Bobo playing chess. Mister Bobo was in Rodin's *The Thinker* pose, and

---

17 Men's vocal cords tend to be thicker than women's, so they produce a deeper tone in exactly the same way that a thick rubber band makes a deeper sound than a thin one when you twang it. You might need to stretch the rubber bands over a biscuit tin to get the full effect.

Darwin had thrown his hands up in defeat. The Pirate Captain had drawn the picture himself, and was proud of his effort. Before he became a pirate he was going to be an architect, and he had used his knowledge of perspective and foreshortening to make Mister Bobo's massive monkey behind seem a lot smaller than it was in real life. And he'd managed to give Darwin a genuine look of exasperation at having been bested by a chimp. The only thing about the picture that slightly disappointed the Pirate Captain was Darwin's hands, which looked more like lumpy starfish – for some reason the Pirate Captain had never got very good at drawing hands. Above the picture were the words:

One night only - Mister Charles Darwin will be showing off his fantastic hirsute new friend Mister Bobo - the world's first Man-panzee! Royal Society Lecture Rooms, admission free.

In very small print it was noted that Mister Bobo did not actually play chess to a particularly high standard.

'These are very good, Captain,' said the scarf-wearing pirate, already applying a cherry-coloured lipstick. The Pirate Captain waved away the praise, and mumbled something about how he didn't think it was that good a picture, even though it was obvious how proud he was.

'Now, I hope I can trust you pirates with this. I'm afraid I've got a prior engagement, so I won't be around to help out,' said the Pirate Captain, giving his sternest look to his men, which involved lowering his eyebrows and pursing his lips together.

'What's that, Captain? asked the accordion-playing pirate, having some difficulty with his bra strap.

'I received a letter this morning, inviting me to attend a Pirate Convention at Earls Court. I'm one of the guests of honour.'

The other pirates occasionally wondered how it was that these letters found their way to their itinerant captain, but somehow they always did.

'A Pirate Convention? You're certain this isn't another of those Royal Navy schemes to trap a whole bunch of pirates?' said the scarf-wearing pirate, his brow furrowed with concern.

'Remember that time they said there was going to be a pirate beauty contest on Mozambique, and we had to shoot our way out?'

'Remember it? Of course I remember it! I still say I was robbed,' pouted the Pirate Captain. His crew nodded – certainly none of them had ever seen another pirate as attractive as their chiselled Captain.

'But, anyhow, the letter came with our secret pirate symbol marked on the envelope. See?' The Pirate Captain pointed to the Jolly Roger[18] stamped on the seal. 'So it must be the real deal. I'm quite looking forward to it. With any luck I'll be able to sign a few autographs for the kids, and pick up some pirate equipment at bargain prices.'

'All due respects, Captain,' said the pirate in green, feasting on a bowl of cereal, 'but have you really got time to be going off to a Pirate

18 Though the name 'Jolly Roger' would lead you to expect a picture of a happy-looking man, it is actually a scary skull above two crossed bones.

Convention? We're sort of bang in the middle of an adventure here.'

'It's a fair point,' replied the Pirate Captain. 'But I have my reasons. For a start, what with Black Bellamy pulling a fast one on us, the boat's finances aren't looking too healthy, and this could be a chance to make a doubloon or two. Good deeds won't keep us in ham, you know. Secondly, a few of my pirate contacts might come in useful in figuring out just what this Bishop is really up to. And thirdly, I'm the Pirate Captain and I can do whatever the hell I please!'

'Are you planning on wearing that hat to the convention?' asked the pirate in red. The Pirate Captain thought he could detect a certain amount of disapproval in his tone.

'Yes, I am. It happens to be my favourite hat. You may notice that the blue of the trim brings out the blue of my eyes,' the Pirate Captain pointed to the blue trim and then at his blue eyes to emphasise the point.

'Ah. Well, then. I'm sure you know best, Captain.'

'Are you trying to say there's something wrong with my hat?'

'Not at all, Captain. It might not be the most up-to-date choice, but I'm sure there's nothing wrong with that,' said the pirate in red, sounding very much like he thought there was a great deal wrong with it.

'This is a perfectly good pirate hat. It's a tricorn.'

'Exactly.'

'Your point being?'

'It's just . . . nowadays . . . a more Napoleonic design seems to be the choice of the successful pirate. It's generally held to have a touch more . . . *je ne sais quoi*. I'm only saying, is all.'

'My hat has plenty of *je ne sais quoi*. Not to say *joie de vivre*.'

'If you say so.'

'Fine. Hands up who likes my hat?'

Most of the pirate crew loyally stuck their hands in the air. The pirate in red just shrugged and pretended to be reading a book. Satisfied that the mutinous swab had been put in his place, the Pirate Captain helped himself to another bowl of Coco-Pops.

Nine

ENTER THE
PIRATE KING!

By twelve o'clock the scarf-wearing pirate and the pirate with an accordion were already sweltering under their multiple disguises. You could hardly hear the clanking of their pirate buckles beneath the layers of lab coat and lady's dress each man wore. They didn't know exactly what it was they were meant to be looking for at the sinister circus – the Pirate Captain had simply told them to keep an eye out for anything suspicious. Looking through the glossy circus brochure the pirate with a scarf thought that it all sounded pretty suspicious – a man with no face, a lady with a phobia for tin foil, an out-of-control teen . . . he was worried that they wouldn't know where to start. The queue to get in stretched all the way down the Mall.

'That's a fetching eye patch. Is it just for show?'

It took the pirate with a scarf a few seconds to

realise that the question was being directed at him, and by the young lady just ahead of them in the queue. Looking up, he was so taken aback by how pretty she was he almost forgot to answer in a high-pitched voice instead of his normal pirate voice.

'It's . . . that is . . . I've got an astigmatism,' he stuttered. 'The optician says I have to wear the patch until it goes away.'

'You poor thing,' said the girl, with a look of real concern. 'Would you like a sandwich? It's Serrano ham.'

The pirate with a scarf gratefully took the proffered sandwich. He thought he had better make introductions. 'Thank you. I'm . . . Francine. And this is, erm, Daphne,' he said.

'Jennifer. That's a very shiny accordion you have there, Daphne.'

The pirate with an accordion just grunted, because his lady voice wasn't particularly realistic.

'You're extremely rugged. For a girl,' said Jennifer, turning back to the pirate with a scarf.

'Thank you,' said the pirate, unconsciously

flexing the muscles in his back, and knitting his eyebrows together in what he hoped was a suave manner.

'Are you here to see the Mer-maid?' asked Jennifer. 'I've heard it's a bit disappointing. Just the top half of a monkey stitched to the bottom half of a fish.'

'Erm, no. That is, not in particular.'

'The albino then?'

'Actually, one of our friends is an albino,' said the pirate brightly.

'Ooh! Is it true that if you ever look directly into their eyes, you turn into an albino yourself? And that they can only eat white things, like vanilla ice cream and Milky Bars?'

'I don't think so. I'm not entirely sure.'

'I wonder if they can eat mallow?'

Jennifer seemed to be lost in her deliberations about albinos. If the pirate with a scarf had been more poetically minded he'd have thought that her eyes were like a thousand emeralds, glittering in a far-off pirate treasure chest. But he wasn't, so he just thought that she had really *really* green eyes, a bit like seaweed.

'What about you? What are you here to see?' asked the pirate quickly, anxious to keep the conversation going. 'The Elephant Man?'

'Not really. Between you and me,' at this point Jennifer put her mouth alarmingly close to the pirate with a scarf's ear, 'I think something sinister is going on at the circus. My sister Beatrice visited it last week, and that's the last we ever saw of her.'

'I think you could be right,' said the pirate, completely forgetting the undercover nature of their mission because of the shape of her neck. 'In fact, we're here to investigate. I'm not even really a lady.'

The pirate with a scarf briefly raised his dress.

'You're a scientist!'

The pirate remembered to lift up his lab coat as well.

'You're a pirate!'

'Yes, but don't tell anybody.'

Half an hour later Jennifer and the two pirates were through the turnstiles and inside the circus itself. The pirate with an accordion pretty quickly started to feel more like the pirate who was a gooseberry, so he wandered off to look at an exhibit that claimed to be 'the dog that wore sunglasses', and left Jennifer and the scarf-wearing pirate to their own devices. The circus was sprawled across St James's Park, and a blanket of thick London fog hung between the various tents. The pair decided to start their investigations with the Elephant Man. He was sitting in the centre of a little hut looking a bit forlorn, whilst a man with a tuba played a few bars of 'Nellie the Elephant' over and over again.

'He doesn't look big enough to have eaten my sister,' said Jennifer. 'But he might know something.'

'We should try to gain his confidence by carrying on a pleasant conversation,' whispered the pirate.

'I'll have a go,' nodded Jennifer. She took a few steps towards the creature and cleared her throat.

'Wow!' she said. 'So you're the Elephant Man! That's some face!'

It wasn't exactly the opening gambit the pirate

with a scarf had in mind, but he bit his lip because the closest he had come recently to having any success with a girl was the time a few weeks before when he had drunk too much rum, and ended up thinking he was in love with the pirate boat's figurehead. The boat's figurehead was certainly attractive, and extremely well carved, but it left him with nasty splinters whenever he tried to give it a hug.

'I'd – uh – prefer it if you called me John,' said the Elephant Man, trying to crack a smile. 'My name is John Merrick.'

'Okay, John it is. So let me get this straight . . . you got turned into an elephant *man* by being bitten by an actual elephant, is that right? Was the elephant radioactive in any way?' asked Jennifer.

'Ah . . . no. I suffer from a rare genetic condition. It causes the rapid growth of bony tumours. There are no elephants involved. Several unfortunate children are born with it every year.'

'Children are born with it? Is that because their mothers have been bitten by an elephant whilst pregnant? Are you saying that if I got pregnant, I shouldn't visit a zoo?'

'No. Really, the condition has nothing to do with elephants.'

'Would the baby only be affected if the mother was bitten in the belly by an elephant? Or would a bite to the leg do it too?'

'I don't think you're really listening . . .' said the Elephant Man with as much patience as he could muster.

'I can tell you're from India, because of the shape of your ears,' added Jennifer triumphantly. The Elephant Man just sighed and shook his head.

'Tell me, John,' Jennifer went on, swiftly changing tack. 'Do you know why this circus has so many ladies' nights? I mean, they're virtually every night! It's suspicious!'

'No. No, I don't. I . . . I don't even know what you're talking about,' said the Elephant Man quickly. The pirate with a scarf thought he saw a flash of fear in the wretch's eyes, but it was hard to tell because his face was such a funny shape.

'Listen. Why don't I sing you a song?' said the Elephant Man, obviously desperate to try to change the subject. He even got up and did a little ungainly jig as he sang.

I look like some ex-pe-ri-ment!
But please believe me I'm a proper gent!
I seem like a monster, but whatcha don't
    know is,
I got a scorching case of neurofibromatosis![19]

Jennifer and the pirate with a scarf gave up on getting a straight answer, and went to search for any clues that might be evident at the other exhibits. But they had no more luck with the Man Who Could Eat A Bicycle, or the Lady Who Had Had Hiccups For Forty Years, or even with the Girl From Chesterfield Who Would Repeatedly Go

---

19   Or possibly Proteus Syndrome. There is still some debate in medical circles. Contrary to popular belief, Michael Jackson never did purchase the Elephant Man's skeleton from the Royal Hospital. This is a good example of how you shouldn't believe everything that people tell you.

Out With Idiots When She Could Do A Great Deal Better For Herself. The pea-soup fog was starting to make their eyes sting, so Jennifer and the pirate ducked inside a tent that was simply marked 'A Special Exhibit For The Ladies'. It didn't seem very special – it was just an empty and badly lit tent as far as the pirate with a scarf could make out.

'It's very dark in here. I can't even see what we're meant to be looking at,' said Jennifer, slipping her hand through her companion's arm. The pirate with a scarf's heart skipped a beat. He couldn't believe how well it was going. Usually by this point with a girl he'd have said something idiotic, or spilt drink all down his front, or chewed with his mouth open, but he'd managed not to do any of those things so far, and he even seemed to be impressing her with some of his nautical anecdotes.

'It must mean a good deal of responsibility, being the first mate on a pirate boat,' said Jennifer, shivering at a sudden breeze that seemed to blow through the tent.

'It's not easy. But I try to look after my crew,'

said the pirate. 'I saved a man's life the other day. He got attacked by a huge jellyfish, and I neutralised the sting by pouring a bucket of wee all over him.'

He instantly wished he had instead told her about the time he fought a monstrous manatee, because it cast him in a slightly more heroic light, and didn't involve big buckets of wee. Jennifer had gone very quiet, and looking up from his shoes – he was terrible at making eye contact with girls he liked – the pirate with a scarf was surprised to see her slumping unconscious to the floor. For one frightened moment he thought his conversation might have sent her into a daze, so he was pretty relieved when he felt a chloroform-soaked rag press against his mouth, and blacked out himself.

The pirate with a scarf opened his eyes groggily. His vision seemed to go cloudy, but then he realised it was just his breath condensing on the inside of the massive glass tube in which he now found himself trapped. The tube was attached to some kind of improbable contraption, fashioned of wood and brass and covered in cogs, pipes and hissing gaskets. Looking to his left, he saw that Jennifer was held in an identical predicament. With a sinking feeling, he realised that yet again a date with a pretty girl had gone horribly wrong. He could just make out that they were in some kind of big square room, with what looked like gigantic stained-glass windows for walls. He gave a peevish sigh – he certainly wasn't enjoying this adventure as much as, say, the Pirates' Adventure On The Island Of Rum And Amazons.

'So, young scarf-wearing lady! You and your pretty friend are awake!'

The room was so dingy, and so cluttered with menacing-looking bric-a-brac, that the pirate hadn't noticed a figure dressed all in black robes[20] busying about in the corner. It was the

---

20 Black looks best on persons who have black in their features (hair, eyes, brows and lashes), although black can be worn by most people for very dramatic occasions.

iniquitous Bishop of Oxford himself! The pirate with a scarf could tell it was the Bishop because he was wearing a bishop's hat, just like the chess pieces that he had seen the Pirate Captain play with on occasion. The pirate with a scarf preferred Ludo or Snakes and Ladders himself.

'What's all this about, you beast?' asked Jennifer from inside her big glass tube. The Bishop fixed her with a beady stare.

'How old would you take me for?' he asked, as if by way of explanation. Jennifer had never been particularly good at estimating this sort of thing, but she hazarded a guess anyhow.

'Mid to late forties?'

'Hah! I'm actually fifty-one years old.'

The Bishop gazed at the pair of them expectantly. Jennifer and the pirate with a scarf just looked blankly back at him. He seemed a bit annoyed that he had to explain things further.

'I keep myself so fresh-looking by using this devilish machine to distil the very life-essence from young ladies such as you!' he added impatiently.

'So you're responsible for all these grisly murders! I had my bets on it being a member of the Royal Family. Or maybe gypsies,' said Jennifer, wide-eyed and fuming. 'You villain!'

'I must say, Bishop,' said the pirate with a scarf – remembering to keep up his lady voice – 'the sack and the drugs. It's not the sort of behaviour I'd expect from a man of the cloth.'

The diabolical Bishop looked almost sheepish.

'I realise that my methods leave a lot to be desired,' he replied with a rather forlorn sigh, 'but you have to appreciate the climate I'm working in. Anyone will tell you how difficult it is to meet a nice girl in a big city like this. So you can understand that in my case, where I need to meet about a dozen nice girls a week in order to synthesise my ghastly concoction . . . well, it's virtually impossible.'

'I can see why you're not a girl's first choice,' said Jennifer with a sneer. 'If a lady is looking for anything to be planted on her mouth at the end of an evening, it's a kiss, not a dirty old cloth soaked in chloroform. The least I'd expect of a fellow who intends to drain the youthful life-force out of me would be flowers and conversation.'

'Yes, it's a bit much. Do you really need the sinister circus and the swirling fog and the kidnapping? Have you tried a nice coffee shop? I hear that they're great places to pick up us women,' said the pirate helpfully.

'Of course I have!' replied the Bishop with an air of despair. 'But it just never works out. I meet a girl, I laugh a booming maniacal laugh at their anecdotes, just like I've read you're meant to, and I make sure to pay them a compliment – "you've got a lovely hairline, I won't need to shave your temples when I attach you to my nightmarish device" – something like that. But more often than not it's a swift peck on the cheek, thanks for a lovely evening, and I'm home alone in my macabre lair. I just don't have time for it! I'm not getting any younger, you know. Well, I suppose in a manner of speaking I am, but you see my point.'

'I doubt that funny little moustache is doing you any favours,' said Jennifer with an arched eyebrow.

'It's an evil moustache, not a gay moustache,' replied the Bishop with a pout.

'That's why you're so bothered by Darwin's Man-panzee!' exclaimed the pirate. 'You're worried that if Mister Bobo is a roaring success then all the crowds will forget about the Elephant Man, and they'll flock to see him instead! Without a constant supply of young ladies visiting the circus for you to kidnap, you wouldn't be able to fashion your evil elixir!'

'It's not really an elixir. It's more a sort of facial scrub,'[21] said the Bishop. 'But listen, I'm not about to let you gab your way out of this. On with the show!'

The Bishop threw an enormous lever, and his horrific machine roared into life. Sparks bounced off the walls, pistons smashed up and down, lights flashed and bells rang. But just as

---

21   The Bishop of Oxford was widely known as 'Soapy' Sam Wilberforce. However, if you look this up on Google, chances are it will ascribe the nickname to his 'slippery ecclesiastical debating skills' rather than because he turned ladies into bars of soap.

the contraption seemed to be building to a crescendo there was a sickening metallic gurgle, a belch of acrid black smoke, and everything fell silent.

'Oh, for pity's sake!' moaned the Bishop, giving an apologetic look to his captives. 'Honestly, this has never happened before.' He spent the next few minutes trying fruitlessly to find a fault with the various gears and pulleys and bits of wire that made up his machine. The pirate with a scarf took this opportunity to attempt a bit of romantic small talk with Jennifer, but she seemed a little preoccupied and he could sense that the moment might have passed.

'There's no reason why this shouldn't be working. It's brand new,' said the Bishop tetchily. 'Unless . . . one of you isn't really a lady!'

The pirate with a scarf gulped, and tried to do his most winning lady smile, but then he realised that this just showed off more of his gold teeth.

'There's only one way to find out,' said the Bishop, a nasty reptilian grin playing across his face as he advanced upon Jennifer and the disguised pirate.

Forty minutes later, the two of them reluctantly handed the Bishop their completed psychometric test papers. He pored over the results, and then pointed an accusing finger at the pirate. The scarf-wearing pirate hung his head in dismay – his skill at spatial awareness and numerical pattern identification compared with his comparative weakness at colour differentiation and verbal reasoning had given away his secret.

'You're no lady!' said the Bishop with a scowl. 'In fact, these test results suggest you're a pirate! Goodness knows what you've done to my machine. It's only designed to work with ladies aged nineteen to twenty-six. You've probably invalidated my warranty, you lousy bum.'

The Bishop unhooked the pirate from his infernal apparatus, and rolled him in his tube over to what looked for all the world like a massive metal cog. Then he opened up the top of the tube, slid the bound pirate out and fastened him to one of the notches between the cog's gigantic teeth. The Bishop looked at his watch irritably. 'I've got an appointment with a man and his monkey,' he said, turning his attention to Jennifer. 'But I expect you to be a lifeless husk by the time I get back, young lady. No funny business.'

With that, he pulled the big lever again, and went off whistling a show tune. The pirate with a scarf looked on in horror as the life started to drain from what was the first girl in ages who looked as though she might actually have put out for him.

Ten

A DEAD MAN'S
CHEST!

Halfway across town the Pirate Captain strode along with big piratical strides. He didn't stare down at his feet and scuttle through the sudden downpour like the sorry rubber-necks who shared the narrow streets with him; he held his head high and seemed almost to be snarling at the sky, willing it to do its worst – he was the Pirate Captain, and he wasn't bothered by a bit of rain.

Just a few minutes later – he walked at quite a pace, and had been known to swing his cutlass at ditherers who blocked his way – the Pirate Captain arrived at the Hotel Metropolitan where, according to his letter, the Pirate Convention was being held. The concierge, a slight and sweaty man, greeted him in the swanky lobby.

'You must be here for the Pork Convention,' he said with an exaggerated wink.

'Pork Convention? Are you mad? I'm here for

the Pirate Convention!' said the Pirate Captain, dumbfounded.

'Ha-ha! A Pirate Convention!' laughed the concierge, nervously brushing some of his few remaining hairs across a shiny scalp. 'Imagine! If you were an otherwise respectable hotel, and you were to hold a pirate convention, why . . .' the concierge gave a meaningful pause '. . . you'd probably pretend it was a Pork Convention, or something like that.'

'What's this blathering about pork?'

'I think that's what you're looking for.'

'I'm looking for no such thing! And stop winking at me! I've run men through for less!'

'I was simply saying the word "pork" instead of "pirate" so as not to draw any unwanted attention to the proceedings. It's a kind of clever code. It doesn't really matter any more,' whispered the concierge, a touch irritably.

'Ah! Yes. I'm here for the Pork Convention," said the Pirate Captain in a loud voice, adding quietly with a wink of his own. 'I see what you're doing now.'

'If you'll just follow me.'

'Certainly. Is there anywhere I can leave my gammon?'

'I'm sorry?'

'My gammon. It's clever code for "cutlass". I just made it up.'

The concierge led the Pirate Captain through the lobby, which had been smartly decked out with big misleading papier-mâché models of different kinds of pork products – including chops and sausages – across an expensive-looking carpet, and into the hotel's main conference hall. It was full to the brim with pirates from all over the globe. Several of them were roaring, so it was quite noisy, and there was a distinct smell of seaweed about the place. Scanning the room, which read like a *Who's Who* of the nautical underworld, the Pirate Captain recognised a familiar figure. He threaded his way through the crowd.

'Raagh! You lubber!' roared the Pirate Captain.

'What's that? Lubber! Who's calling me a lubber! You cur!' said the pirate, spinning round angrily. He must have been a good seven feet tall, with hands the size of the hams the Pirate

Captain usually ate for dinner. Several of the other pirates in the immediate vicinity fell silent, their hands on their cutlasses, expecting trouble. But the giant pirate held up his arms and proceeded to squeeze the Pirate Captain in an embrace that would have crushed the breath out of lesser men with a more limited lung capacity.

'Why! It's my old friend the Pirate Captain!' bellowed the pirate.

'Scurvy Jake!' said the Pirate Captain, evidently glad to see his former comrade. 'I haven't seen you since that incident on Madagascar!'

'Aaarrr! I was sure they were girls!' said Scurvy Jake with an apologetic shrug.

'What are you doing here, you salty old dog?' laughed the Pirate Captain, giving his friend an affectionate slap on his oversized biceps.

'I'm in the nostalgia business!' said Scurvy Jake, indicating the convention buzzing on around them. 'I mean, after I hung up my eye patch I tried my hand at a few things, but what with the Industrial Revolution, it's all factory work. I'm not cut out for all that fiddly business, haven't got the fingers for it.' Scurvy Jake indicated his fingers, which were the size of bananas.[22] 'But then I found out how lucrative going on the Pirate Convention circuit can be. You sign a few books, tell a couple of stories, there's plenty of grog in return, and you get free board and lodging to boot. I'm actually a lot better at reminiscing about pirating than I ever was at doing it in the first place.'

Scurvy Jake helped the Pirate Captain to a complimentary glass of rum.[23]

'Let me show you the ropes,' the giant continued. 'There's a panel quiz later on where fans can ask us a few questions, and everybody tends

---

22 Edible bananas may disappear within a decade if urgent action is not taken to develop new varieties resistant to blight, according to recent studies published in *New Scientist*.

23 Rum is the oldest distilled spirit in the world. After he was killed at the Battle of Trafalgar, Lord Nelson's body was preserved in a barrel of his favourite rum. To make a good Mai Tai, you need 1 oz. Dark Rum, 1 oz. Light Rum, 1 oz. Triple Sec, ½ oz. Lime Juice, ½ oz. Grenadine, ½ oz. Orgeat Syrup. Garnish with a pineapple wedge and cherry. Serve in a High Ball.

to hit the bar after that. But right now I'm going to sign a few photos of myself. I charge a doubloon a time. Care to join me?'

As it happened the Pirate Captain had stopped off at a Victorian Snappy Snaps, and was clutching a stack of black and white six-by-eights, in which he was doing a very debonair face indeed. He settled down at a table next to Scurvy Jake and pretty soon had a queue of asthmatic-looking kids and creepy middle-aged men lining up in front of him. He'd been sort of hoping that groupies might prove to be a problem – girls who wanted nothing more than to annoy their respectable families by throwing themselves at a handsome Pirate Captain, but it was immediately obvious that they were going to be in short supply.

'Could you sign it to Paul,' said the first fan to come shambling up. 'And maybe put something like "Arrgh! Here be treasure!". I was going to stick it on top of my money box, you see.'

'Certainly. That's very clever.'

'My money box is shaped like a pirate boat.'

'Even better,' said the Pirate Captain, handing him his picture with a grin.

'You're fantastic!' said another eager young boy.

'Ah, I don't know if I'd go that far . . .'

'No, really, you are. I was even going to buy a resin model of you swinging on some rigging, but I only had six shillings, so I got Black Bellamy instead. Have you ever met Black Bellamy? He's my favourite pirate ever!'

'Is that a fact?'

'Oh yes. He's terrific. You're almost as good, though. But why are you wearing a hat like that?'

'This happens to be a very stylish pirate hat.'

'Black Bellamy has some brilliant hats. You should talk to him to find out where he gets his hats from.'

'How would you like to be run through by a genuine pirate cutlass?'

Ker-chunk!

Back in the Bishop's gloomy lair the pirate with a scarf was starting to realise the nature of his predicament. Every few minutes the massive

135

cog to which he was tied clicked on a few inches. It meshed with another gigantic cog, and he estimated that in a couple of hours he would reach this second set of metallic teeth and be crushed to a pulp of bone and gristle and bits of scarf. The only consolation was that he had found Erasmus Darwin, who was tied between two teeth a little further round, and would be crushed to death several minutes before him. And as the Bishop's monstrous contraption continued to chug away, Jennifer would probably be worse off even sooner. Neither fact was actually much consolation at all.

'Are you okay?' said the pirate to Jennifer.

'My fingertips have started to shrivel up a bit. It's like I've been in the bath too long.'[24]

---

24 There's no need to be frightened when your fingers shrivel up after being in the bath. Normally your skin is lubricated with a thin layer of sebum – an oil which acts to waterproof the surface of your body. With prolonged exposure to water the sebum is washed away, which allows water to penetrate into the epidermis by osmosis. The skin becomes waterlogged, resulting in a wrinkled appearance – rather like a monster or an old woman.

'Listen. Assuming we get out of this, how would you like to come out to dinner with me?' The pirate gave what he imagined to be a sexy wink.

'Oh. Well . . . I've sort of got plans,' said Jennifer. Erasmus made a sound like a plane crashing. The pirate with a scarf shot him a bit of a look, and started to wonder why he had bothered getting out of his hammock that morning.

Just then there came the wheezy sound of an accordion. It was an odd little tune that, had he been alive exactly one hundred and fifty years later, the scarf-wearing pirate would have recognised as the first few bars from 'Theme to Bergerac'. Out from behind a gigantic bell stepped the pirate with an accordion. The others were unanimously glad to see him.

'Rescue!' cried Erasmus.

'Daphne!' said Jennifer.

'What took you so long?' asked the pirate with a scarf, in a bit of a strop.

'You two wandered off, so I went to the hall of mirrors,' said the pirate with an accordion defensively. 'It was fantastic! One of the mirrors made me look like a little dwarf, but with a big long head! I laughed for ages! And then I got bored of that, so I played a bit of "What shall we do with the drunken sailor?" on my accordion, which happens to be my favourite shanty. Then I tried to find you and your girlfriend.'

'She's not my girlfriend,' said the scarf-wearing pirate with a scowl.

'Bad luck. Anyhow, I noticed the pair of you going into that Special Exhibit For The Ladies, and when you didn't come out for ages I thought perhaps you were teaching Jennifer about tying knots.'

'Knots?'

'You must have noticed how whenever there's a lady onboard the pirate boat the Pirate Captain will always disappear into his cabin with her for a while and, afterwards, when any of us ask what they were doing, he tells us he was just teaching the lady how to tie knots, because most girls don't know much about nautical matters. Between you and me, I think he must tell funny anecdotes at the same time as showing them how to tie knots, because quite often I've heard a lot of giggling. But that's not to say the Captain doesn't take his knot tying seriously – he obviously puts a lot of effort into it, as he tends to come out from a knot-tying lesson looking quite exhausted.'

The pirate with a scarf wondered if it were perhaps time to sit down with some of the crew and set them straight on a couple of matters.

'So eventually I decided to follow you into the tent myself,' continued the pirate with an accordion. 'But you were nowhere to be seen! It was completely empty, except for a half-used-up bottle of chloroform. I looked about for a while, and then I found there was a trapdoor hidden in the floor, which led to some steps. And the steps led to a creepy-looking tunnel. Well, that all seemed rather rum. I think it was part of an old sewer system, and you know how you're always reading about people flushing away baby alligators which then grow to gigantic proportions, so – given that alligators and us pirates have got a bit of a troubled history – I was pretty frightened, but I played the most upbeat shanties I could think of to keep myself calm. The tunnel went on for a few hundred yards, and then I got to more stairs, lots of them this time, and they led up here. Now I've found you I suppose I should probably—'

But, without saying another word, the pirate with an accordion died of scurvy, right there and then.

'Blast,' said Erasmus.

'I wasn't expecting that,' said Jennifer miserably.

'Idiot!' said the pirate with a scarf. 'I told him what would happen if he just ate chocolate all the time instead of limes.'

Scurvy Jake and the Pirate Captain had gone on signing autographs for most of the afternoon. Occasionally the Pirate Captain got a bit annoyed to hear Scurvy Jake passing off one of the Pirate Captain's exciting anecdotes as if it was his own, but he decided to let it slide. After they had both run out of photographs – the Pirate Captain was pleased to have pocketed over sixty doubloons for his efforts – they decided to wander over to the part of the convention where several stalls were selling piratical equipment at trade prices. There was a lot of good-natured bargaining going on, as pirates jostled each other for the best deals. The Pirate Captain picked up a job lot of thirty portholes for just twenty-eight pounds – less than a pound per porthole! He also bought a barrel of tar, six bottles of Pirate Rum, and a few tricorn hats just to spite everybody. Satisfied with his purchases, he and Scurvy Jake headed over to the Metropolitan's bar to drink and reminisce.

Pretty soon Scurvy Jake was a bit worse the wear from all the grog.

'I was a terrible pirate,' he said, in a cracked voice. 'You were always a much better pirate than me.'

It was true, thought the Pirate Captain. Scurvy Jake had always been a rubbish pirate. With his lumbering lack of coordination and his giant hands, he was no good at tying knots, and he was famous for repeatedly burying treasure and then forgetting where he'd left it. But the Pirate Captain didn't like to see his old friend upset.

'Pfft! I've made a few mistakes myself,' said the Pirate Captain, trying to console him. 'Like that time I let a cannibal join the crew. And that other time when I said "Well, I don't see any hurricane." I'm not perfect.'

'But I'm the worst pirate ever. I'm so clumsy,' sobbed Scurvy Jake.

'What about Courteous Frank? He was easily a worse pirate than you ever were. I heard he refused to let his crew cure the ship's meat with salt, because he'd read that a high sodium intake had been linked to heart disease. Died eating a slice of rancid ham. You're not even close!'

'It's kind of you to say so, Pirate Captain. You know, if there's anything I can do to help, you just have to ask. Are you on holiday, or are you on an adventure?'

'Adventure. And you can help, Scurvy Jake!' The Pirate Captain's beard glittered with piratical cunning. 'Do you know where I could get hold of a big white sheet?'

Eleven

MAROONED!

'He's not just evil! He's insane! A 100 per cent Grade-A lunatic!' shouted Darwin, flinging the evening edition of the *Mail* at the Pirate Captain, who had returned from his Pirate Convention and was helping set up the stage of the Natural History Museum's lecture room for the evening's performance. 'The Bishop of Oxford has persisted with his ridiculous scare-mongering. Now he's saying that if I go ahead with my Man-panzee demonstration, the Holy Ghost – the Holy Ghost! – will personally make an appearance at my lecture, and wrestle me and Mister Bobo to the ground! Really, it's too much!'

'It's not the Bishop's work. It's mine,' said the Pirate Captain, chewing the end off a fat cigar, and looking smug. Sometimes the Pirate Captain found himself thinking what a fantastic, hard-bitten and wily newspaper mogul he would have made, had he not taken up piracy instead. Darwin slumped into one of the auditorium's seats.

'I'm not sure I follow,' he said weakly.

'I'm the one who started the rumour. And – even though I say it myself – it's a stroke of genius.'

'For pity's sake, why?'

'Listen, Charles. You've got a lot to learn about this science business. It's not all about test tubes and creatures and bits of gauze.'

'It isn't?'

'No, it isn't. The whole thing became clear to me when I was talking to an old friend of mine. He was telling me how great at pirating he always thought I was,' explained the Pirate Captain. 'And the fact is, I have made something of a name for myself in nautical circles. But why do you think that is?'

Darwin scratched his head thoughtfully. 'Your luxuriant beard?'

'Aaarrr,' said the Pirate Captain. 'That probably plays a part in it. But more than that, I think it's because of my gift for showmanship. Like the way I drink rum mixed with gunpowder, even though it tastes disgusting. And the way I run people through in such a grisly manner.'

'Surely,' said Darwin, 'it's not possible to be run through in any manner other than a grisly one?'

'Now, a lot of people will tell you that. But it's not the case. You take the pirate with a scarf. He's such a proficient swordsman that I've seen him run a man through without spilling a drop of blood,[25] and the fellow on the receiving end dies in a speedy and humane fashion. Me on the other hand, I'm forever making a mess of it, hacking about all over the shop, getting my cutlass stuck in a particularly tough bit of gristle. Yet, quite inadvertently, this has all added to my fearsome reputation! And with pirating, reputation is everything.'

'I'm *still* not sure I follow you,' said the puzzled young scientist.

---

25 There are roughly eight pints of blood in the average human. Blood contains red cells, white cells and platelets suspended in a proteinacious fluid called plasma. The first dog biscuit to be made entirely out of blood was invented by Tamsin Virgo, a young woman from Stoke, England.

'Mister Bobo is a fantastic achievement. But there's a thousand other scientists out there trying to make a name for themselves. So if you're going to stand out and impress the stony-faced Victorian establishment, you need a gimmick! A bit of controversy! It's all about the presentation.'

So the Pirate Captain explained his latest plan. Though perhaps it was a little more complicated than his usual plans, which tended to involve how much ham to eat, the Pirate Captain was confident of success. Darwin was less certain.

'I don't know, Pirate Captain,' he said with a sad shake of his head, once the Captain had finished. 'It all seems such a risk. This lecture is expressly against the Bishop's wishes. I can't help but think something truly terrible will befall my poor brother.'

'Well, I'm in the same boat myself,' said the Pirate Captain with a shrug. 'Two of my pirates never returned from investigating that sinister circus. There's a good chance the Bishop has some evil fate planned for them too. I'm not really that bothered about the swab with the accordion, but that other fellow . . . the one with a scarf –' the Pirate Captain really never seemed to be able to remember the names of any of his crew – 'the truth is, I'm at a bit of a loss without him. He cleans my hats, keeps me up to date with all the latest shanties, and he even knows all the proper nautical terms for things. I bet you didn't realise that on a sailing boat you're not even meant to say "upstairs" or "downstairs" or "left" or "right". It's all "port" this and "starboard" that and "galley" instead of kitchen and goodness knows what else. How am I expected to remember that kind of thing? Anyhow. What was the point I was making?'

'I'm not really sure,' said Darwin.

'Well then,' said the Pirate Captain, flashing the scientist his most winning grin.

The Royal Society's grandfather clock struck a quarter past ten. It was just a few minutes to go until Darwin's big moment, and the lecture hall was fast filling up. Most of the audience had read the evening papers' controversial head-lines, and there was an excited buzz of anticipation throughout the room. The Pirate Captain's ploy had certainly done the trick in bringing in the crowds, thought Darwin. He stood at the door, greeting people as they arrived, whilst Mister Bobo paced backstage taking nerv-ous swigs from a flask of whisky.

'Nice that you could make it. Hi. Hello. Thanks for coming. Glad you could be here. Nice to—'

Darwin froze. He found himself face to face with the Bishop of Oxford.

'Darwin.'

'Bishop.'

'So you're going ahead with this?'

'I – uh – that is . . . it looks that way.'

'What a pity your brother Erasmus couldn't be here.'

'You villain! What have you done with him?'

'Mr Darwin . . . Charles. I haven't the slight-est clue what you're talking about. I just hope his health isn't suffering,' said the Bishop, waggling his bushy brows and grimacing to show that he meant the exact opposite of what he was saying. 'It's not too late to reconsider,' he added as he took his seat in the audience, unwittingly right next to the Pirate Captain, who was back in scientist disguise.

The lights dimmed, the thick velvet curtain went up and Darwin and Mister Bobo came out to enormous applause.

'Ladies and gentlemen. He's hairy! He's scary! I would like to introduce you to the world's first fantastic . . . Man-panzee!'

The spotlight fell on Mister Bobo, who was so well turned out, with his hair slicked back, a breath mint in his mouth and his best dress shirt tucked into a pair of handsome trousers, that it looked like he was going on a first date. In actual fact, Mister Bobo had never so much as kissed a girl. The audience clapped again. Darwin coughed nervously, and started to explain how he fed Mister Bobo on a diet of pituitary glands taken from the cadavers of baby seals.

'One might expect the pituitary gland to have some effect on the language capabilities of the simian brain, but I can't detect any. Mister Bobo just seems to like the taste,' said Darwin.

Ker-chunk!

The gigantic cog clicked on another notch.

'Shall we have a game of animal, vegetable or mineral? To take our minds off things?' suggested Erasmus brightly. The scarf-wearing pirate would have enjoyed a game of hangman more, but seeing as they didn't have any chalk, and their hands were all tied up anyhow, he nodded reluctantly.

'I'll go first,' said the pirate. 'Okay, I've thought of something.'

'Are you a mineral?' asked Erasmus.

'Nope.'

'Animal?'

'Sort of.'

'Sort of?'

'All right, yes. Animal.'

'Are you a hoofed animal?'

'No.'

'Claws?'

'No.'

'Not claws or hoofs? What does that leave? Trotters?'

'Yes!'

'So you're a pig?'

'Not exactly . . .'

'Not exactly a pig? Then a bit of a pig? Are you bacon?'

'No, but you're getting warm.'

'Ham?'

'That's it! I'm a succulent piece of ham! But you took too many guesses, so I won, and I get to choose again.'

Darwin had finished his introduction and explanation of his training methods, and now he was leading Mister Bobo – who was doing his best not to knuckle-walk, because he knew just how vulgar that looked – over to a carefully laid out dinner table in the centre of the stage.

'Mister Bobo – would you be so kind as to show these ladies and gentlemen exactly which of these spoons you would use to eat a dessert?'

Mister Bobo held up the correct spoon almost instantly, and the audience let out some 'oohs' and 'aahs'. His confidence building, Mister Bobo proceeded to run through the rest of the routine with aplomb. Shown pictures of two different girls he correctly identified which one was more attractive, he made a selection of cocktails called out by the audience, and he played 'God Save the Queen' and 'Crockett's Theme' on the piano, without hitting a single wrong note.

Ker-chunk!

'So you're not actually a cow?' said Jennifer, rolling her eyes in exasperation.

'No,' grinned the pirate with a scarf.

'Are you a steak?'

'No!'

'I give up.'

'I'm a sausage! But one made out of beef

instead of pork. Right – I've thought of something else!'

'Is this going to be meat-based again?'

'It might be.'

Darwin and Mister Bobo were building up to the grand finale. The lecture had gone well, and the audience seemed politely impressed, but it clearly needed something more to whip them into a frenzy. With a pre-arranged signal from Mister Bobo, a clattering noise came from off stage, and then a lumbering figure appeared.

'Wait a minute! Who's this?' said Darwin, looking surprised. 'Oh my goodness! Ladies and Gentlemen . . . it's the Holy Ghost!'

'Wooo! Raaah!' said the Holy Ghost, a bit muffled, sounding a lot like Scurvy Jake with a sheet over his head. There was the plink-plink of gentlemen dropping monocles into their drinks and the gentle rustle of several ladies fainting.

155

'He's come to get me, because my theories are so blasphemous!' shouted Darwin, in mock terror. Nobody noticed the twinkle in his eye. 'The Holy Ghost is attacking me! Look at the Holy Ghost!'

'Rah!' said the Holy Ghost, in a booming voice. 'The science you are doing is too shocking by half! I've come to wrestle you! I will lay the smackdown on your wicked ways!'

Gasps shot round the auditorium, and Darwin was pleased to see he had the audience on the edge of their seats. He just had time to notice the Pirate Captain lean over to the Bishop and whisper something in his ear, before his attention was diverted by the Holy Ghost picking him up and hurling the young scientist straight through the middle of the dining table. [26]

*   *   *

26 Wrestlers today are highly trained professionals, and obviously you should never try smacking people about the head with chairs or throwing them through tables at home. Even the best wrestlers get injured – Mick Foley, three times WWF champion, has broken most of the bones in his body during his career, lost several teeth and even an ear.

'Dear me! The actual Holy Ghost!' the Pirate Captain was saying to his neighbour. 'If I'd done any sins, I'd probably want to get them off my chest right about now. Like that time I kidnapped somebody. I'm really sorry about that. What about you, Bishop? Have you ever done any sins? Like kidnapping?'

'That's not the Holy Ghost,' snorted the Bishop dismissively.

'Yes it is!' said the Pirate Captain, a bit put out. 'Look how tall he is! He's a giant! And he's covered in a big sheet! Just like it describes him in the Bible.'

'The Bible says nothing of the kind. Where on earth did you get the idea that the Holy Ghost is a giant? He's the same size as Jesus. That's the point – he's just a creepier version of Christ.'

'Are you sure?' frowned the Captain, wondering if his research had let him down. 'Doesn't he fight Goliath at some point? I'm sure he does. He throws a leper at his face.'

'No. I've no idea where you've picked all this up from.'

'It's just after the bit where he hides in that gigantic wooden horse. Isn't it?'

'I think you're a trifle confused.'

'Ah well. Plan B,' said the Pirate Captain with a disappointed shrug. He whipped his cutlass out from under his lab coat and jabbed it in the Bishop's ribs. 'I'm not really a scientist – I'm the Pirate Captain! Tell me what you've done with Erasmus!'

The Bishop didn't miss a beat. 'Why! Look over there! Is that a treasure chest?' he said.

Even though he knew better, the Pirate Captain looked over to where the Bishop was pointing. The villain took this opportunity to bolt from the lecture room. 'I just can't help myself,' thought the Pirate Captain irritably. 'Damn my piratical nature!'

He leapt to his feet, pulled off the cumbersome lab coat and, seeing the stricken look on Darwin's face, gave the scientist a reassuring thumbs-up to show he had it all under control. Then the Pirate Captain chased as fast as he could after the despicable cleric, pausing only briefly to give his card to a striking blonde sitting in the second row.

Darwin, having little option but to hope the Pirate Captain knew what he was doing, went on hamming it up as he pretended to be desperately trying to make a wrestling tag with Mister Bobo. After a great deal of gurning and grunting he slapped the monkey's hand, and Mister Bobo leapt into centre stage and swung a folding metal chair at the head of the Holy Ghost, who promptly collapsed in a heap. Darwin held up Mister Bobo's hand triumphantly.

'Hooray for science!' he shouted. 'Tell your friends! Tell your family! And don't forget that Mister Bobo merchandise can be purchased from the museum shop!'

And with that, the audience were on their feet, giving Darwin a spectacular thunderous ovation.

The Pirate Captain skidded to a halt in the museum's cavernous main hall, realised he had lost sight of the fleeing Bishop and said a terrible salty pirate oath. It occurred to him that the

Bishop might be hiding inside the gigantic Armadillo shell that was one of the Pirate Captain's favourite exhibits, but before he could check it out he was alerted by a scuffling sound from the balcony above, and so he began to charge up the marble staircase, four steps at a time, only to find an enormous slice of Californian Redwood[27] rolling straight towards him. A full twenty feet in diameter, the Redwood came within a whisker of crushing the Pirate Captain flat, but he just managed to dive out of the way with an athletic leap. The monstrous Redwood still knocked off his pirate hat though.

'That's my favourite hat, Bishop! You're not doing yourself any favours!'

The Pirate Captain bounded to the top of the stairs and saw the Bishop disappearing into the Hall of Fossils. Waving his cutlass and roaring, for effect more than anything, he careered

---

27 The California Redwood is the biggest and most majestic tree in the world. Some of them can grow as high as 367 feet (13 London buses) and as broad as 22 feet in diameter (4/5 of a London bus). Their flowers are cones and they can live for over 2,000 years.

inside, and almost found himself smashed in the face by a trilobite. The Bishop had a whole armful of trilobites and was flinging them at the Pirate Captain like prehistoric discuses. The Captain did his best to bat them away with his cutlass.

'Stop throwing trilobites at me!' shouted the Pirate Captain, because it was the only thing he could think of to say given the situation. Luckily for the Pirate Captain they were not having their climactic fight in Prague Natural History Museum, which is full of trilobites and not much else, and the Bishop quickly exhausted his supply of fossils. He dashed into the adjoining room, and the Pirate Captain followed at full tilt, even though it contained the museum's collection of stuffed birds, which the Pirate Captain had always found especially creepy.

The Bishop swung a dodo at the advancing pirate, sending his cutlass flying. In return the Pirate Captain picked up an albatross and flung it squarely at the Bishop.

'Ooof!' said the Bishop, his mouth full of albatross wing. He clambered onto a balustrade and leapt from the balcony. For a moment the Pirate Captain thought the Bishop had decided to end it all, but then he realised that the wily cleric had landed on the skull of the enormous brontosaurus that was the museum's centre-piece, and was now sprinting down its bony neck to safety. The Pirate Captain jumped over the balcony himself and decided to slide down the skeleton's neck like it was a banister on the pirate boat, a decision he pretty quickly regret-ted. It took a moment for him to get his breath back and for his eyes to stop watering, by which time the Bishop had fled into the Mineral Room. The room's curator was surprised to see anybody coming into the Mineral Room, arguably the most boring room in the whole museum, let alone the Bishop of Oxford hotly pursued by an angry-looking pirate.

The Bishop smashed open a display case, sending a cloud of dust into the air, and flung a hefty rock at the Pirate Captain. The Pirate Captain squinted – it looked like a piece of iron as it hurtled towards his luxuriant beard. Moving lightning fast the Pirate Captain scanned the display in front of him, found a big chunk of nickel and hurled it back towards the Bishop. The nickel hit the iron and knocked it into a thousand splinters.

'Ha!' cried the Pirate Captain. 'Nickel! Atomic weight 58.71 – beats your iron, atomic weight 55.85. In your face, Bishop!'

'So let's see you deal with this!' shouted the Bishop, hefting a lump of Ruthenium at the pirate.

'Ruthenium! Atomic weight 101.07! Goodness me!' cried the Pirate Captain, though perhaps in slightly saltier terms than that. He barely found a slab of Osmium – atomic weight 190.2 – in time.

Several elements later they were still dead-locked, and fast running out of periodic table.[28]

'Give up, Bishop!' said the Pirate Captain, a nugget of Selenium whizzing past his ear.

---

28   Mendeleev is widely credited as being the first person to produce a 'periodic table of the elements' in 1865, but that, you'll notice, is a full thirty years after these events are supposed to be taking place. I leave the reader to draw their own conclusions.

'Oh, give up yourself!' shouted the Bishop, unimaginatively.

The Pirate Captain was momentarily put off when he picked up a lump of what he took to be gold, before realising it was actually iron pyrite – fool's gold, the dreaded nemesis of pirates everywhere – and his pause gave the Bishop an opportunity to escape the Mineral Room and head into the Hall of Mammals. The Pirate Captain charged after him relentlessly, but the Bishop had managed to snap the tusk off a shabby-looking walrus, and as the two men grappled he slowly inched his makeshift weapon towards the Pirate Captain's neck. The Bishop was unexpectedly strong.

'Do you work out?' asked the Pirate Captain through gritted teeth.

'A little,' said the Bishop, his face turning red. 'And yourself?'

'When I have the chance.'

'What do you bench-press?' hissed the Bishop.

'Around a hundred and ten pounds. How about you?'

'Oh . . . a hundred and twenty . . . hundred and twenty-five . . . or thereabouts.'

'Damn.'

The trouble, reflected the Pirate Captain, was that the pirate boat's gym was covered in mirrors, so whenever he worked out he would glimpse himself pulling a ridiculously strained face, which just made him laugh and not be able to take it all that seriously. As a result he had failed to keep up with the weights regime which had been set out for him by the pirate who was a jock. But he was paying for it now. The Pirate Captain genuinely thought he was done for. The tusk pressed against his throat, cutting off his pirate breath, and as consciousness began to slip away the Pirate Captain felt like he was starting to hallucinate – it seemed as if the very exhibits behind the Bishop were writhing and coming alive! Then he realised that the exhibit behind the Bishop really *was* moving. A hairy arm reached out, there was the distinct sound of monkey fist smashing into bishop skull, and the Bishop of Oxford collapsed in a daze. The walrus tusk clattered to the floor, and the Pirate Captain looked up to see that what he had taken to be part of the stuffed chimpanzee display was actually Mister Bobo!

'Thanks for that, Mister Bobo,' said the Pirate Captain breathlessly, shaking him by the hand.

'Aaargh! Me. Beauties!' said Mister Bobo with his cards, laughing a monkey laugh.

Twelve

SWINGING FROM
THE YARD-ARM!

Darwin helped the Pirate Captain to his feet, and gave him back his hat.

'It's a good job I cut that question and answer session short,' he said. 'Looks like me and Mister Bobo only just got here in time.'

'No need,' said the Pirate Captain, gingerly rubbing his neck. 'I had the fiend just where I wanted him.'

'You'd started to turn blue.'

'Aaarrr. It's an old pirate trick,' said the Pirate Captain defensively. 'Not something lubbers would understand. But enough about me – how did the lecture go?'

'It was fantastic!' said Darwin with a big grin. 'I got five phone numbers from pretty girls! Five!' He waved some scraps of perfumed paper at the Pirate Captain. 'They couldn't get enough of Mister Bobo! And you were right, when he smashed that chair over the Holy Ghost's head, they almost jumped out of their seats! I'm sure they'll go home and tell everyone how shocking it all was, and how science is in the infernal pocket of Lucifer, but secretly they loved it. I've been invited to do a tour of the American universities! And Mister Bobo is going to appear on the cover of *Nature*.'

Mister Bobo gave a sheepish shrug, but you could tell he was pleased.

'Look, shall we grab a coffee?' asked Darwin. 'My shout. I've got to tell you all about the bit when I thought Scurvy Jake was actually going to sit on my head!'

'I rather think we should find out what this wretch has done with your missing brother first,' said the Pirate Captain, giving the Bishop a quick kick in the gut.

'Erasmus!' Darwin slapped his uncommonly large forehead with his palm. 'In all the excitement I'd clean forgot!'

The young scientist knelt down and shook the dazed Bishop by his bushy sideburns. 'Where is he? What have you done with my brother, you brute? I'll cut your pretty face!'

'No! Not the face!' cried the Bishop, holding

up his hands to protect his beautiful skin. 'He's tied to a big cog inside Big Ben! But you're much too late – as soon as Big Ben chimes midnight, he'll get another cog right in the chops!'

The unlikely trio hurried down to Parliament Square.

'Look! Only twenty minutes to go! How are we ever going to reach them in time?!' wailed Darwin.

'Aaarrr,' said the Pirate Captain, because he couldn't think of anything more helpful to say.

Darwin tried to look resolute. 'Climbing! It's the only way. One of us will have to climb up there!'

Big Ben loomed forbiddingly out of the fog. The Pirate Captain craned his neck, and felt a bit ill just looking up at the towering clock.

'Oh, well,' he shrugged. 'I'm afraid us pirates are notoriously rubbish at climbing up tall buildings. It's like that old shanty says . . . if a-climbing you need to go, leave those pirates down below, they're no good at it yo ho ho . . .'

It sounded to Darwin suspiciously like the Pirate Captain was making this shanty up as he went along.

'What about monkeys? They're always climbing up tall buildings! How about it Mister Bobo?' said the Pirate Captain, giving him an encouraging slap on his hairy back.

Mister Bobo chose his flash cards carefully.

'No. F*!$%ng. Way.' signed the monkey.

'Well, Charles. It is your brother.'

Darwin squinted at the distant clock face, and shivered.

'Ah . . . you know, me and Erasmus were never that close. He was a very solitary child. Not much of a brother at all.'

But Mister Bobo was holding up his cards again. 'What. About. FitzRoy. And. His. Airship?' he spelt out.

'Ah-ha!' cried the Pirate Captain. 'The little *pan-pongidae* fellow has it! We could steal the airship, pop it with my cutlass, and fashion a big rope from all the silk!'

'Or we could float up there in the airship. Because it's an airship.'

'Yes. Yes, we could do that instead. Either way's good. I'm not bothered.'

They hailed an oldendays taxi – which back in those topsy-turvy times used horses instead of electricity – and hurried back to South Kensington as fast as they could. Sprinting into the Natural History Museum the Pirate Captain quickly grabbed his men, who he found in the gift shop buying dinosaur masks and roaring at each other.[29]

'Raagh!' roared a pirate. 'I'm a triceratops!'

'Grraagh! I'm a brontosaurus!'

It was like the usual pirate roaring, but even better. They all stopped and paid attention when the Pirate Captain burst in.

'Stop mucking about, pirates!' he shouted. 'We've got a bit of traditional pirate boarding to do!'

---

29 To this day one of the best things you can buy in the Natural History Museum gift shop is a lenticular dinosaur ruler. When you waggle it back and forth, the dinosaurs appear to attack each other in an exciting fashion.

The pirates all flung off their scientist disguises, but several of them kept on their dinosaur masks because they figured it made them look even more fearsome than they already were. Into the gentlemen's club they charged.

'Dino-pirates!' cried a scientist, dropping his pipe in surprise. 'It's my worst nightmare!'

The Pirate Captain waved his pirate cutlass at FitzRoy and Glaisher, the airship scientist, who were sitting in a corner arguing over what the best bit about being a meteorologist was.

'It's the clouds,' FitzRoy was saying. 'Clouds are easily the best bit about meteorology.'

'Nonsense!' said Glaisher. 'It's the barometers.'

'We're boarding your airship!' bellowed the Pirate Captain. 'Prepare to be overrun! By pirates!'

FitzRoy and his friend reluctantly took the pirates round the back of the museum, to where the airship was parked. Its enormous gas-bag billowed in the wind, attached by a series of sturdy ropes to a luxurious-looking gondola. The pirates all clambered aboard.

'I think this may be a first. We're taking pirating into a whole new era. They'll probably put
us on stamps,' whispered the Pirate Captain to
the pirate dressed in green.

'How does it float?' asked Darwin, turning to
FitzRoy and Glaisher and pulling a face to show
how sorry he was to be responsible for the
pirates stealing their beloved airship.

'Initially we used helium as the lifting agent,'
replied FitzRoy with a grimace. 'But it turned
out to have a terrible and dangerous flaw.'

'Which was?'

'The pilots were always so busy larking about
with the gas cylinders, making their voices go all
squeaky, that they kept on smashing into trees and
buildings.[30] So now I've switched to hydrogen. I
can't see any sort of dangerous flaw when it comes
to good old reliable hydrogen,' said the young
captain, moving several boxes of fireworks out of
the way so that he could get to the steering wheel.

---

30   Much like bananas, supplies of helium may also
run out within the next twenty years. Helium is not just
used in party balloons, it is also important for the
manufacture of superconductors.

'It's certainly impressive. You can tell no expense has been spared. I like what you've done with that roaring log fire next to those spare cylinders of hydrogen in the lounge,' said the Pirate Captain politely as they wandered about the gondola.

FitzRoy, busy throwing out ballast and letting loose the anchor rope, though annoyed to find himself being hijacked by pirates for the second time in the space of one adventure, still appreciated their compliments nonetheless.

'Be sure to check out the splendid smokers' gallery,' he said. 'You'll find it affords tremendous views of the billowing bags of hydrogen gas. And help yourself to the chops which are cooking on the airship's flaming barbecue.'

After some chops, the pirates all helped to shovel coal into the blazing furnace that powered the airship's engines.

'It's a lot quicker than a boat,' said the pirate in green appreciatively, once they were airborne.

'And that scientist is right. You *can* see down ladies' tops. Look!' exclaimed the albino pirate excitedly.

'I think I like this better than sailing. You don't get wet, and I haven't been sick once,' said the pirate who chain-smoked, lighting his cigarette and tossing away the match.

'It does have its drawbacks, mind,' cautioned FitzRoy. The albino pirate was just about to ask what sort of drawbacks there could possibly be, when a low-flying crow smacked right into his face. FitzRoy sighed and shook his head sadly.

Above the ever-present fog they could see the dim lights of the city stretching out in all directions. The dirigible bobbed across central London at quite a rate, and soon they had Big Ben in sight. The Pirate Captain did a pirate gob on one of the tourists below, and was pleased to see his aim was still good.

'Heavens to Betsy!' cried Darwin. 'We've only got three minutes! We haven't time to try to find purchase on the roof. One of us will have to jump across!'

There was the unmistakable sound of several pirates staring at their fingernails.

'Honestly!' bellowed the Pirate Captain, very

disappointed at his lads. 'I've been attacked by jellyfish with more backbone than you lot! Well, then. If none of you lubbers will volunteer, we'll just have to settle this the old pirate way.'

The crew looked deathly serious – the Pirate Captain could mean only one thing!

A few moments later the albino pirate took a deep breath, counted to three, and held out his clenched fist. He tried to look apologetic, but a big grin spread all across his face.

'Sorry, Captain. Pirate stone blunts your pirate scissors.'

'Whatever,' said the Pirate Captain tetchily, thinking for a moment about trying to pretend that the two fingers he was holding up were actually supposed to represent a narrow piece of paper rather than a pair of scissors. But ancient pirate tradition was ancient pirate tradition, and there was no use arguing with it. He bent down to make sure his bootlaces were done up, checked he had as big a run-up as possible, let out a mighty roar, and leapt the gap between the airship and Big Ben.

The Pirate Captain had been expecting to smash right through the gigantic glass clock face, thereby making one of his famously dramatic entrances, but he just slapped against it with a sound like a side of beef hitting a chopping board, and slowly began to slide down in a daze. Luckily the Pirate Captain had the presence of mind to grab at the huge cast-iron minute hand, and there he hung, his coat-tails flapping. He took a deep breath to relax himself, but the buffeting winds were doing nothing to calm his nerves and even though he didn't mean to, he glanced down. The people on the streets below looked just like ants, thought the Pirate Captain, but not regular ants, more like some kind of sinister super-ants that wore clothes and hats and carried newspapers instead of bits of leaf. Noticing the worried looks on his crew's faces as they leant anxiously out of the airship's gondola he felt like he ought to make some sort of wisecrack in an effort to look hard-boiled and nonchalant, possibly involving a play on words with 'time', something like: 'I'm not having the TIME of my life!' But he didn't, he just grimaced a bit instead. With an effort he managed to twist himself about, and give one of the glass panels in the clock face a big kick. To the Pirate Captain's relief the panel shattered with the first blow and, after some grunting and sucking in of his gut, he was able to clamber inside.

The Pirate Captain rushed over to help Jennifer first, because she was the prettiest. He hefted the top off the big glass tube and helped her climb out. Jennifer flung her arms round his sturdy shoulders.

'Thanks! I thought I was going to end up as a bar of soap for sure! My name is Jennifer.'

'And I'm the Pirate Captain. It's a pleasure to meet you.'

'Likewise.'

'I have my own pirate boat, you know.'

'Really?'

'It has twelve cannons.'

'Goodness! That's a lot of cannons. Your beard is fantastic, by the way.'

'That's nice of you to say so. You yourself have a lovely face.'

'Oh! You're sweet.'

'Us pirates aren't just the weather-beaten rogues we're portrayed as. We have a soft side too. Also, my boat has silk sheets.'

There was a sudden sickening crunch of metal against bone, and an alarmed yelp. The Pirate Captain pulled a guilty face and slapped his forgetful forehead. He rushed over to the gigantic cog and dragged Erasmus Darwin from between its monstrous teeth.

'Sorry about that,' said the Pirate Captain with an apologetic grin. 'I'd forget my own head if it wasn't nailed down.'

'Oh! My arm!' wailed Erasmus.

'Aaarrr. Let's not get too precious about an arm,' said the Captain. 'Some of my crew don't even have legs! Just little wooden pegs. I swear, half of them are more like chairs than pirates!'[31]

---

31 Loss of limbs was an occupational hazard for

The Pirate Captain began to untie the ropes attaching the pirate with a scarf to the huge cog.

'I wish you wouldn't get yourself into trouble like this,' he scolded his trusty number two. But he meant it in an affectionate manner. You could tell this because when the Pirate Captain scolded somebody in a manner that wasn't affectionate they tended to end up with a cutlass in their belly. 'You're definitely the best one out of my whole crew. You're worth ten of any of the rest of them . . .' the Pirate Captain paused and fought back a grin '. . . because you have so many gold teeth!'

The pirate with a scarf laughed. The Pirate Captain always made that exact same joke, but they both knew that he really would be sorry to see anything happen to his able second in command. For a start, without help from the scarf-wearing pirate, the Pirate Captain probably

---

pirates. As a result most ships offered a degree of compensation for pirates injured in battle. Loss of an eye would net you 100 pieces of eight. Loss of a right arm 600 pieces of eight, and loss of a left leg 400 pieces of eight.

wouldn't have remembered where they had left the boat.

The Pirate Captain turned to give Darwin, FitzRoy and the rest of the pirates bobbing about in the dirigible a wave through the shattered bit of clock face to show them that everything was fine, and in the process almost tripped over the pirate with an accordion, who was sprawled across the floor.

'What's up with *this* swab?' asked the Pirate Captain, nudging him with the toe of his shiny pirate boot.

'He died of scurvy, sir,' said the pirate with a scarf.

'Aaaarrr. I hope that's proved a useful lesson to you. Ham is all well and good, but make sure you get your vitamins! Scurvy is no laughing matter,' said the Pirate Captain. 'Except in those rare instances when a fellow's head swells up like a gigantic lemon,' he added as an after-thought. 'Which I grant can bring a smile even to my salty old face.'

Thirteen

TO THE
PIRATE COAST!

'. . . Seven . . . eight . . . nine. Nine hams. Nine juicy hams.'

The Pirate Captain made a note on his clipboard. 'Well, that's just about everything.'

The pirates were back in Littlehampton Docks, and they had just finished loading up the pirate boat with fresh supplies of meat and grog. The only thing that remained to be wheeled on board was the pirate with an accordion, who the other pirates had decided to have stuffed and nickel-plated, because they thought it was what he would have wanted, and besides which the pirate boat could never have too many lucky mascots. Jennifer, who the Pirate Captain had made an honorary pirate, reckoned it was a bit on the creepy side, but pirates were a superstitious bunch.[32]

---

32 There are several seafaring superstitions. It is widely believed that redheads bring bad luck to a ship, though this can be averted if you speak to the redhead

Darwin, Erasmus and Mister Bobo had come down to wave them off. Darwin was almost unrecognisable from the callow youth the Pirate Captain had first met on this adventure – he had started to grow a little beard, his clothes were of the best Savile Row cut, and he had his arms round two vivacious-looking brunettes.

'Good luck then, Charles. I hope all the science goes well,' said the Pirate Captain, shaking him warmly by the hand.

'I think I'm really getting the hang of it,' said Darwin eagerly. 'I've got a lot more ideas to keep the audience on their toes. I'm going to fit a soundproofed box in the corner of my lecture theatres where I'll invite scientists too frightened to hear the shocking conclusion to my nightmarish theories to sit out the rest of the talk. And I'm offering life insurance policies to everybody in case my terrifying ideas scare them to death. I'm trying to work out a way to make all the seats vibrate. I'm calling it "Evolvovision".

---

before they speak to you. Flat-footed people are also considered best avoided, as is dark-coloured luggage.

Me and Mister Bobo are going to be the smash-hit of Victorian science – and I owe it all to you and your pirates, Pirate Captain!'

'Aaarrrr! Don't mention it! It's been a pleasure,' said the Pirate Captain. 'I have to say, when I first saw you, I thought – there's a man whose face isn't really big enough for the size of his head. But you've proved me wrong. Oh, and by the way . . .'

The Pirate Captain paused.

'Indian, North Pacific, South Pacific, Antarctic, Arctic, North Atlantic, South Atlantic. I'm not a complete idiot, you know.'

The pirate boat slowly pulled out of the shabby dock, and all the pirates waved the steadily shrinking trio goodbye. The Pirate Captain smiled. There were good bits about the land, he reflected, like the shops and the way it didn't wobble about all the time, but he'd missed the ocean. The Pirate Captain actually became quite lost in his thoughts about how much he liked the crashing waves and seaweed and being a pirate and that, until an indignant cough jolted him back to the moment.

'And what do you propose to do with me?'

said the Bishop of Oxford, who had been lashed to the boat's mast.

'We'll find an uninhabited island someplace,' said the Pirate Captain, 'and then we'll maroon you. It's the pirate way.'

'I don't much like the sound of that.'

'Oh, it's not so bad. For some reason Pirate Law says you're allowed to take a few records. And the odd book. I think it's eight of each.'

'Can I take the Bible?'

'Oh, you get that anyway. And the complete works of Shakespeare. But the rest is up to you. Don't be clever and choose *Robinson Crusoe* – everybody does that.'

The Pirate Captain turned back to watch Littlehampton's amusement arcade fade into the distance.

'That went pretty well, don't you think, number two?' he said to the pirate with a scarf.

'Yes, Captain. Though maybe our next adventure should be a little less episodic? And not be so confusing at times?' said the pirate with a scarf, leaning on the boat's safety railings and enjoying the spray of the sea on his face.

'Aaargh. You're right. And towards the last half of this adventure, I don't know if you noticed, but we stopped having half as many feasts. That was a pity.'

'And we didn't really end up with much treasure,' said the albino pirate sadly. 'Which is usually the best bit about our adventures.'

'Oh, I didn't come away completely empty-handed,' said the Pirate Captain with a grin. He rummaged about in the silky folds of his beard where, amongst the ribbons and the luxuriant hair, something shiny seemed to be lodged. The Captain eventually prised it free. He held up a large nugget of metal. It gleamed white in the evening sun, and the pirate with a scarf whistled in admiration.

'Ruthenium!' said the albino pirate.

'Aaargh. That it is. Atomic number forty-four. Most valuable metal in the world.[33] Better than gold – and you know how highly I rate gold, so that's saying something.'

---

33 Ruthenium is one of the ultra-rare 'Platinum Group metals'. It has a melting point of 2250°C and a boiling point of 3900°C, 44 protons, 44 electrons and 57 neutrons.

All the pirate crew cheered their Captain, and then they went downstairs to do some shantying.

And with that, the pirate boat sailed about for a bit.

Comprehension Exercise
Answer all questions to the best of your abilities

1. What do you think the themes of this book were? Several commentators have described the main theme as 'pirates'. Another theme might be said to be 'ham'. Would you agree?

2. Which do you think is more important to the Pirate Captain – ham, or his luxurious beard? If you had to choose which was more important to you, which one do you think you would pick?

3. On *The Late Show*, one of the critics, who has a face that looks like it's made of mallow, said to Germaine Greer, 'I wish there were more of Black Bellamy in *The Pirates! In An Adventure With Scientists*, he was the best character ever.' Would you agree with this assessment?

4. Apart from Brian Blessed, who do you think should play the Pirate Captain if they were ever to make a movie of this book?

5. Do you think the section in Chapter Five when the Pirate Captain forces several pirates to walk the plank is included to show that life at sea had a harsh edge to it? Or do you think the author has some other motives?

6. Choose the letter that best represents your feelings:
'Upon completion of *The Pirates! In An Adventure With Scientists*, I would describe my mood as _____.'

    (A) angry   (B) restless   (C) excitable
           (D) sleepy   (E) afraid

7. Scientifically speaking, who do you think the tallest pirate in the world is?

THANK YOU

WORDS TO KNOW:

lubber   pirate   starboard

ham   sloop   galley

ACKNOWLEDGEMENTS

Firstly, to Richard Murkin, because this book is the product of us knocking about for the last ten years. Thanks also to Helen Garnons-Williams for her ace editing, Claire Paterson for her ace agenting and Caitlin Moran for actually sending it to Claire in the first place. I should mention that David Cordingly's *Life among the Pirates* and Bodenstandig 2000's *Maxi German Rave Blast Hits Vol.* 3 both came in very useful when I was writing this.

Plus (for a load of different reasons): my mum, Sam Brown, Chloe Brown, Rob Adey, Nicola Hughes, Dr Jack Button, Danny Garlick, Sherhan Lingham and Rebecca Andrews. And Ruth.

THE PIRATES! IN AN ADVENTURE WITH COMMUNISTS

He's conquered the seven seas, hunted Moby Dick and rescued Charles Darwin; now the Pirate Captain and his crew are off on another adventure. Their mission this time: to sail to London, buy a new suit for the Pirate Captain and maybe have some sort of adventure in a barnyard.

But nothing is ever straight forward for the hapless pirates. In no time at all, the Pirate Captain is incarcerated at Scotland Yard in a case of mistaken identity. Discovering that his doppelganger is none other than Karl Marx, the Captain and his crew are unwittingly caught up in a sinister plot involving communists, enormous beards, and a quest to discover whether ham might really be the opium of the people.

BLOOMSBURY

THE PIRATES! IN AN ADVENTURE WITH NAPOLEON

The Pirate Captain has finally had enough. Still reeling from the crushing disappointment at the Pirate of the Year Awards, he decides it's time to hang up his hat and ditch his cutlass. Begrudgingly followed by his sceptical but loyal crew, the Captain fixes his sights on a quiet life on the island of St Helena.

But his retirement plan is rudely disrupted by the arrival of another visitor to the island – the recently deposed Napoleon Bonaparte. Has the Pirate Captain finally met his match? Is the island's twenty-eight mile circumference big enough to contain two of history's greatest egos? And will the Pirates be able to settle the biggest question of all: who has the best hat?

✱

'Little slabs of super-concentrated funny'
ANDY RILEY

✱

'It's supreme silliness is its charm'
DAILY TELEGRAPH

✱

'Deliriously Funny'
ARDAL O'HANLON

ORDER YOUR COPY:
BY PHONE: +44 (0)1256 302 699; **BY EMAIL:** DIRECT@MACMILLAN.CO.UK
DELIVERY IS USUALLY 3–5 WORKING DAYS.
FREE POSTAGE AND PACKAGING FOR ORDERS OVER £20.

ONLINE: WWW.BLOOMSBURY.COM/BOOKSHOP
PRICES AND AVAILABILITY SUBJECT TO CHANGE WITHOUT NOTICE.

WWW.BLOOMSBURY.COM

BLOOMSBURY